SONS OF THE
FATHERS

First published 2015 by DB Publishing, an imprint of JMD Media Ltd, Nottingham, United Kingdom.

ISBN 9781780914831

SONS OF THE
FATHERS

IAN C. SIMPSON

DB PUBLISHING

'I could take out of my life everything except my experiences at St Andrews and I would still have a rich, full life.'
Bobby Jones, 9 October 1958, at the ceremony when he was given the Freedom of the Royal Burgh of St Andrews.

For Annie without whose encouragement this would not have been written.

AUTHOR'S NOTE

In this book I seek to weave an entirely fictitious murder mystery into an authentic account of the 1927 Open. The non-golfing plot lines are also fictitious. Most of the characters and all the main suspects, lawyers and policemen are creatures of my imagination. Any resemblance to persons living or dead is coincidental.

When Provost Boase, Laurie Auchterlonie, Jim Barnes, Larry Nabholtz, Charlie Mayo, Stewart Maiden, Bob Jones (Senior) and Jack McIntyre appear, I have tried to make them act in character as well as I can. That goes for Bobby Jones as well. In his case, I have been greatly helped by the numerous quotes from him reported in my sources.

I have allowed myself much more licence with O.B. Keeler. About him Bobby Jones wrote: 'Whatever the mood, Keeler was the ideal companion. He had read almost everything and remembered most of it; he could, and frequently did, recite verse for hours...he was an acutely sensitive, instinctively gallant, and wholly unselfish friend whose loyalty and devotion could never once be questioned.' I hope I have done him no disservice.

I have relied on archive material from *The Scotsman* and *The Times*; *Golf is my Game*, Bobby Jones; *The Bobby Jones Story*, O.B. Keeler; St Andrews, Home of Golf, J.K. Robertson; Golfers' Gallery, Frank Moran; *Masters of Golf*, Golf World Anthology; *Maestro Henry Cotton*, Peter Dobereiner; *A Wee*

Nip at the 19th Hole, Richard MacKenzie; *The Winged Foot Story*, Douglas La Rue Smith; *The Glenalmond Chronicle*; and Gordon Simmonds' *History of the Scottish Universities Golfing Society*. I have consulted numerous books in the library of the Royal and Ancient. I am grateful for the help given by Laurie Rae and Hannah Fleming of the British Golf Museum. Thanks also to Steve Caron and all at DB Publishing. However with all errors the buck stops with me.

Ian C Simpson.

List of characters you will meet and those associated with them:

The Drummond household:
Sheriff Hector Drummond
Lavender Drummond, his wife
Marie and Charlotte Drummond, his daughters
Jake Taylor-Smith, his stepson
Mrs Alves, their housekeeper
Alf Tindall, their gardener
Jim Tindall, his son

The Jones party:
Bobby Jones
'Colonel' Bob Jones Senior, his father
O.B. Keeler, his biographer
Eleanor Keeler, O.B.'s wife
Stewart 'Kiltie' Maiden, Jones' coach
Jack McIntyre, Jones' caddie

The police:
Inspector McTaggart, Cupar
Sgt McNeill, St Andrews
PC Gemmell, St Andrews

The courts:
Sheriff Principal Crichton 'Fatty' Fairweather, KC,
    Hector's superior
Forbes, Hector's bar officer
Newton, the Cupar procurator fiscal, who prosecutes
Wilson, an Edinburgh solicitor

The local caddies:
Tommy Addison
Jeannie, his sister
Wullie Kay
Martin Kay, a greenkeeper and Wullie's cousin

In St Andrews for the Open:
Ralf Murnian, a wealthy New Yorker
Enid Murnian, his wife
Paul Murnian, his golfing son
Enda Murnian, his non-golfing son
Vera Murnian, Enda's wife
Gloria Van Dyke, a New York socialite
Benny Sabbatini, a wealthy New Yorker
Dick Robinson, his protégé
'Long' Jim Barnes, a professional golfer
Larry Nabholtz, a professional golfer
Charlie Mayo, a professional golfer
Lord Terry Coates-Moulton, an aristocratic English
    amateur golfer

St Andrews citizens:
Provost Norman Boase
Tomkins, manager of the Grand Hotel
Mary, a receptionist/telephone operator in the Grand
Billy, a bellboy in the Grand
Jean, a chambermaid in the Grand
Dr Henry Madsen, a university lecturer
Jocelyn Varvell, a university lecturer
Willie Auchterlonie, 1893 Open Champion and clubmaker
Laurie Auchterlonie, a clubmaker
Hamish McCann, a clubmaker

Peter Nugent, a chef
Esme Hamilton, a battleaxe
'Bean' Hamilton, her husband

Also:
Mo 'Molasses' Evans, Ralf Murnian's New York attorney

A number of other names, which are not important to the story, come up in the text. Some readers will doubtless recognise many of these as eminent golfers of the time.

PROLOGUE

Columbus, Ohio; 10 July 1926

He'd walked miles yet the anger still gripped him, knotting his gut, making him shake. He kicked a stone on the rough path and watched it disappear into the darkness of a thorn bush.

The wind had dropped since the bruising afternoon. It whispered among aspens and made their long shadows waltz over the golf course.

Ahead and round a bend, wheels rattled. Going fast, a boy on a bicycle saw the man, swerved sharply, skidded and fell with a clatter. The man glared. 'Sorry, sir,' the boy said, though he hadn't hit him.

The boy was thirteen or fourteen with dark, wavy hair. Good-looking.

'Let me help you.' The man reached down.

'Thank you, sir.'

'Let me brush the dirt off your clothes.'

'Don't bother, sir. I'd best be on my way.'

'Oh but I must.' The man's voice was an octave higher. With his hand he brushed the boy's shoulders, back, butt. Moving quickly, he stuffed a handkerchief in his mouth and twisted an arm up his back. 'You're coming with me,' he said, and he pushed the boy into the aspen wood.

Above the wind, muffled howls reached the path. The sun set and the shadows ceased to dance. A hobo, long deaf to others' suffering, tripped over the bicycle.

'Never look a darn gift horse in the mouth,' he muttered as he picked himself up. It had been a while since he'd ridden a bicycle but he managed.

1927

FIFE, SCOTLAND

1

Monday 4 July

'When I saw the medals above the fire I went straight out.' The speaker was a thin lad of seventeen, standing in the dock of Cupar Sheriff Court. Below a tangle of ginger curls his freckled face was weather-beaten to a reddish brown. Defiance gave an edge to the anxiety in his voice.

Sheriff Hector Drummond reined in his anger. He scratched his forehead where, a decade ago, the lining of his helmet had rubbed. 'By then you'd given a war widow a very nasty fright,' he said.

Though fear flickered in his eyes, the lad held his gaze.

There was no one remaining on the public benches to support this boy. He was not an ordinary housebreaker, Hector thought. He had fled, taking nothing from the widow's home in Queen's Gardens, St Andrews, but had gone on to break into a house just round the corner. The family silver and money he had taken from there had not been recovered.

The spotty, buck-toothed *Dundee Courier and Advertiser* reporter sat beside the dock smirking, his pencil poised in anticipation. Hector cleared his throat.

'Thomas Addison, housebreaking is an activity that will not be tolerated.' He paused, cleared his throat again. He wanted to be reported accurately. When the badly-chewed pencil stopped moving he continued. 'Men did not fight and die in the trenches so that rascals like you might invade their homes, frighten their women, and steal. I sentence you to one year's borstal training. Take him away.'

The youth stiffened then consciously jutted out his chin as the clerk read out the sentence and the dock policemen led him out of the courtroom. It was the last case of the day. Forbes, the bar officer, shouted 'court!' and the officials stood up, bowing deeply towards the bench. The reporter gave a casual nod. Hector heaved himself out of his throne-like chair, padded with sleep-inhibiting leather upholstery, bowed, then followed Forbes through the door at the back of the bench to his chambers.

'Do you think borstal will sort out that lad?' Hector asked as he removed his horsehair wig and placed it on the stained mahogany table he used as a desk.

'I'm not sure he needs much sorting, my lord.' Forbes helped Hector out of his robe and hung it in the cupboard.

Hector looked at him, puzzled. A retired policeman, Forbes had strong views on crime and punishment. His disapproval at the leniency of some of Hector's sentences was almost palpable.

'You know about him?' Hector asked, taking a cigarette from his case and tapping loose tobacco from the end. He flicked his scuffed lighter a couple of times before it produced a large flame.

'He lives round the corner from us in Bridge Street. You know his faither, Kenny. You've jailed him a few times.'

'Doesn't ring a bell.'

'Drunken breaches of the peace, but that's just the tip of the iceberg. Young Tommy's been the real man of the house.'

'How?'

'He works as a caddie. And he protects his mum. There's a wee girl, too, with a weak chest. Kenny gets handy with his fists, specially at home when he's in his cups. After he's drunk all the money there's only what Tommy earns.'

'Is that why...?'

Forbes nodded.

'Why didn't he say?'

'Pride, my lord. He'd rather go to borstal than have his dirty linen washed in public.'

Hector went to the window. Sucking in smoke, he looked down the main road leading to St Andrews. He thought for a moment then turned abruptly. 'Get him in here, could you? Quick, before they take him away.' When Forbes left, he stubbed out his cigarette violently, then sat at the table, wishing he had known the background earlier. Once a prisoner had left the building, his escort holding the clerk's warrant, there was nothing Hector could do.

Heavy footsteps in the corridor and a knock on the door told him he was not too late. Handcuffs rattling, the lad came in between two policemen and stood in front of the table, his shoulders stooped.

'I believe your mother relies on you, Addison,' Hector said.

'Yes, sir.'

'To protect her from your father, apart from anything else?'

The boy raised his head and looked steadily at Forbes, who avoided eye contact. He said nothing.

'Has the cat caught your tongue?' Hector asked. 'I'm seeing you in here so you can speak freely.'

The lad shook his head then stared at the floor. Softly he said, 'You obviously know, sir.' He shot a resentful glance at Forbes.

Hector saw the boy had character but he could not allow him to remain so stubborn. He rested his elbows on the leather armrests of his chair and made an arch by touching his fingertips. After a moment's silence he spoke quietly. 'I want to hear it from you and I want to hear it now. Otherwise you might as well set off for borstal.' He sat back and waited.

Why did the sheriff need to know this, Tommy asked himself. Could he have changed his mind? Close up, he didn't seem frightening any more, as he had in court. His eyes looked red and he wheezed, like Jeannie. 'I did it for my mam,' he said as steadily as he could. 'She was starving. Our Jeannie too. I had to do something.'

'So you went housebreaking?'

'That was the first time, sir. Honest.'

'And money isn't the only problem in the house?'

Tommy's shoulders twitched and he looked up at the ceiling. He wanted to cry, but not in front of the sheriff. 'He wis always hitting them, both of them, their heads, their faces even.' He hung his head.

'Does he hit you?'

'Of course. Or he did.'

'What do you mean "he did"?'

Tommy sensed that, in a strange way, the sheriff was on his side, that he could tell him things. 'When he wisnae in jail, he never lacked drink. He didnae care if we ate or not. One night I'd had enough.' He breathed deeply. 'He wis taking his belt to my mam. To my mam. I held his arm and he punched me with his other hand. Then it started. I knew I had tae beat him. He broke a chair on my back, and I broke another on his heid. It wis a right dirty fight. Then he stood facing me. I wis hurting and wanted to stop, but I knew I couldnae. He says to me, "So yer a man, are ye?" and he held out his hand. I just picked up a chair-leg, ready for more. He called me a name and walked out.' The boy clamped his mouth shut and searched for some reaction from the sheriff.

Hector frowned. 'When was this?' he asked.

'Three, four months ago.'

'What happened after that?'

'He hasnae lifted his hands. But he's no' paid us a penny.'

'So you support your mother and your sister?'

'I tried, but there were debts...' His voice trailed off.

'Some blasted tally-man?' Hector's usual leniency deserted him any time he sentenced a loan-shark.

Tommy nodded.

'Can you get the silver you stole back?'

Tommy shifted from foot to foot. 'Maybe.'

'You'd better.' Although Hector had seen many tearaways benefit from the harsh regime of borstal, he knew it would do nothing but harm to this lad. He sat back in his chair then spoke with great deliberation. 'I'm going to reconvene the court then I'm going to put you on probation. A probation officer will supervise you. You must take his advice, whether you like it or not. If you let yourself down, you'll let me down, and it'll be two or three years' borstal. Do you understand?'

Tommy blinked. For a moment he hesitated then said, 'I understand, sir.'

Always wanting to do something positive, but surprised by the boy's coolness, Hector allowed himself a smile. 'Well, good luck. Do you have a bag for the Open?'

'No, sir. I wisnae going to try before today. I'll go straight to the course now.' Slowly, a grin spread over his face.

'I understand Bobby Jones arrives this afternoon, but he'll probably have someone lined up.' Hector smiled again. He was due to meet the defending champion that evening. 'Right, let's

not waste time. Forbes, could you send the clerk in? He's not
going to be very pleased with me.'

*   *   *

A swirling fog, known as *haar* on the east coast of Scotland,
grey, chilling and wet, had swept in from the North Sea, blan-
keting the links and reducing visibility to a few yards. Round
the entrance of the Grand Hotel, the majestic red sandstone
building, a chip and run from the first tee of the Old Course,
a small crowd had gathered. Tommy joined it. Still shaking
with relief when he got off the train from Cupar, he had seen a
lot of people round the first class carriages. He guessed whom
they were there to greet, and where he would stay for the
championship.

The crowd round the entrance of the famous hotel grew
restive.

'All that rain's made it too easy for them. We need the wind
to blaw,' a grizzled local in a flat tweed cap stated loudly.

'That'll sort the men from the boys. Maybe Jones will tear
up his card again.' Under a similar cap, thin lips formed an
inhospitable fissure in a stony face.

Behind them but in front of Tommy, a youth spoke up. 'Mr
Jones can play in the wind. It wis blowing last year.'

'What do you know, sonny?' asked the second man.

Jack McIntyre stuck out his chin. 'I wis...' His voice tailed
off. A car's headlights approached down Golf Place. Its brakes
squeaked as it drew up outside the hotel. Those nearest were
reluctant to surrender their spot and, puffed up with self-im-
portance, the chauffeur required to push them aside. First on
to the pavement from the back came a short, wiry man. His face
wore a slightly puzzled frown. If he welcomed the attention he

did not let it show, but the crowd's attention was focused on a younger man, short of stature but stocky, who slid gracefully from the front passenger seat and held the door behind him for the oldest of the three. The familial resemblance was unmistakable. Bobby Jones' father looked round, inhaling deeply. He held in the damp, salty air as if savouring fine but unfamiliar wine.

Jack broke free from the crush round him. 'Mr Jones, sir! Mr Jones!'

A broad smile creased Bobby Jones' face. 'Jack! I guess you must have gotten my wire.' The soft southern drawl was as smooth as warm honey.

'I'd be here anyway, sir.'

'Well, collect the clubs from the trunk and come on in.'

'Into the Grand?'

'Sure. You're with us.'

Like a mother lifting her baby from a cot, Jack took the famous golf clubs from the boot while the chauffeur and two porters hefted heavy leather suitcases. They followed the three men into the hotel.

'Dad, meet Jack McIntyre. It seems he wants to caddie for me again. Jack, this is Colonel Jones, my father.' Jones smiled as his father stretched out a hand and Jack wiped his on his trousers before taking it.

Jones turned to the third man. 'This gentleman taught me to play, Stewart Maiden. He comes from Carnoustie, so he's not far from home.'

'How do you do,' Jack stammered. Maiden looked him up and down before giving a not unfriendly nod.

While these introductions were being made, a tall young lady sashayed into the hotel lobby and joined the throng at the reception desk. Her long, blonde hair cascaded on to the collar of the red fox fur coat that remained fastened as she waited imperiously, her delicate nose wrinkled as if she had smelt a bad smell.

'Go ahead, ma'am. I guess you'll be quicker than us,' Jones said, bowing slightly.

A false smile that showed off her scarlet lipstick was her only acknowledgement. She approached the ruddy-cheeked lady receptionist. 'Mrs Van Dyke. I trust you're expecting me,' she said. Her voice came from somewhere that was a few degrees north of Jones' and many degrees colder. She drummed her long nails on the desk as the receptionist searched a card index system and became increasingly flustered.

With a sigh of relief she drew out a card. 'Yes, I have it here, madam.'

Mrs Van Dyke nodded.

The receptionist turned to get the key from its pigeonhole. 'Rab will show you to your room, madam. I hope you enjoy your stay with us.'

Mrs Van Dyke favoured her with a second false smile. 'Please tell Mr Murnian, Mr Paul Murnian, that I have just arrived. It'll be a surprise for him.' She followed the elderly porter towards the stairs, his arthritic frame racked by the weight of her two enormous suitcases.

As the receptionist struggled to find Mrs Van Dyke's reservation, an elegantly dressed lady who looked as if she might be in her mid-forties came down the stairs, treading delicately. She also was tall and blonde, but puffy coarseness spoiled a face that might once have been beautiful. She surveyed the crowded lobby and, when she saw the new arrival, froze. For a few seconds her hands gripped the banister. Then she slowly turned and, her head high, went back upstairs.

Outside the hotel, his face pressed against the glass of one

of the lobby windows, Tommy took in this scene. He needed
to find a bag for the Open, make some money. He wondered
if his housebreaking activity had come to the ears of the cad-
die-master, beside whom Sheriff Drummond was definitely a
soft touch. He rehearsed what he would say.

*　　*　　*

Not far from the Grand Hotel, *haar* drifted round the weathered sandstone ruins of the castle and the cobbled streets to
its landward side. In a poky, terraced house in one of those
streets, Dr Henry Madsen, a gangly man with piercing eyes and
an untrimmed beard, stooped to avoid the lintel as he entered
his sitting room.

'Enjoy your walk?' Jocelyn Varvell, whose fresh complexion made him look about twenty, glanced up from the heavy
book on his lap. 'You've got wet,' he added.

'When the *haar* wrapped itself round me, I felt completely
at one with nature. But nature's cold. I need a bath.'

'Shall I...?' Varvell raised his eyebrows.

'I'll just wallow and contemplate, this time. I'll be back for a
drink in half an hour.' The hair beside Madsen's mouth twitched
as he smiled and turned to go.

Varvell shrugged. Then, noticing marks on the carpet, he
shouted after him: 'There's something on your shoes.'

*   *   *

Nearby, in a one-room flat, Alf Tindall pulled back the greasy hem of the lop-sided curtain above the sink, but could see nothing except *haar*.

'Where is that boy?' he muttered, more angry than worried. His hand went to the buckle of his belt. If Jim had gone to see his pal Hamish without telling him...

2

'Everyone's so excited about the Open. There was a real buzz about the town this morning before the *haar* came in.' Lavender Drummond inspected herself in the oval mirror on the serpentine-fronted dressing table and dabbed her nose with her powder puff. 'Will the American ladies be the most frightful swells?' she asked Hector, frowning.

'Exotic, maybe, darling, but you'll be tops in swellishness, if there is such a thing.' He took a sip of his whisky and soda before looking over his wife's head to check his bow tie and his hair. As usual, the tie was immaculate. He adjusted his parting so that it concealed as much of his scalp as possible.

'Do they ever have bow tie-tying competitions?' Lavender asked. 'I'm sure you would win by a street. I don't know how you get it right every time without a mirror in front of you.'

'It's the only practical skill the Scottish bar teaches you. If you might be late for court, you learn pretty quickly. When it comes to bow tie tying, the Faculty of Advocates could take on allcomers.' He put down his drink and gently massaged under the broad white collar of her floral dress. She reached for the gold chain her parents had given her for her twenty-first.

'I read in *The Scotsman* that the Earl of Silloth and Solway has offered a hundred pounds as a reward for getting his emeralds back,' she said.

'The Eyes of the Fox. Do you think they'd be worth as much without the fancy name? It's rather obscene that two bits of rock can be worth thousands of pounds. I wonder if they were stolen to order or if an ordinary burglar got lucky – or not. He'll be for the high jump if he's caught.' As he fastened her chain, in the looking glass his brown, blood-shot eyes met her clear blue ones.

'We won't need to be late, darling, will we?' she asked.

'I don't imagine so. The golfers will want to get to their beds.'

'It'll be interesting to watch how they drink,' Lavender mused. 'Do you think they'll feel guilty about drinking in public?'

'Some of them will be used to ninety percent proof hooch and others will get squiffy on a dry sherry. It might be rather fun to watch.'

'I'm dying to see Bobby Jones. He's not very tall, is he?'

'Not very.'

'Maybe I should wear flat heels.' She eased her feet out of her shoes and went to her wardrobe.

'Don't worry. If Walter Hagen can't intimidate him, your high heels certainly won't. He's what the Americans would call a tough cookie and he has a temper. The first time he was here he tore up his card, a poor show, if you ask me.'

'Well, they say he's a complete gentleman, so I should be considerate towards him.' She brought out a pair of flat-heeled brown shoes and slipped them on. Hector beamed at her, shaking his head. He had adored her since their teenage years in St Andrews. There had been well-chaperoned dances during the winter, and daring, goose-bumped midnight swims on the West Sands in summer. Alone together they had kissed and, on one unforgettable evening, she had let him feel under her dress.

During school terms they wrote regularly. Then he introduced her to his best friend from Glenalmond, John Taylor-Smith, and immediately felt the electricity between them. As their love grew he tried not to let his envy show, particularly on their wedding day when he was best man. But then John had been killed at Ypres. Hector spent his leaves with his mother in St Andrews trying to comfort Lavender, who had gone to live with her parents. In those days it seemed that life had drained out of her as, hollow-cheeked, she devoted herself to John junior, her two-year-old son.

Mustard gas ended Hector's war. His skin blistered, his lungs scorched, blinded for a few horrific days, he came back to St Andrews to recuperate. He and Lavender often walked together, John junior, now known as Jake, toddling beside them, gabbling away and happy in his own safe little world. Once the War to End All Wars was over, Hector proposed and she accepted. After their marriage, Hector went to the bar and Marie and Charlotte arrived in 1921 and 1923 respectively. After a few years as an advocate, Hector received a summons to see the Lord Advocate, who offered him the chance to return to his home town as the sheriff. He knew he was a lucky dog, and the feeling in his heart of hearts that he was not, and never would be, John Taylor-Smith melted year by year.

He drained his glass. 'Well, if you're adequately shod I think we should hit the trail,' he said. They visited the nursery to say goodnight to Marie and Charlotte who were listening enthralled to Mrs Alves, their housekeeper/nanny, reading about Peter Rabbit's adventures in Mr McGregor's garden. Their parents' departure was of no consequence to them.

'I don't know what we'd do without Mrs Alves,' Lavender said.

'It cuts both ways, I think. We're the nearest thing to family that she has. Remember how upset she was when Jake went off to board at Glenalmond?' With a crunch of gravel, Hector drove out of the front gate of their home, Ballochmyle, and steered his pride and joy, a blue Morris Oxford Bullnose, at a stately twenty miles per hour past the new houses of Buchanan Gardens, down streets of stone houses, as grey and spooky as the pervasive *haar*, then turned into Golf Place. He parked on the Scores and they stepped into the lobby of the Grand Hotel, whose manager had spotted the happy coincidence of Bobby Jones arriving on the Fourth of July. Sparing no expense, he had organized an Independence Day party to welcome his American guests. An assortment of famous golfers and local big-wigs, including the sheriff, had been invited to drinks and dinner.

The drinks were being served in a long, rectangular first-floor lounge. A large Stars and Stripes adorned one wall. On the long wall opposite picture windows, dramatic Highland scenes were depicted in dark, thickly applied oils. On the sofa table, beneath a gory painting of a newly shot stag, was a photograph of a bleak-faced man with a prominent nose and eyes that stared downwards. Calvin Coolidge, 'Silent Cal', did not take a good photograph, Hector thought. There was more life in the eyes of the stag than in those of the thirtieth president of the United States. The room was already crowded. Everyone had dressed for dinner. A few American men wore white tuxedos but most wore black dinner jackets. Their ladies were more distinct from the Scots, with sleeker lines, more eye-catching lipstick and no floral patterns. Hector smelled Havana cigars and musky perfume. 'Deep breath, darling,' he whispered, placing a hand on the small of Lavender's back. He sensed the timidity that sometimes overcame her when confronted with unfamiliar company.

'Sheriff Drummond, good of you to come. Mrs Drummond, good of you to come,' Tomkins, the manager, gabbled at them. Hector could not tell where his hair pomade ended and sweat from his brow began. 'Do come and meet Mr Ralf Murnian, a gentleman from New York who's been with us for the last few days. His son's playing in the championship. Mr Murnian, Sheriff and Mrs Drummond.'

As Tomkins bustled away, they shook hands. Murnian was short and pudgy, one of those in a white tuxedo. His quick movements suggested impatience. He held his whisky glass and his cigar in his left hand with practised ease. He had a heavy growth on his jowls and a ski-jump nose. His dark eyes darted about, passed over Lavender then settled intently on Hector.

'A lawman, huh?' He sounded less than friendly. Hector thought it might just be the strong New York accent.

'Not your sort of sheriff, I'm afraid. I'm the local judge and I don't carry a six-shooter.'

'You should. Can't be too careful. Till recently, I carried a 1908 Colt, but for a year or two I've been more comfortable with a little Derringer. Lighter, hard to spot.'

A waiter carrying a salver of drinks approached. Murnian finished his then stopped himself from seizing another before Lavender had made her choice.

'Thank you so much,' she said, to Murnian as much as to the waiter, and picked up a dry sherry. 'I see someone I've been meaning to have a word with over there.'

Murnian did not give her a second glance. He took his whisky and looked quizzically up at Hector. 'Do lawyers here wear these long grey, curly wigs that make them look like sheep?'

'Occasionally. In court we wear shorter wigs that leave the ears exposed.'

'So you can hear the evidence?' Hector wondered if the way he tilted his head had led this strange little man to pick up on his slight deafness.

'Mr Murnian, Sheriff Drummond, this is Mr Sabbatini. He has just today arrived for the championship. Another passenger on the *Transylvania*.' Tomkins was determined to make everyone feel welcome.

As Hector shook hands with the stooped, silver-haired newcomer he noted his swollen, arthritic knuckles and cold, claw-like fingers that gripped his own with surprising strength. The lined, walnut-coloured face twisted into a warm smile which changed to a sneer as he turned to Murnian. 'Your boy's driving straightened out yet, Murnian?' he rasped, also in a gritty New York accent.

'He'll be just fine. There's a lot of room on these fairways. I don't know why you took the trouble to come. The greens are as big as Central Park and your protégé can't putt.' He pronounced the word 'pro-tay-jay'.

'We'll see. Good to meet you, Sheriff. I hope this man doesn't keep you and your deputies too busy.' He nodded at Murnian then moved off slowly.

'S.O.B.,' Murnian muttered.

'You two are not exactly old friends?' Hector asked, he hoped lightly.

'We've been at each other's throats since the turn of the century. When my boy, Paul, turned out to be a fine golfer it made him mad, so he found a kid with talent but without a dime to his name and he's paying for him to play the tournaments. Tell the truth, I feel sorry for the boy. Sabbatini doesn't let him out of his sight. That's him there.' Narrow-eyed and insistent, Sabbatini was lecturing an unhappy-looking youth at least a foot taller than himself; either rosy-cheeked or blushing, he had a glass of sherry in his hand. Sabbatini summoned a waiter, put the sherry glass on the salver and handed the youth a long glass of ginger beer. Having struck this blow for temperance he carefully wrapped his fingers round a glass of whisky and took a mouthful.

'See what I mean?' For the first time, Murnian looked as if he was enjoying himself.

'Do you play golf?' Hector asked.

'Sheriff, you are speaking to one of the founder members of Winged Foot Golf Club. We built it on Indian hunting land and it's only four years old but it'll soon be one of the greatest places to play golf in the world.' He took a gulp of whisky.

'Can I ask how Prohibition affects a club like that? I find it hard to imagine a golf club where a fellow can't relax with a beer or a whisky after a round.'

Murnian chuckled. 'You don't have to imagine such a thing, Sheriff. Winged Foot was christened with a bottle of your best Scotch whisky, wrapped in tartan. Lawmen mostly realize if they get too unreasonable over Prohibition, folk will stop supporting them when real crime's involved. A group of us call ourselves "The Niblicks". We always have something for medicinal purposes, snakebite maybe, hidden away somewhere. We get by.'

'A wise precaution.' Hector raised his glass.

'I'm glad I'm not shocking you, Sheriff. In Manhattan we have to be more careful. I visit the Leash Club. Every member has his own locker, just big enough to hold a bottle, I might add. Each locker has a brass plate with the member's dog's name on it. We go to the club to discuss our dogs and if we get a little thirsty....' He shrugged his shoulders expressively. 'If the law enforcement authorities come calling they're just as likely to join our discussion as try to figure out who owns what dog...'

'Ralf, it's time for dinner.' The tall, expensively clothed

woman who addressed Murnian in glacial tones was certainly a swell. Without affection she added, 'You have that poor man cornered.' Hector's back was to the wall. He hated being talked at by people who crowded him.

Murnian's face darkened. Nearly a head shorter than the lady Hector supposed was his wife, he did not even glance at her. 'I'll go eat when I'm good and ready,' he growled. 'Good meeting you, Mr Lawman. There's a guy I must see over there.' He nodded to Hector and pushed his way towards a young man carrying a salver of drinks.

'I'm Enid Murnian.' The tall lady held out a white-gloved hand.

'Hector Drummond. Delighted to meet you. Do you?' He offered her a cigarette. She accepted and inserted it into the longest holder he had ever seen. She raised an eyebrow at the battered lighter which needed several flicks. The two inch flame, when it came, made her step back with a slight stagger that made Hector wonder if she was less sober than she appeared to be.

'You have an interesting lighter, Mr Drummond,' she said doubtfully.

'It was my best friend's. Killed at Ypres. I'm afraid it behaves a bit erratically.'

'I like erratic. You could use that flame-thrower to burn heretics. You sure have some history right here on your doorstep.'

With her drawl and his deafness in a crowded room, Hector had difficulty catching all that she said, but he got the gist and started to tell her about the Covenanters and the murder of Archbishop Sharp when Tomkins, red-faced and sweating, swung a brass bell up and down with exaggerated energy. He soon commanded the attention of his guests, and announced that Provost Boase of St Andrews would say a few words.

A distinguished looking man with an upright bearing and a dark, luxuriant moustache stepped forward. Hector knew and respected Norman Boase. As well as being Provost he also chaired the Championship Committee. He wore the trappings of his office, a red gown trimmed with ermine and a gold link chain round his neck.

By now, the *haar* had retreated out to sea as stealthily as it had crept in, revealing on cue the broad expanse of light green turf comprising the first and eighteenth fairways of the Old Course and the snake-like meandering of the Swilken Burn. Squinting into the setting sun, Boase read out his prepared speech in a loud, clear voice. He welcomed the competitors in the Open Championship, in particular on Independence Day, those from the United States. He extended a special welcome to the defending champion, Bobby Jones, and wondered if he would care to say something.

Jones stepped forward slowly and, half smiling, half grimacing, looked round the room. He could tell from their expressions that the hard-to-impress Scots were assessing him.

'Provost Boase, Ladies and Gentlemen, I am sure I speak for my compatriots when I say how grateful we are to Mr Tomkins for laying on this celebration of our Independence Day. I think we're particularly grateful that he did not follow the example of Boston and make this a tea party. Speaking for myself, I am enjoying the spirit of Scottish hospitality.' Amid laughter he raised his whisky glass. 'When I first came here, six years ago, it is well known that I found the Old Course difficult. I have learned quite a bit since then and I now hold it to be a great course. What I like about it is that you haven't got your play prescribed for you when you step on the tee. You can have your own ideas about playing the hole, and you're usually wrong. If I don't score well this time, I certainly won't blame it on the Old Course.

'I know the weather will have an effect on the play. Personally, I am happy that the wind should blow, as long as it's behind me at most of the holes.'

Laughing with the rest of the company, and impressed that he should make oblique reference to tearing up his card in the 1921 Open, Hector found Jones' quiet, self-deprecating authority remarkable in a man of only twenty-five. During the War he had witnessed the maturing effect of great and traumatic events on young men, but it was Jones' own achievements that had made him older than his years. When he finished speaking there were noises of approval and the muted applause that comes from a crowd standing with glasses in their hands.

As Hector turned to Enid Murnian, he saw Sabbatini bowing his head towards them.

She aimed a wry smile in Sabbatini's direction. To Hector, she said, 'It's been a pleasure meeting you, Mr Drummond. Now I'm going to find my husband and go have dinner with or without him.'

'I hope you have a pleasant time here, Mrs Murnian,' Hector responded.

'So do I, Mr Drummond. So do I. Goodbye.' Stepping deliberately, she joined a young couple near the door. He was lanky, with a ginger tint to his fair hair that a generous application of pomade failed to mask. A thin moustache darkened his upper lip but did not strengthen his face. She was small and mousy and gripped his arm with curious intensity.

Hector looked round the room and recognized several famous golfers. The very tall 'Long Jim' Barnes, the 1925 champion, was talking to an older man of similar height, the lugubrious James Braid, who had won five times. Beside the window stood the robust Cyril Tolley, the main British amateur hope for the Open, pointing out something on the course to the great Harry Vardon.

Hector spotted Lavender beside the president's photograph, and moved towards her. She was with Bobby Jones and an owlish man with round, gold-rimmed glasses. The owlish man was in the middle of a story.

'...so she went up to Silent Cal and said, "Mr President, my husband has bet me five dollars I can't get three words out of you." He looked at her and said, "You lose."'

Hector joined in the laughter and took Lavender's arm.

Sparkling and happy, she turned to him. 'Darling, there you are. You must meet Mr Jones and Mr Keeler.'

'Your wife tells us you are the local judge, sir,' Jones said as he shook hands. 'This is my friend and Boswell, O.B. Keeler. He's come here straight from his honeymoon. His wife, Eleanor, is over there.'

'The lady in the dark red dress,' Keeler explained. 'I told her she was like a "red, red rose that's newly sprung in June". Seeing we're in Scotland, we've been reading Robert Burns in bed.'

Jones turned away, grinning as he lit a cigarette. 'Give him half a chance and he'll start on about "wee, sleekit, cowrin, tim'rous beasties",' he said, mangling his imitation of a Scottish accent.

'*To a Mouse* has much in it for golfers, including champion golfers,' Keeler retorted, wagging an admonitory finger.

'I understand you also are a lawyer, Mr Jones,' Hector said.

'I was admitted to the Georgia State Bar and the Federal Bar this year,' Jones replied with more pride than he allowed when talking about his golf. For a moment there was a shift in status as the Open Champion became a young lawyer talking to a senior member of his profession.

'Fortunately, Bob has found himself an understanding employer.' Keeler's eye twinkled. 'But Big Bob, over there, tells me he has gotten some real mean cases lined up for his junior partner this fall.' Hector saw the man he presumed to be Jones senior in earnest conversation with Provost Boase.

'I'm glad to see you gentlemen are taking advantage of the availability of our national drink,' Hector said. 'I was speaking to Mr Murnian earlier. He was telling me Prohibition's a law more honoured in the breach than in the observance.'

Keeler snorted. 'He should know. He's made as much out of it as anyone.'

Jones shook his head. 'It's a bad law that makes rich men out of crooks.' He looked sharply up at Hector, who shrugged.

'"Chatham House Rules," I believe is the new saying. You can use the information but must not reveal the source.'

'And if you want someone to disappear in New York, Murnian's your man.' Keeler, less circumspect than Jones, was careless of who might overhear. He drained his glass. 'And if he's Tweedledum, that's Tweedledee over there.' He nodded towards Sabbatini, who stood next to them with his back turned.

Jones looked away. Hector and Lavender tried to hide their surprise.

'Oh, and see that broad who came in late and is floating round Big Bob and the Provost?' Keeler pointed towards a younger woman dressed in a sequin-covered sheath of lime green with an orange collar. 'That's Gloria Van Dyke, Paul Murnian's mistress. She got rich on her first divorce and has young Paul lined up for her second. She sure didn't get that outfit from a Sears catalogue.'

'It's strange how sheriffs in Scotland are so different from sheriffs in the States,' Jones interjected.

'Sheriff-substitute is my proper title, actually, though

I'm generally called Sheriff. My court is in Cupar, eight miles inland.'

'Our train passed through Cupar this afternoon. I guess there won't be too much serious crime round these parts?' Jones asked.

'I believe I heard about a man going to jail for improving his lie in a bunker,' Keeler said in a solemn voice, but with a glint in his eye.

'Just as well that's about as bad as it gets. McNeill, the local police sergeant, is not over-burdened with brains. Chatham House Rules,' Hector added quickly.

In answer to Lavender's enquiry about his family, Jones spoke about his wife, Mary, and their baby boy, Robert Jones III.

'Is he going to be another golf champion?' Lavender asked.

'I'll try to discourage him all I can for I want him to have a quiet life and no worry,' was the moving but slightly surprising reply.

It was time for dinner. Jones and Keeler said a courteous goodbye and left to join their table. Hector and Lavender had been assigned to a table of six, the others being Sabbatini, his protégé, Dick Robinson, and the town clerk and his wife. Long-faced and straight-laced, they said as little as possible. Hector wondered if they competed with each other to see who could maintain an expression of gloomy disdain for the longest time. A tiny movement of Lavender's eyebrow told him she was as unenthusiastic about the company as he was. However there would be no awkward silences with Sabbatini at the table. Whisky had dulled his pain and loosened his tongue. Insisting on being called Benny ('short for Benito, like Il Duce') he talked constantly, mostly about himself. He did not let eating interrupt the flow, disregarding the morsels he sprayed around his place setting.

'I give money to an orphanage,' he explained. 'The supervisor told me he had this kid who had the best natural golf swing he'd ever seen. So I had a look at him.' He smiled at Dick. 'I was real impressed and kept track of him after he'd left the orphanage. Last year I saw him play at our National Open at Scioto and we wound up talking. I used to be pretty good myself, I might add, so I know what to look for. I can't play these days.' A look of regret passed across his face. 'Dick was cleaning cars and shining shoes so he could go play tournaments, but I've made a pile of dollars so I help Dick out till he's established in his profession. Tell the truth, I get what you'd call a vi-carious pleasure out of seeing him hit a ball into the next county. He's going to be a great champion one day. Last month, he tied fifteenth in the National Open at Oakmont. I'm hoping he'll go fourteen better here at St Andrews.' Like all Americans, he emphasised 'Saint'.

His blush intensifying, the lad took a spoonful of soup which he slurped noisily. The neck of his white shirt was too big, one of its studs had come out, the arms of his jacket were short and the knot in his bow tie might keep a liner at anchor. Hector wondered if the stock of dinner wear the hotel kept to spare guests' embarrassment caused more than it saved. He decided to pour Dick some wine but got no more than a drop into his glass when Sabbatini intervened.

'No thank you, Sheriff. This boy needs a clear head for his golf. We don't drink much wine in the States, but I'd be happy to take a glass and give you my opinion on it.'

'Dick?' Hector ignored Sabbatini.

'Well, one glass isn't going to hurt, I'm sure.' Dick's voice squeaked. He avoided the glare Sabbatini aimed at him.

'There are those round here who swear that drink helps your putting,' Hector purred as he filled Dick's glass. He put the bottle down on its coaster. 'Oh sorry, Benny,' he said as Sabbatini reached out a claw. Hector took the bottle and carefully poured a smaller quantity into Sabbatini's glass. Impervious to the slight, Sabbatini swallowed a mouthful and started to talk about somewhere he called 'Noo Joysey'.

The Murnians' table was on the other side of the room. At either end, Murnian and his wife avoided looking at each other. Facing Hector were the ginger-haired man and the mousy woman. Neither looked relaxed or happy. Murnian appeared to be haranguing a dark-haired young man with broad shoulders. Two tables away from them, dining alone, Gloria Van Dyke blew delicate smoke rings in the direction of the Murnians, a superior, disdainful smile on her lips.

Her back to the room, Lavender reflected that the influx of Americans made her more conscious of the history of her home town. She gazed out over the green grass of the Scores where the Martyrs' Monument formed a grey, accusing finger pointing at the sky. Between that and the sea there had been, centuries earlier, the Witch Lake. Women suspected of being witches were cast into it. If they swam, that proved they were witches and they were burned at the stake. The way to prove innocence was to drown. Lavender shuddered at the thought and looked west towards the golf courses and a blood-red sunset. Some people said the eighteenth green of the Old Course had been a Pictish burial site, and blamed missed putts on malevolent influences from below. Hector would laugh at her, but she wondered what the spirits of the dead would make of these intruders from the twentieth century.

As they ate their pudding, Murnian approached their table unsteadily. He glared first at Dick, then at Sabbatini. Wrinkling his nose, Dick pointedly lowered his head over his plate. Sabbatini looked up defiantly.

Murnian wagged his finger. 'Make no mistake, Sabbatini, an amateur is going to win again this year.'

'Well, my boy here will finish ahead of yours any roads.' Sabbatini jutted out his chin.

'Paul will take on Robinson any day before the championship and he'll beat him hollow.' He turned to the dark-haired young man. 'Won't you, son?'

'Make it tomorrow afternoon, and five hundred bucks says Dick wins.' Sabbatini glared at his old rival.

'We're in Britain, so make it pounds. Five hundred too much for you?'

'I'd prefer a thousand. I just didn't want to embarrass you.'

Murnian swayed on his feet and grabbed the back of a chair to steady himself. He clenched his jaw. 'A thousand it is, then. Two o' clock on the first tee. Match play or stroke?'

'Make it match. We don't want to spend all day looking for every ball your boy puts in the bushes.'

While this exchange was going on, Paul caught Dick's eye, grinned and shrugged his shoulders. Sheepishly, Dick shook his head and gave a half smile in return.

*   *   *

While Hector tried not to make the front door squeak as he shut it, Lavender sensed something was wrong. As well as the lamp on the half landing, there was a chink of light under the sitting room door. As they approached it, Mrs Alves emerged, her face contorted.

'Oh, Sheriff, Mrs Drummond, it's terrible,' she panted, her voice low.

'The girls...' Lavender cried.

'They're fine, Mrs Drummond.'

'Come in here.' Hector strode into the sitting room and stood by the fireplace. Shaking, Lavender joined him. 'You'd better sit down, Mrs Alves,' he said.

She sat on an upright chair, her hands on her lap, and sniffed. 'It's Tindall's boy, Jim. He's been found murdered. It's horrible. The telephone rang an hour ago. It was Sergeant McNeill. Tindall insisted he told you. He willnae be able to face his work tomorrow.'

'Of course not.' Hector was stunned. Alf Tindall had been their gardener for nine years. He had survived the War only to watch his wife and two daughters succumb to the influenza epidemic of 1919. With the help of his mother-in-law, he had brought up his sole remaining child. A year younger than Jake, Jim had sometimes come with his father and the boys had played together. Hector silently rebuked himself for the snobbishness which had once prompted him to tell Tindall to bring the boy less frequently after Jake had pronounced a few words in a broad Scots accent.

'Do you know what happened?' he asked, keeping his composure with an effort.

'Well, sir, it seems Jim went to his gran's after school. He was attacked walking home. Somewhere near the castle. I don't know any more, but Sergeant McNeill told me Tindall's in a terrible way.'

'I must go and see him.' Hector felt the heavy numbness in his stomach that had been an everyday sensation in the trenches.

'I'll come with you,' Lavender said, taking his arm. 'Will you be all right here?' She turned to Mrs Alves, whose face was buried in a handkerchief.

'Yes, Mrs Drummond,' she replied tearfully. 'The girls are asleep. Tindall will appreciate you calling, I know.'

* * *

From the Grand Hotel the Scores climbed then led to the castle ruins. On both sides of the road substantial buildings sat behind high walls. Hector parked opposite the castle. Beyond, the road narrowed and a single row of small houses looked out over St Andrews Bay. Ill-lit, a glimmer in the northern sky helped Hector and Lavender find Tindall's front door. Lavender squeezed Hector's arm. He took a deep breath then gave a loud knock.

'Sheriff, Mrs Drummond, thank you for coming. Thank you.' It had taken time for the gardener to answer. He was dressed in a shirt, trousers and socks. Staggering slightly, he led the way upstairs. The air was thick with sweat and whisky. On the mantelpiece was a faded photograph of the Tindall family at the end of the War. It was hard to recognize the now broken man in the proud and erect soldier. The wooden frame, chipped and unglazed, had deteriorated with the family.

Beside the fireplace, a tired-looking man rose and made his excuses. Tindall wrung his hand and thanked him for visiting. As the man saw himself out, Tindall offered Hector and Lavender drinks, nodding towards a nearly empty whisky bottle on the table. Both refused. Lavender sat on a wooden chair beside the table, leaving Hector to occupy the stained and lop-sided armchair, the place of honour where Tindall sat his guests.

It had been a standing joke with Lavender that every Christmas when Hector delivered a hamper to the Tindalls, and sat with them for a chat, he wore old clothes. For the second time in the last half hour he felt diminished by his own superiority. Opposite him, on a second wooden chair, Tindall sat with tears running down his stern, weather-beaten face, desolate and inconsolable.

'We were so sorry to hear about Jim,' Hector said inadequately.

'Why, Sheriff? Why?'

'I can't answer that, Alf.'

'Have I no' suffered enough?' Lavender put her hand on the scratched, brown sinews of his arm. 'Have you heard what he did to him?' His voice choked.

'No.' Hector winced in anticipation.

'Dirty, dirty, ken? Then strangled him. Sorry, Mrs Drummond.'

'That's appalling.'

'You'll get him, Sheriff. Please say you'll get him, and before he hangs I'd give anything for half an hour with him, alone.' Tindall's chair creaked as he shook with rage.

'He won't get away with it, Alf, I'm sure. But it's up to the police, not me, to catch Jim's killer, and when they do, I'll be involved only at the start. He'll go to the High Court for trial before a High Court judge. I can't sit there.'

Tindall's shoulders drooped. 'But he will hang?'

'Unless he's mad, almost certainly.'

'What happened, Alf? When was he found?' Lavender asked softly.

'He was at his gran's as usual after school and she gave him tea. I'd told him to be back by six, but he was late. I thought maybe he wis visiting a friend.' He sniffed loudly. 'About seven the *haar* lifted and I went looking for him. His gran had given him a bag with scones and strawberry jam. I found it near the castle. The jam jar was smashed. There was shouting from a driveway. A man with a dog had found him. In bushes. Like a rag doll. His trousers and underpants off.' He buried his head in his hands and his whole body shuddered. 'They have to get who did it. They have to.'

Lavender turned to practical matters but it soon became clear that Tindall could not begin to deal with them. He gave her the address of his mother-in-law. She would try to see her in the morning. Hector sat back, depressed and impotent, as he had felt after a man under his command had been killed. They stayed for a while, mostly in silence, then rose to go.

As Tindall, full of gratitude, wrung his hand, Hector said, 'Don't worry about paying for the funeral, Alf. I'll do that. Come and see me about it when you're ready.'

The gardener was too choked to reply.

Back in the car, Hector looked at the outline of the castle, just visible in the dark. 'In the sixteenth century they desecrated Cardinal Beaton's body and displayed it from these walls,' he said. 'I sometimes think the human race is becoming less civilised as the years pass.'

3

Tuesday 5 July

'Will Jum see Gamagio in Heaven, Daddy?' Charlotte asked earnestly as she finished her boiled egg.

Before Hector could think up an appropriate reply, Marie sniffed loudly and corrected her younger sister. 'Don't be silly. Tortoises don't go to Heaven.'

'You can't be sure of that,' Hector said, finding bizarre comfort in the image of Jim feeding celestial lettuce to the tortoise who had failed to survive the previous winter's hibernation.

'But why Jum, Daddy?' Marie asked, dabbing her eyes.

'Jim,' he corrected automatically. It was a question he had asked himself many times during the night.

Lavender spoke firmly. 'It's not for us to understand why some things happen, but God demands that we accept them, and continue to do our best.' It was a mantra she had clung to during the darkest times of her life. Head down, she crunched a piece of toast.

Sensing her distress, Hector rang for Mrs Alves. It was time to get the girls ready for kindergarten. He said he would take them in the car and explain the situation to the motherly lady who ran the little school both girls attended.

An hour later, he arrived at court. His mood did not improve when he saw the case down for proof. Two intransigent neighbours disputed the right of one to gain access to his property using a narrow track owned by the other. After an hour of mind-numbing evidence Hector intimated that he would see both parties and their solicitors in chambers and stomped off the bench.

With no shorthand writer present, Hector pointed out the hazards and expense of continuing the battle. He told them that he would have a cigarette and a cup of coffee and suggested they should use the time wisely.

Alone, his thoughts turned to Jim's murder. He reached for the telephone he had reluctantly allowed into his chambers and asked to be connected to Inspector McTaggart, the senior police officer for the area. They had not spoken since, some months earlier, he had publicly disbelieved the inspector's evidence in a theft case.

'Good morning, Sheriff.' The tone was icy.

'Good morning, Inspector. That was a terrible murder in St Andrews last night, young Jim Tindall. I called on his father. He's my gardener. He's quite devastated. The boy was the only member of his family he had left.'

'Quite so. Absolutely tragic.'

The man sounded as emotional as a codfish. Hector pressed on: 'I wonder if you've made any headway with your investigation? Tindall's understandably desperate for the man responsible to be caught.'

For a moment, Hector thought the pompous ass was going to refuse to discuss the case. Then his voice came down the line, slow and deliberate. 'It's too early to say, Sheriff. But...I can tell you, in confidence of course, that there are two university lecturers, one a Doctor of Philosophy, who live in the same house in North Castle Street, three hundred yards or so

from the crime scene. We have been wondering for some time
if there might be a case against them under the Criminal Law
Amendment Act 1885. I'm sure you'll get my meaning. We're
looking very carefully at them.'

'Did you get any worthwhile fluid samples?'

'Some items have been sent to Dundee, yes. I don't think I
can tell you any more, Sheriff.'

'Well thank you, Inspector. If I can help in any way, I'd be
happy to do so.'

After replacing the earpiece on its hook he once more
regretted curtailing Jim's visits. He pictured him running with
Jake to the back door to taste Mrs Alves' freshly made ice cream.
He remembered setting up a treasure hunt for the boys with
clues in doggerel which had made them scream with laughter.
Jim's death would come as a dreadful shock to Jake. He hoped
Lavender had thought to contact the Warden at Glenalmond.
News of the murder would be certain to hit the press the next
day, and it would be an inevitable talking-point for the boys at
the prestigious school in Perthshire.

As he sat thinking about Jim, his anger grew. He imagined
the boy walking home. Had it been a sudden attack, or had the
boy's initial apprehension turned to fear and then to terror?
He probably experienced extremes of shame and pain before
he ceased to feel anything. He totally understood Tindall's wish
to be left alone with the murderer, so he could at least get the
visceral satisfaction of kicking and beating him senseless. Mere
hanging was far too good for him.

Forbes knocked at the door. The parties wanted more time
as they had hopes of reaching agreement. This was promising. Hector lit a cigarette and tried to concentrate on his newspaper. The sports columns were dominated by Bobby Jones,
and Hector felt proud of having talked with him the previous

evening. But after half an hour he began to fret in case his optimism regarding the negotiations had been misplaced. At length Forbes knocked again. He came in grinning broadly. The protagonists had worked out a compromise that was tolerable to both. Hector wasted no time in completing the formalities. His day's work over, he drove home thinking he had done the parties as much of a favour as he had done himself. The prospect of writing a judgment in that case had been distinctly unappealing. His thoughts returned to Jim Tindall.

'It sounds a bit unlikely to me.' Lavender screwed up her face when, over lunch and after the girls had left the table, Hector told her what McTaggart had said. 'If two intelligent homosexuals are defying the law I wouldn't expect them to dirty their own doorstep.'

'I see your point,' Hector said, picking up his last lamb chop. 'On the other hand, whoever did something so evil must have been driven by some awfully powerful inner compulsion, something he couldn't resist. I understand why the police should start by looking at these two men. They are deviants.'

'But if one of them wanted to do something like that he must have known that he and his friend would be prime suspects. I feel rather sorry for them, actually.'

'You've been thinking too much about these frightful Bloomsbury people. Homosexuality is criminal for sound reasons.' He threw down his bone emphatically.

'Maybe so. I don't know, but it would be terrible if the police looked no further than two local homosexuals when the real culprit was someone quite different.'

'I agree it would be easy for the police if they could charge one of the obvious suspects. But we just have to trust them to do their job properly. And this afternoon, I'm jolly well going to watch some golf.'

＊　＊　＊

That week the Open competitors played practice rounds. On the following Monday and Tuesday the qualifying rounds would be played, one on the Old Course and one on the adjacent New, a fine test in its own right. All competitors, however eminent and however far they had travelled, had to be among the top hundred and those tying. If they failed their championship would be over before it had begun. The qualifiers would play two rounds, one on the Wednesday and one on the Thursday. The field would be cut again, the leading players playing the third and fourth rounds on the Friday, leaving the course free for normal play on the Saturday.

Hector arrived in time to see Bobby Jones complete his practice round. Before putting on the eighteenth, he looked round the crowd and on spotting Hector, touched his cap. Conscious of curious glances from those near him, Hector returned the compliment. As he watched Jones putting, Hector felt a nudge at his elbow. It was O.B. Keeler.

'Bob and I enjoyed meeting you and your charming wife last night, Sheriff,' he whispered.

'We greatly enjoyed meeting you,' Hector replied. 'He's an impressive young man.' He nodded towards Jones, who completed his round by knocking in a tiddler one-handed.

'It's a good thing to have a sporting hero who doesn't have feet of clay. He's always had an exceptional talent. I've followed his progress for a decade, and I find myself liking and respecting him more each year.'

'We all hope for a British winner, but he's a wonderful golfer.'

'He's coming to love this place, Sheriff. I know he didn't make a great impression six years ago, but he meant what he said last night.' Keeler looked down and shuffled his feet. 'I don't like to bring this up, but Jack, Bob's caddie, told us this morning that a boy was found murdered near here last night.'

Hector looked at him sharply. 'I'm afraid so.'

'Jack also said he had been, well, violated.' He raised his eyebrows expressively.

'That's correct.'

Keeler took Hector's arm and led him away from other people. 'I feel I ought to tell you something. Last year, our National Open was at Scioto. That's in Columbus, Ohio. After the championship a boy of fourteen was found strangled, and he had been, well, raped. Do you understand what I'm saying?'

Hector was taken aback. 'I think so. I hope not. Did they not catch the murderer?'

'It got real nasty. A hobo was caught trying to sell the boy's bicycle and he was nearly killed by a lynch mob. He denied the murder but the jury convicted and the last I heard there was only the appeals process between him and Old Sparky.'

'Did you think he was guilty?'

'Hell, Sheriff, you just hope they've gotten the right man. If they have, he deserves all that's coming to him, or has come to him. It's just that this latest murder makes me wonder. The boy in Scioto was heading home in the evening when he was jumped.'

'It's difficult to believe someone connected to golf could be a child killer.'

'If we've a bad apple, we gotta get him out of our barrel. Golf is growing all the time, but something like this could kill it stone dead. Sorry, I could have put that better.'

'I just want to see that boy who was killed last night avenged. He was my gardener's son.'

'I'm sorry.'

'And it's up to the police to investigate. I know they have a

lead, but I'll certainly tell the inspector in charge of the case.'
He hesitated then decided he owed it to Keeler to warn him. 'If
the police follow this up, you could find a lot of people in the
Grand Hotel complaining about having to answer questions,
you know.'

Keeler did not flinch. 'I've thought of that, but we have to
get this S.O.B. before he kills any more kids. If it's the same
guy.'

'Are you suspicious of anyone in particular?'

'As you know, I don't care for Ralf Murnian.' He shook his
head and his mouth opened then shut as if the words were
stuck in his throat. 'I was passing through the hotel lobby yesterday and saw him go out in the fog. For all that I detest him,
I can't see him doing this. I can't imagine anyone I know doing
this.'

'What time did you see him? Can you recall what he was
wearing?'

'It would have been about half past four, maybe a touch
later. The people who'd arrived from the station had been in the
hotel for a good half hour. And he was wearing a light coloured
raincoat. That attracted my attention. I remember thinking it
strange he should have gone out when he could only see a few
yards.'

'That is strange.' Hector rubbed his forehead. 'Do you think
you could compile a list of those who were at Scioto and are
here this week? I'm sure Inspector McTaggart will find that
helpful.'

'I'll do that now.'

'Thank you for telling me this O.B., if I may call you that?'

'That's what my friends call me, and you are Hector?'

'Absolutely. I'll telephone the inspector now. Don't hesitate
to contact me if you want to.'

Thoughtfully, Hector went into the Royal and Ancient and, citing confidentiality, persuaded the secretary, Henry Gullen, to let him use the telephone in his new office at the back of the building. Sitting in the spacious, finely appointed room, he asked to be connected to the district's main police station in Cupar. The inspector was in the building but it took a long time for him to come on the line. Hector drummed his fingers on the secretary's huge desk. When McTaggart did answer, he sounded equally impatient.

'Inspector, I know you must be busy, but I've just received remarkable information. At the American Open last year a boy about Jim Tindall's age was violated and strangled. A man was convicted but he denied guilt. It's possible that Jim's killer is in town for the Open.'

McTaggart allowed several seconds of silence to elapse. 'Thank you, Sheriff. I shall note that, but as a man has been convicted in America I doubt if it helps my inquiry. As I said this morning, that is progressing well and I have personally been questioning the two gentlemen I told you about.' He gave the word 'gentlemen' undue emphasis. His tone became brusque. 'In fact, I was called away to speak to you on the telephone.'

'But this must change things, don't you see that?'

'Frankly, Sheriff, I don't. Serious crimes happen all over the world. Very few of them are linked to crimes in other countries.'

'Well, if you do decide to take this further, you should speak to Mr O.B. Keeler, an American gentleman who is staying in the Grand Hotel. He's compiling a list of those who were at Scioto last year and are here this week. He can also tell you about someone who was near the crime scene at the material time.'

'Thank you, Sheriff. I'll bear that in mind. Now, if you'll excuse me?'

Seething, Hector replaced the receiver, sat back and smoked

a cigarette. Then he took the most direct route to catch up with the Robinson/Murnian match, which had started earlier.

Beside the first fairway of the New Course he encountered a bent figure with a stick, limping in the opposite direction.

'Sheriff Hector! Have you come to see Dick give young Murnian a whipping?' Benny Sabbatini wore the baggiest pair of Lovat green tweed plus fours Hector had seen. His jacket and an enormous flat cap were both cut from the same cloth. Red white and blue check socks with black and white shoes completed his attempt at dressing appropriately for British golf. The brim of the cap came over his face, as if he wanted to conceal his identity, but to anyone who knew him he was unmistakable.

'Good afternoon, Benny. Yes, I thought I'd try and catch them. Are you heading in?'

'Goddammit, yes. I watched the first three holes but I can't keep up with these young guys. I figured I'd take a seat at that bumpy little ladies' putting course and I'll catch them playing seventeen and eighteen, if Dick hasn't won by then, of course.'

'I'm sure the ladies will be happy to see you,' Hector said, wondering what any ladies who happened to be there would make of him. Then, remembering that Sabbatini had seen Dick at Scioto, he visualised claw-like hands, strong despite arthritis, round Jim's neck. He told himself to keep his imagination in check.

Dick and Paul were half way up the long fifth when Hector caught up with them, a small crowd in their wake. News of the remarkable wager had spread. Paul was first to play his second. His swing was violent, incorporating a lunge through the ball. Hector had become a keen student of the game, consulting Harry Vardon's *How to Play Golf* more often than *Gloag on Contract*. His first sight of Paul as a player did not impress him.

Thirty yards further, Dick and his caddie were in earnest

consultation. Hector moved closer. It was evident that his patron had bought him clothes for the occasion, but what looked absurd on Sabbatini, Dick wore with a certain style. His head high, he carried himself with a confidence that had been absent the previous evening.

'There's a wee bit of wind behind so you can get there with a cleek, but you must be straight,' the caddie said. With a start, Hector realized it was Tommy Addison. Decisively, Dick pulled an iron from his bag. Tommy stepped back, causing Hector to move smartly to avoid his toes being stood on. Dick took a slow, easy practice swing then addressed the ball, which lay on a slight up slope. Two glances at the target then, with a swing combining grace, rhythm and effortless power, he sent the ball straight and true towards the green. It bounced on the top of the bank between the cross bunkers then disappeared from sight.

'That should be well up on the green, sir,' Tommy said approvingly.

Hector smiled as he followed them up the fairway. Sabbatini had arrived the previous day and arranged a big money match for Dick over a course he had never seen before, and which demanded local knowledge like no other. Instead of playing the course that morning they had gone clothes shopping and engaged a caddie who was lucky not to be in borstal. It was becoming more interesting by the minute. He asked a New Club member how the match stood and learned that Paul Murnian was one up.

'Hi, Sheriff! How are you this afternoon?' Ralf Murnian bellowed. Tommy's shoulders stiffened, but he continued to walk without turning to see who was behind him.

'Good afternoon, Mr Murnian. I hear it's a good, close match.' Hector could not avoid shaking the outstretched hand.

Like Sabbatini, Murnian had dressed in tweed, but he favoured conventional slacks and plain brown shoes. But for the newness and creases in the brown tweed he might have passed for a Scotsman. The cream slacks that Paul wore gave him a more transatlantic appearance.

'I'm mighty proud of my boy, Sheriff. He's going to make it big, I'm sure. Some say he swings the club like Hagen.'

'Some compliment,' Hector replied, wondering what Walter Hagen would make of the comparison.

Hector noted the intensity of Paul's concentration as he played his third. He was the sort of golfer who made the most of whatever talent he had.

The fifth and thirteenth holes share the biggest green on the course. While Dick three-putted from long range for a five, Paul holed a fifteen-footer for a birdie four.

Dick won the next, but Paul was still one up when they reached the ninth hole, which shared a wide fairway with the tenth. Unlike the other holes on the Old, there was room for error only to the player's right. To the left lay prickly whin bushes, heather and sand.

It was Dick's honour and he drove straight down the strip of fairway between End Hole Bunker and the wiry heather from which accuracy was impossible. Paul fiddled uncertainly with the woods in his bag. His long shots had been hooking to the left and he would need to be careful. He pulled out a black-headed driver with a big brass sole-plate. It had been well rubbed up and looked like new. When placed behind the ball, its face was skewed to the right. He swung it to and fro to get its feel. His father looked horrified but said nothing. At length he addressed the ball and swung. The impact sounded dull and, despite the angle of the clubface, the ball hooked viciously to the left. Paul banged the club on the ground in frustration.

They found the ball in a deep, difficult bunker surrounded by heather. It was known as Mrs Kruger, whom Hector pictured as an ugly South African harridan. A savage blow with his niblick got Paul out, but only just. He failed to reach the green with his third. An easy par four saw Dick reach the turn all square, the momentum of the match in his favour. He smashed a long, straight drive up the tenth.

Reverting to the driver he had used before the ninth, Paul hooked again and his ball disappeared into heather. For a time it was lost. Players, caddies and spectators spread out, hunting with varying degrees of urgency.

'Found it!' Tommy shouted.

'Well done.' The relief in Paul's voice was clear. He went to where Tommy stood, bent to check it was his ball then swore under his breath. The ball nestled deep among twisted, mature heather stems, strong enough to withstand the sharpest niblick. There were no good lies nearby but this was a stinker. 'Goddammit,' he said more loudly.

'You, caddie, I saw you kick that ball!' Ralf Murnian advanced on Tommy, his finger pointing accusingly.

'I did not, sir,' Tommy stammered, horror written across his face.

'Yes you did. Don't dare deny it,' Murnian thundered. 'Loss of hole,' he said to Dick.

'Did you move his ball, even accidentally?' Dick asked.

'No, sir. I didnae touch it. I saw it right in front of me and shouted straight away. I let Mr Murnian check it was his.'

'I saw you kick it.' Murnian, senior, stood beside the ball, feet apart, daring anyone to contradict him.

'The boy didnae kick the ball. I was beside him when he found it.' The speaker was Paul's caddie, Wullie Kay, a man in his forties and one of the best caddies in the town.

'He lifted his foot. I saw it.' Glaring at Wullie, the elder Murnian was not about to give in.

'Aye, you've got to in that stuff. And he put it straight down.' Wullie was adamant.

'Sheriff Drummond, what do you make of this? I saw that boy kick my son's ball.' The tone was harsh and challenging.

Hector had been impressed by the way Tommy had steered Dick round the course. 'I didn't see anything of that sort going on, but I can't say I was watching closely.' He glanced at Tommy, who looked appealingly at him. 'It would be a very serious matter for any caddie to do such a thing, and I cannot imagine any sensible person kicking a ball with so many people around.'

Murnian scowled. 'But everyone was looking down, not round about to prevent cheating.'

Hector said smoothly, 'I'm surprised you were not too busy searching for the ball yourself. After all, you have most to gain if your son wins.'

His voice shaking with anger, Dick spoke loudly. 'I'm not having it said I won by cheating.' He went close up to Murnian and looked down at him contemptuously. 'I know all about you, the things you've done. If you're so keen for your son to win this goddam hole, you can have it. But you get it because I'm giving it to you. Tommy did not cheat.' Without a backward glance, he strode to his ball in the middle of the fairway, picked it up and made for the eleventh tee. Murnian stood immobile then walked over to Wullie. 'Just who the hell do you think you are to tell me I'm wrong?' Their faces were inches apart. 'Put my son's clubs down right now and get out of my sight.'

'You owe me wages, but I cannae abide a common cheat.' There was a loud clack from the hickory shafts as Wullie threw the bag to the ground. With slow dignity, he started the long walk home.

'You won't get a dime outta me,' Murnian shouted at his back. He turned to the ginger-haired young man, who, with the mousy woman, had been following the match with barely concealed indifference. 'Enda, they're ganging up on us and your brother needs a caddie. You take his clubs.' Obediently, Enda detached himself from the woman's hand and picked up the clubs. As he adjusted the strap on his shoulder his face was full of sullen resentment. There was something far stronger in the woman's expression.

Appearing embarrassed, Paul had not intervened in the confrontation. When he stepped on to the tee of the short eleventh, Dick did not look at him. 'Your honour and you're one up,' he said curtly.

'Sorry about that,' Paul muttered.

'Say that to the caddies,' Dick snarled.

Paul shrugged then, after a couple of practice swings, hit a mashie safely on to the green. Dick's shot was similar. Up till that point the players had complimented good shots and conceded short putts. Now there was no quarter asked or given. Paul's hook cost him the fourteenth, but three putts lost Dick the sixteenth. One down with two to play, he viciously banged his putter against his foot and winced. In a stiff, controlled way, he walked to the fence beside the railway line where the seventeenth tee was placed.

In front of the tee of the famous Road Hole a low stone wall sat at an angle. Behind the wall and out of bounds lay a railway yard where ominous-looking black wooden sheds rose up to confront players and obscure their view of the hole. Wasting no time, Paul struck his drive sweetly. It sailed over the sheds with only a little hook spin. Dick's face twitched as, standing beside Tommy, his fingers went from one clubhead to another.

'You can do it, Dick.' Sabbatini's voice rasped from the gallery.

'See that name, D. Anderson, in big letters on the side of the shed?' Tommy asked.

'That's all I can see,' Dick said sharply.

'Play over the d in Anderson.' It was an order.

Shrugging, Dick teed up his ball. A practice swing and he was ready to play.

'Stop!' Tommy shouted.

'Goddammit.' Dick banged his club on the ground and stepped back.

'Train coming,' Tommy explained. Hissing, chugging and clanking with ever-increasing volume, a passenger train from Leuchars was soon on them, passing within feet of the tee and shrouding them briefly in a cloud of smoky steam. Seconds after it had gone by, a loud hoot warned of its arrival at St Andrews station. 'You can go now, sir,' Tommy said.

'The d of Anderson, is it?' Dick said thoughtfully. The interruption had given him time to regroup. He swung back slowly and kept his eye on the back of the ball. When he looked up it was flying over the e. Clapping from some of the spectators huddled round the back of the sixteenth green reassured him. He walked quickly off the tee, anxious to avoid Sabbatini's encouragement. When he rounded the corner of the sheds, Dick saw the hole stretch in front of him, his ball right of centre, but in the fairway. For his second, Paul struck a good, long brassie into the breeze. His ball climbed on to the top plateau of the narrow green, the road to its right, the Road Bunker to its left. But then a cruel slope sent it swinging off the plateau to the left, so the Road Bunker lay between it and the hole.

'I have to go for it,' Dick said, his hand on the head of his brassie.

'No you don't,' Tommy said, as authoritatively as he could. 'Play short with an iron, and stay to the right of the fairway. You've a better chance of a four that way.'

For a moment Dick hesitated, but again did as he was told. When he reached his ball he turned to Tommy and grinned. 'What do I do now?' he asked.

'Aim six feet right of the pin, take your mashie niblick, land it on the top level and let it run up the green.' Dick took a couple of practice swings then played the prescribed shot. It finished four feet past the hole.

From an impossible position, Paul putted back on to the plateau and narrowly missed a twenty-five footer to take five.

'The line's a full inch left of the hole. And keep yer bloody head still, sir,' Tommy whispered as he handed Dick his putter. Dick went to the side of the green and practised several smooth strokes, not looking up on his follow-through. He stood over the ball for longer than usual before hitting it firmly into the back of the hole. The match was all square.

Both drives bounced over Grannie Clark's Wynd, the road that crossed the eighteenth. Both seconds cleared the dip at the front of the green known as the Valley of Sin. From the right side of the green, Paul putted and missed, his ball stopping directly between Dick's ball and the hole. When he saw what he had done, he smiled then nodded towards his father.

'What a time for a stymie,' Dick muttered.

Tommy got down on his hunkers to read the green. Dick's ball lay fifteen feet behind the hole, Paul's three feet. 'His ball's a good guide for you,' Tommy said, after looking from several angles. 'You want to pass just to its left. Your putt will swing to the right at the end, but it'll have to die into the hole. Don't hit it too hard.'

After more practice strokes and a nerve-jangling wait as

he stood over the ball, Dick struck his birdie putt, his head motionless. It rolled down the green past Paul's ball then, as its momentum slowed, broke sharply to the right. For half a second it hovered on the left edge of the hole then toppled in, just as Tommy had read it. Dick raised his arms in triumph, the spectators applauded, and Paul offered his hand perfunctorily. For the first time in the match, at the time that mattered most, Dick was one up.

'If you pay by cheque, it's S A B B A T I N I,' Benny spelled it out. Beside him, there was a twisted smile on Dick's face. 'But I'll take cash,' Benny crowed, loud enough for Murnian to hear as he crossed the road to the Grand Hotel.

At the foot of the broad stone steps leading up to the Royal and Ancient clubhouse, Enda dropped his brother's clubs, mutely refusing to carry them further. There was a smile on the mousy woman's face as she took his hand and they went off together towards the West Sands. Unusually animated, Dick told his happy sponsor how the match had gone, stressing Tommy's importance. Sabbatini drew a piece of paper from his wallet, unfolded it and handed it to the boy. 'I reward good service, son. We're happy to have you on the team for this championship.'

FIVE POUNDS was written on the paper. Tommy had never seen a five pound note before and tried to mask his shock. He folded it reverently and placed it in his hip pocket, which he carefully buttoned. After arranging to meet Dick the next day, he cleaned and rubbed up the clubs then returned them to the foyer of the Grand. Humming an old tune, he set off up Golf Place. His heart sank when he heard a familiar voice behind him.

'Thomas Addison, you're coming with me.' The heavy hand of Sergeant McNeill grasped his shoulder and he was bundled into the police car.

* * *

Hector had begun to tell Lavender about his afternoon when, from the hall, the telephone rang.

'Mrs Alves will be bathing the girls, dear,' Lavender said.

'Confounded machine,' Hector grumbled as he got up. When he reached the hall the ringing had stopped, but it sounded again.

It was Sergeant McNeill from the police office in Queen's Gardens. 'Sheriff, I've arrested a lad, Addison. I read in *The Courier* that you'd sent him to borstal yesterday, but I found him this evening, bold as brass, walking up Golf Place. And when I searched him he had a five pound note on him. He had some cock and bull story about earning it as a caddie. He swears you'll vouch for him, sir. I told him he'd finish up doing more time....'

Hector sounded as grave as he could. 'You did the right thing to telephone, McNeill, but actually the lad is right. I changed the sentence yesterday, but the reporter had left by the time I did so. And he has been caddying. I saw him myself, and because of his skill an American gentleman won a lot of money. I can well believe he got an exceptionally generous tip.'

There was silence from the other end of the line. 'So you want me to let him go?' the policeman asked.

'I think you'll have to, with an apology.'

'An apology?'

'Well he didn't deserve to be arrested, not today anyway. It's up to you, though.' He knew he shouldn't do it, but Hector could not resist baiting McNeill.

'All right, sir. I'll do as you suggest.'

'Thank you, McNeill, and now you can get on with trying to find Jim Tindall's killer.'

'Inspector McTaggart has that inquiry well in hand, sir. Goodnight, sir.'

'What was that about?' Lavender asked when Hector returned to the drawing room.

'Some people can't stop making asses of themselves,' he said, taking out a cigarette.

*   *   *

As he walked down South Street towards the West Port, Tommy thought how he should spend the five pounds that Sergeant McNeill had grudgingly returned to him. The first priority was food for his mother and sister. Then there was the silver he had stolen. He'd visit Sam McAskill later. In a thieves' bargain, no questions asked, McAskill had paid Tommy four pounds, a fraction of the true value. Tommy hoped he might give the silver back to him for four pounds, ten shillings. No harm in asking, anyway.

He replayed in his mind the events of the day. It had been the talk of the caddie shed that wee Jim Tindall had been murdered. He had barely exchanged a couple of words with the boy, but it was shocking all the same. That sort of thing didn't happen in St Andrews. From what he had overheard in the police station, they were holding two university types in Cupar. It was a pity they could only hang them.

The day had improved when he met Dick Robinson. He had not dared to hope for a good player, but he had never seen a golfer swing more sweetly or powerfully than the tall young American, and he had his bag for the Open. If he could just hole more putts, he might even win. As his own match had gone up the second, Bobby Jones himself had been playing the seventeenth. Tommy had watched awe-struck as the great man had hit a wooden club for his second. It had looked perfect yet had rolled on to the road. That had given him the confidence to tell Dick to go short and right. If Jones could not be relied on to hit the green, ordinary mortals should certainly play safe. Dick's swing was more upright than Jones' but, to Tommy's eye, no less pleasing. He was still beaming as he reached the door of his house near the Kinness Burn.

A pungent smell of tobacco in the hallway told him instantly that something was wrong. No voice greeted him, which was unusual. Saying nothing, he went quickly to the kitchen door, threw it open, and stepped inside. A fist hit him very hard in the face and he fell back, dazed.

When he came to, he saw his mother and sister cowering on the other side of the room. Two burly men wearing dark suits and Trilbys stood in the middle. Tommy had seen one of them before. The other had a pipe in his mouth.

'Mam, Jeannie, are you all right?' He tasted blood as he spoke and one of his teeth hurt.

'We're fine, son, but your faither's gone away and he owes these gentlemen a lot of money.'

'Gone? Where?'

'I don't know, son. He said something about Edinburgh.'

'He knew fine we were coming, and so did youse. He owes thirty-one pounds, eight and five pence, and it's going up all the time it's no' paid.' Tommy remembered the coarse voice. He guessed the men came from Dundee.

'So you settle up for him, or you get what we'd have given him.' The pipe-smoker's voice, though less broad, was more menacing. Its owner punched his left palm with a loud smack to emphasise the point.

'What have you got on you?' The first man stepped towards Tommy.

'Nothing.'

'Nothing. That's no' a word we like, is it?'

'Don't like it at all,' said the man with the pipe. With a swift movement he grabbed Jeannie's hair and twisted it until she cried.

'No, no,' Tommy shouted.

'So you do have something?' The first man stood on his foot and twisted his heel.

'Yes.' Tommy gasped in pain.

'What?'

He had only the five pound note. He unbuttoned his hip pocket and drew it out. The first man took it, his eyebrows raised.

'If that's nothing, so is this.' A second punch knocked Tommy's head against the wall.

'We'll give you a month to find thirty pounds, or you know what to expect, all of you.' The cold eyes of the pipe-smoker looked at them in turn. 'And we don't care how you get it.'

'But it's just gone up,' Tommy's mother wailed.

'Interest.' The first man spat out the word as they left.

Together in the middle of their kitchen floor the little family hugged each other, sobbing with despair.

*   *   *

'I can't get over the narrow-mindedness of that policeman.' Lavender took a last spoonful of sago pudding.

'I saw plenty of his type during the War. Everything done by the book, no imagination, no originality. You get a deviant crime so look for the nearest deviants and assume they're guilty till something different is proved.' Hector swallowed a mouthful of claret. 'Of course, maybe one of them is guilty.'

'Well I just hope that if he doesn't get anywhere in his interviews, he widens his net before all the Open people leave town.'

'I wouldn't bet on it, so let's hope he's got it right first time and collects enough evidence,' Hector said.

4

Wednesday 6 July

'There's a letter from Glenalmond,' Mrs Alves said, setting a tray down on the sideboard. As Hector attacked his boiled egg, Lavender read her son's letter.

'Jake wrote this on Sunday,' she commented. 'He's still enjoying cricket. He had a good innings last Saturday. Thirty-four's good, isn't it?'

'Depends on the bowling, but yes, it's good.'

'He's looking forward to Commem. Says he wants lots of smoked salmon sandwiches and chocolate cake for the picnic.'

'And we'll need bags of jelly,' Charlotte piped up, earning Marie's most grown-up frown and a beaming smile from her father.

'You never forget your first Commem,' he said, then added wistfully, 'The place is completely transformed for a day.'

'Memories of John?' she asked lightly.

'We got squiffy on champagne, but no one seemed to mind too much.' They exchanged smiles.

Lavender turned the page. 'This is strange. He wants to speak to us before the end of term. He says it's important. Can we take him out after chapel this Sunday?'

'Don't see why not. What's bothering him?'

'I've no idea. I'll write today and say we'll take him out for Sunday lunch. Or maybe I'd better telephone, check that he's all right after hearing...you know.'

Neither had slept well. When they got up they adhered to an unspoken agreement to behave as normal, particularly in front of the girls. Frowning, Hector applied a thick layer of butter to his toast. 'It's a pity he'll be at school next week so he'll miss the Open. Talking about missing things, you really don't mind not going to the Royal Garden Party?'

'Really. I'd far rather you saw the last day of the Open. What's the King thinking of, picking that Friday? Anyway, according to *The Scotsman* they've invited about seven thousand from all over Scotland to Holyrood, and I don't fancy queuing for hours to catch the ferry home.'

Hector shuddered. 'As long as you don't mind, I'm happy to miss it.'

'And I'll be happy if you enjoy the Open. You have arranged to take that Tuesday off for Commem?'

'It's been scored off in the court diary for months. Did I tell you James Irvine said to me the other day that he's going to make the speech?'

'The university principal? That should be good. I'd assumed they'd have some boring old general. By the way, will you be in for lunch?'

'I don't think so, darling. Because that dreadful case settled yesterday I don't need to be in till the afternoon, so I'll go to the course then have lunch in the club.'

She shook her head. 'You have organized things well this week.'

'It's just good luck,' he said defensively as she passed Jake's letter to him, removed the knitted cosy from her egg and deftly cut the top off.

After Mrs Alves had taken the girls to get ready for kinder-garten, Lavender spoke earnestly. 'Hector, do you think any-thing is wrong with Jake?'

He picked up the letter and looked at it a second time. 'I wouldn't have thought so. He seems quite cheerful.'

'Commem will be very important for Jake. He's very aware that you were at Glenalmond. He does regard you as his father, you know.'

He turned his head and exhaled, careful not to blow smoke over Lavender. 'He's a fine boy. You should be proud of him.'

'We should both be proud of him,' she corrected.

Catching the rebuke, he said, 'Of course. I didn't mean...'

'It's not easy for Jake. He has his life with us, all the time knowing he's the heir of Lammerstane.'

'Complicated, I agree,' Hector said. His memories of Lam-merstane were bitter-sweet; holidays spent there as a boy, with John, playing war games in the long corridors, building hide-outs in the woods, casting for salmon in the brown waters of the Tweed; later standing back, helpless as his girl fell in love with his best friend. Built by Jake's great-grandfather, the Taylor-Smith family home was just outside Coldstream, on the Scottish side of the river. Their weaving business had pros-pered, but John's father, broken-hearted by the loss of his son, had died before the end of the War. He left the house and a small fortune to Jake, subject to a number of conditions. The boy would inherit on his twenty-first birthday. In the mean-time, the estate was administered by trustees.

Hector was relieved when a knock told him the girls were ready to go. 'Right,' he said in his jolliest voice. 'Kiss Mummy goodbye.' Before Lavender kissed him, she shook her head slightly and smiled.

*   *   *

When he saw the town's police car outside D. & W. Auchterlonie's shop, a group of excited bystanders peering through the window, Hector's curiosity was aroused. He parked round the corner in Golf Place and went to see what was happening. 'It's the sheriff,' someone said, and the crowd parted to let him pass.

Inside, Sergeant McNeill appeared to be pointing out various things to Constable Gemmell, a young man Hector thought had a promising future so long as he did not learn too much from McNeill. Gemmell paused in his note-taking when he saw Hector.

'Has something happened?' Hector asked.

'Oh, Sheriff. It's you.' McNeill said, his voice quavering. 'There's been a murder. Another terrible murder.'

The main area of the shop looked as it always did, drab, with sparse displays of hand-crafted clubs at different stages of construction. It was quality and reputation rather than salesmanship that attracted customers. Behind the desk on which business was done, two men sat. One was elderly with a white moustache, the other in his twenties with a huge, hooked nose. Both looked shell-shocked.

'It's Hamish McCann, Sheriff. He was one of our best craftsmen.' Laurie Auchterlonie, the younger of the two, spoke. Dressed as usual in a shirt, tie and plus fours, he gestured with a meaty hand towards the door at the back of the shop which led to the workroom. Beside him, Willie, the 1893 Open Champion and Laurie's father, shook his head sadly.

The door was ajar. Hector pushed it open and immediately caught his breath. A man dressed in a stained shirt and slacks was bent over the workbench, his head and arms at unnatural angles. His right hand, calloused and rough, was clenched round a metal file seized in his death throes. Lifeless eyes stared at the wall. Beside the twisted mouth, a congealed bloodstain darkened the light-coloured wood. On the left side of McCann's back his shirt was saturated with blood. A long metal spike with a wooden handle that gave it the shape of a T protruded from the stain. Hector immediately recognized it. Willie had been proud to show off his collection of golfing artefacts. This awl had been used to make feather balls, long before the era of the rubber-cored ball.

Willie loved to describe how the ball-maker would boil up enough feathers to fill a top hat. He then compressed them into a leather casing using the sharp metal point of this two foot awl, pressing the wooden handle against his chest as a brace. In a corner of the workroom beside the door, the other tools of the old ball-maker were displayed, smaller awls, cutters, a pot of white paint and a top hat filled with white feathers. The process was known to have damaged the lungs, but not the sort of damage suffered by Hamish McCann. The biggest awl had been thrust right through his chest from behind and now pinned him to his workbench.

'When was he found?' Hector asked.

'Eight this morning when Laurie Auchterlonie arrived for work,' McNeill said.

'Have you any idea who did it, or when he died?'

'He was cold when we got here. I'm waiting for the photographer. Inspector McTaggart said he'd be here soon.'

Steeling himself, Hector felt the dead man's limbs. *Rigor mortis* was almost complete. His curiosity satisfied so far as it could be, he tried to console the Auchterlonies before leaving. As he struggled to find words that were appropriate, one of the caddies burst into the shop.

'Sergeant McNeill, Sergeant McNeill. There's been another murder,' he gasped.

The colour drained from McNeill's face and he leaned against a wall. 'What,' he asked weakly. 'Who? Where?'

'Out at the far end of the course, sir. In the bunker at the ninth, Mrs Kruger. He's wearing a white dinner jacket so someone said it was an American gentleman.'

Seconds passed before anyone spoke.

'Do you know where Mrs Kruger is?' Hector asked.

McNeill shook his head.

'Why don't I take you out there? I'm sure we can leave PC Gemmell to look after this body until the inspector and the photographer get here.'

'Thank you, Sheriff. That would be very good of you.' McNeill smiled gratefully.

With McNeill in the front seat, Hector drove out the West Sands road as far as he could then led the way across rough ground and the New Course towards the Old. They passed high sand dunes bound together by silver-grey marram grass and whins whose sharp, green needles gained strength as their yellow flowers died. By the time they reached the narrow path through whins that took them to the ninth green of the Old, both men were breathing heavily. Hector stopped for a moment, taking in the scene. There was something odd about the limp white flag and the angle of the ninth pin, but, looking towards the Estuary, their attention was drawn to a group of four men standing in a semi-circle in the heather.

The men were staring down into the bunker that had trapped Paul Murnian. One, a tall, stooped man whom Hector recognized as a greenkeeper, spotted them and said something. The rest stepped back.

The body was face down in the middle of the sand, legs and arms outstretched as if performing star jumps. He wore black dinner trousers and his white tuxedo spread behind him like a pair of wings. He was thick-set, with dark hair flecked with grey. The skin round the mouth was dark and mottled. Grains of sand remained stuck to the bulging, blood-shot right eye. There was a small, round hole, blackened but curiously bloodless, in his right temple.

'He's been shot in the face,' one of the men, a golfer, said with gloomy satisfaction. 'Colin Fyfe went in to get a good look and lost his breakfast.'

Hector saw a trail of vomit leading from beside the head to a sticky pool beside the turf wall. The sand round the body had been smoothed over, but a set of footprints followed the trail of vomit.

'The body's all stiff,' the youngest of the golfers muttered. From the shame on his face, Hector deduced his must be the breakfast in the bunker.

'Does anyone know who he is?' McNeill asked.

Hector said, 'I'm almost certain it's Ralf Murnian. He is, was, American and he's been staying with his family at the Grand. His son, Paul, is playing in the Open.'

There were murmurs of surprise that he should know this. Hector could see McNeill did not have much of a clue what he should do, and hoped Inspector McTaggart would be more inspired. He tried to commit the details of the scene to memory.

'Who found the body?' Hector asked.

'Young Colin, here.' The gloomy-looking man who had first spoken to them indicated the lad. 'We were having a quick foursome before they start practising for the Open. I think there were two games in front of us. We would have passed right by only Colin hooked off the ninth tee. Bill Thomson's back on the tee, by the way. He's telling everyone to go straight over to the eleventh, missing out nine and ten. We sent a caddie from the following match to fetch the sergeant.'

'What time did you find him?' McNeill asked.

'Ten, quarter past eight.'

'And only Colin Fyfe's been in the bunker?'

The four men nodded.

'And you are?' McNeill turned to the decrepit-looking greenkeeper, who was leaning on the long bamboo switch he used to clear the greens of dew.

'McSwegan, sir. I wis switching the greens on the New when I saw there was something going on here.' Hector had often seen him trundling round the course, bent, slow-moving and wearing the same tattered old coat and cap whatever the season.

'You,' McNeill addressed Colin Fyfe, who was the leanest of the four, and the fittest looking. 'Run in as quick as you can, go to D. and W. Auchterlonie's shop and tell Inspector McTaggart what's happened. I'll stay with this body.'

Fyfe shuffled his feet but made no move.

'Before you go, Colin, is it? You'd better tell us exactly what you did earlier.' Hector tried to sound encouraging.

'Well, sir, as this bunker's so far off line we wouldnae have seen him at all if I hadnae hooked.' He demonstrated an exaggerated roll of the wrists. 'I thought the gentleman had been drinking. He wouldnae have been the first to sleep it off in a bunker. I didnae think about footprints and I jumped in and shook him. But he was stiff. Then I scratched the sand away from his face.' He paused and put a hand to his mouth. 'The sight turned my stomach, sir, I'm sorry, but it came on me so quick. Then I climbed out of the bunker. That's my ball, there.' He pointed to the far side of the bunker where a ball lay. 'Can I reach down and pick it up, sir?'

'Certainly not,' McNeill sounded shocked. 'This is a murder inquiry and that ball is evidence. Now, off you go.'

Hector said nothing, although he could understand the

resentful look that returned to the lad's face. There was something familiar about him. Hector struggled to remember where he had seen him before. 'Where did you shake him?' he asked.

'His shoulder.'

'Did you touch anything else in the bunker?'

'No, sir.'

Hector turned to the rest of them. 'Have any of you seen anything at all that was suspicious or unusual this morning, or even last night?'

They looked at each other, heads shaking. McNeill harrumphed.

To Colin, Hector said, 'Please could you go back to town as the Sergeant has asked? It would be a great help.'

'As long as someone takes my clubs. I'll have to get straight up to the shop to do my deliveries.' Colin pointed to the four bags lying nearby in the heather. At the mention of deliveries, Hector realized he was the Aikman Terras grocers' boy who sped recklessly round the streets on his bicycle, struggling to keep brown paper parcels of cured ham, ground coffee and fresh eggs safe in the capacious wicker basket above the front wheel. Two weeks earlier he had narrowly missed colliding with Hector at the West Port, the ancient gateway into the Royal Burgh. He had not stayed at the scene for a ticking-off. Hector fixed him with a beady eye.

A look of alarm spread across Colin's face. 'It's Inspector McTaggart that I ask for?' he asked. Without waiting for confirmation, he set off at a brisk trot.

Hector felt that he should stay to support McNeill until McTaggart arrived, but there was little he could do. As the policeman laboriously noted names and addresses, he wandered up to the ninth green where his eye was caught once more by the angle of the flagstick. He pulled the black and white hollow metal tube out of the hole and discovered that near the bottom it was bent and dented. The cord that secured the white flag at the top was twisted and the flag did not unfurl properly to take the easterly breeze. With the championship imminent, the course was kept in pristine condition and a pin like that would be replaced as soon as a greenkeeper saw it. When he returned to the bunker and told McNeill what he had found, the sergeant's face registered nothing.

Half an hour later, Inspector McTaggart arrived. He showed no sign of having hurried over rough ground. His black shoes gleamed and his trousers and tunic boasted creases fit to grace a parade ground. He greeted Hector with chilly politeness, his expression of superior disapproval barely changing when he looked down on the body.

Hector did not want to stay longer than necessary. Addressing McTaggart in his best army officer's voice he said, 'I suggest you should have a look at the pin on the ninth green, Inspector. It's been damaged recently.'

The policeman gave him a thin-lipped smile. 'That's very interesting, Sheriff. One of my men will have a look at it.'

Incensed by his patronising tone, Hector turned on his heel and tramped back to his car.

Still fuming twenty minutes later, he drove to the Royal and Ancient where he ordered a whisky and soda. He did not talk about his morning but news of the murders had reached everyone. At lunch one of the younger members, too young to have fought in the War, told the old, black joke about the St Andrews golfer who dropped down dead on the ninth green. His partner carried him all the way in. When asked if this had not been a great weight, he said: 'Not really. It was picking him up and putting him down between shots that was tricky.' While the rest of the company laughed, the image of the two

dead faces he had seen that morning swam chillingly through
Hector's mind.

*   *   *

Hector was subdued and pensive as he drove to Cupar after
lunch. Police reinforcements from West Fife had arrived in
St Andrews, their presence unsettling rather than reassuring.
Soon the place would be crawling with newspaper reporters,
most of them even less appealing than the *Dundee Courier*
man. The Open itself would be stained by association with St
Andrews, which in the last twenty-four hours probably had
more murders per head of population than New York.

When he arrived at court, Forbes greeted him with a
Cheshire Cat grin. 'First appearances, my lord. The two men
they say killed that boy in St Andrews. They've only got them
on acts of gross indecency with one another, but they think one
of them might crack later and confess.' As an ex-policeman,
Forbes had access to behind the scenes information which he
disseminated with an air of contrived confidentiality.

Under Scottish criminal procedure, someone accused of
serious crime would first appear, with their solicitor, in private
before a sheriff 'for examination'. But very little examining was
done. Before the sheriff, and in the presence of the procurator
fiscal, the local prosecutor, the accused would appear. Usually
he would say nothing except to give his name, but it was an
opportunity for his solicitor to move for bail, except in cases of
murder or treason. The accused might give a declaration stating
his position, but most took their lawyer's advice and kept silent.

In Cupar, first appearances took place in the sheriff's chambers, the accused safely manacled to a sturdy policeman. Some
accused were blasé, others overwhelmed and petrified. Hector

had, he thought, seen all sorts, but he struggled to conceal his surprise when Dr Henry Madsen and Jocelyn Varvell were led in together.

The first accused, Madsen, appeared to have modelled his appearance on the Bloomsbury writer, Lytton Strachey. His light blue tweed suit was crumpled and stained, his beard untrimmed. But he held his head high with the expression of a ham actor playing a martyr on his way to the stake. Varvell, by contrast, was clearly in despair. Seeming to strain against his handcuffs, he tossed his head to get his floppy blond hair out of his eyes. Once he had succeeded, he gazed beseechingly at Hector.

The procurator fiscal's petition, brought under the Criminal Law Amendment Act 1885, which had been the downfall of Oscar Wilde, charged them with acts of gross indecency in the house they shared near to where Jim was killed. It described a variety of activities involving, in legal parlance, the mouths, naked private members and naked hind parts of both men. Hector's lip curled as he read it.

A solicitor from Edinburgh named Wilson represented both accused. His pink cheeks and camp manner reminded Hector of a pantomime dame. After making no plea or declaration, he moved eloquently for bail. The accused were upstanding members of the university community, he said, causing the policeman holding Madsen to smirk. After five minutes he reached a passionate crescendo then subsided.

Dull and dry by comparison, Mr Newton, the procurator fiscal, opposed bail; there was a real possibility that a further charge, for which bail could not be granted, might follow. Further inquiries in relation to that were necessary.

Hector rubbed his forehead. Normally he would grant bail on the indecency charge, the only one before him. His judicial oath enjoined him to 'do right to all manner of people after the laws and usages of the Realm, without fear or favour, affection or ill-will'. He knew he should release Madsen and Varvell on bail.

But in America the hobo had to be rescued from a lynch mob. He had been safer in custody. St Andrews was not America. You would not get a lynching in Fife. Or would you? Goodness knows what indignities they might be made to suffer in jail, but there would be at least some protection for them.

Hector cleared his throat. He glanced at each accused then fixed his gaze on the papers in front of him. Varvell's breathing was audible and harsh. Hector shook his head then spoke slowly: 'I shall refuse bail and continue the case for further examination.' He was glad he was not obliged to give his reasons.

Madsen's loud sniff expressed disappointment and contempt. Varvell burst into tears, shouting 'no, no'. The escorts ushered them roughly out of the room. Hector heard Varvell shouting in the corridor, 'I'll be raped, I tell you. I'll be raped'. Forbes smiled his approval but that did not make Hector feel any better.

*   *   *

'It was the lesser of two evils,' Hector explained to Lavender. 'If Tindall believed they were guilty and living just round the corner from him, anything could have happened. Remember, he can be a bit hot-headed. Anyway, they'll almost certainly have to go to prison for what they've done with each other. The case will come before me and I'll take the time on remand into consideration. I have to do my public duty, you know.'

She waved his cigarette smoke away from her face. 'You're smoking too much,' she said. 'You know it's not good for you.'

'I was no more out of puff than McNeill when we rushed to find Murnian. And our own doctor chain smokes.'

'Neither of them has been half choked to death by mustard gas,' she snapped, then turned to stare out of the window. More softly she added, 'I couldn't bear to lose you, you silly sausage.'

He went to the drinks table and poured himself a second whisky with a token squirt from the soda siphon. When he went to refresh her glass, she shook her head. They sat in uneasy silence for a time.

'Do you think all three murders could be linked in some way?' she asked after a while.

'I don't see how they can be as they're so different, but they've happened within such a short space of time. If there's just one killer, that lets Madsen and Varvell out as they were being grilled by McTaggart when Murnian and McCann were killed.' He took a deep swallow. 'I hope McTaggart can see that.'

'Why don't you have another bash at McTaggart, darling, man to man? He's now got three murders to solve and under the tailor's dummy exterior he's bound to be worried.'

'Perhaps I will. I can't stop thinking about poor Tindall. Do you remember how he sort of flopped when I said I couldn't do much?'

'Well maybe you should. Do something, I mean. Ask some questions. The Americans should be willing to co-operate. Remember, you're the local sheriff. They're not to know you're not a sort of Scottish Wyatt Earp.' She sniffed the air. 'I think I smell dinner.'

Lavender's nose was right. They had just sat down when the back door bell sounded. Mrs Alves' manner was hesitant as she came in.

'It's Tindall, Sheriff. He's come out on his bicycle. He says it's about the funeral.' She coughed and pulled herself up straight.

'I said you were in the middle of your meal, but I thought I should tell you.'

Hector was already up. 'I'll see him now,' he said. 'Is he in the kitchen?'

5

Thursday 7 July

Somewhere near a shell explodes. The duck-board under him shakes. In front of him a line of corpses, big bluebottles crawling over glazed eyeballs, in and out of gaping mouths.

Field Marshal Haig himself comes down the line, glaring. McTaggart behind him, not a hair out of place. A bellow from Haig, 'Why aren't these corpses in uniform?' Hector protests, 'They are, sir.' Haig points behind Hector. There, in civvies, two more bodies: the clubmaker and Murnian.

'Hector, wake up!' Lavender grabbed his shoulder. His pyjamas drenched in sweat, he was in the foetal position, whimpering.

He shook himself, wiped the discharge from his eyes. 'Sorry, darling, did I make a noise?'

'It's all right. It's all right.' She hugged him, reassuring herself as much as him. 'You were back there?'

'Yes. There were these dead men...'

'Tell me later, if it will help. It's ten past four. I'll make a cup of tea. Stay there,' she ordered.

By the time she returned he had collected his wits. Sitting up to drink his tea and nibble a bit of Mrs Alves' shortbread, he said, 'I can't stop thinking about these murders. And now I'm to do the eulogy for Jim, once the funeral is arranged.'

'You'll do it beautifully, and worrying won't do any good.'

He smiled. 'You're right, as usual. Let's try and get some sleep. I wish these confounded birds would shut up.' The dawn chorus was in full voice, cooing wood pigeons to the fore.

*   *   *

While Lavender got back to sleep, Hector did not. After replaying in his mind all his dealings with Murnian and his family, he rose quietly and early. A long soak in his bath helped to gather his thoughts. As a surprised Mrs Alves bustled to prepare some breakfast, he telephoned the police office at Cupar.

The St Andrews operator was slow in answering then slower in connecting him. At length he spoke with a sergeant, who confirmed that Inspector McTaggart would be in the office by quarter to nine and could see Hector then.

After twenty minutes on a hard seat in the police station, Hector checked his watch. It was three minutes past nine. Ignoring the sergeant's protest, Hector strode purposefully into the room he knew to be the inspector's office. He did not pause to stub out his cigarette. McTaggart wrinkled his nose and did not rise from his chair.

'Good morning, Sheriff. How may I help you? I'm afraid it's going to be a busy day.'

There was nothing on the inspector's desk except a leather blotter with a pristine sheet of white blotting paper. Without waiting for an invitation, Hector sat on the chair opposite McTaggart's.

'I met Murnian and his family and thought I should give you some important background to what is clearly a difficult situation.'

'Difficult, Sheriff?' He raised his left eyebrow. His black

tunic with its high neck and sharp creases reminded Hector of a bellboy with ideas above his station.

'You've had three different murders within two days. Surely you'll be looking for a connection?'

'Different murders is right, Sheriff. I shall gather the evidence on each and see where it takes me.'

Hector snorted. 'You are aware that Ralf Murnian was a quite unusual man who led a very interesting life?'

'I've heard gossip about him.'

'I think his best friend would tell you he sailed far too close to the wind. His family relationships seemed strange as well. I'm sure one of his sons, Enda, resents the golfing son, Paul.'

'I've heard quite a bit about the match that took place yesterday afternoon. Do you know anything about it?'

'I saw most of it. There was no love lost between Murnian and Mr Sabbatini.'

'I'm particularly interested in the quarrel over the caddie, Addison, kicking Paul Murnian's ball.'

'I'm as sure as I can be without seeing exactly what the caddie did, that Ralf Murnian was trying to cheat.'

'Whether he was or not, the caddie, who is a local housebreaker who ought to be in borstal, would have every reason to want revenge. Do you not agree?'

'No, I don't agree. He was totally vindicated.'

'Not totally vindicated, surely, Sheriff. Only William Kay supports his claim that he did not kick the ball. It was Ralf Murnian's word against theirs.'

'I'd take the word of that housebreaker plus Kay against the word of an American boot-legger like Murnian.'

McTaggart winced in disapproval. 'Mr Murnian is no longer able to defend himself against allegations that, for all we know, may be scurrilous. Addison wasn't the only one with a grudge. Kay felt Mr Murnian owed him wages.'

'As he did, but Wullie Kay does not cheat and won't work for cheats.'

'Two convictions for assault...'

'The last one was trivial. I dealt with it. The previous one was years ago.'

'And very fond of a drink, I understand.'

'So are lots of people.'

'Sheriff, I am grateful that you should have come forward in this way, but, to be frank, Sergeant McNeill, under my direction and with the help of his constables, is well on his way to making arrests for the murder of Mr Murnian, and I hope that McCann's murderer will be in the cells shortly. You will understand if I say no more at this stage.' His mouth twisted into a mirthless smile conveying nothing but smugness.

Hector did not disguise his frustration and anger. 'Well, I'm not going to tip the wink to any suspects.' He got up. On impulse he threw his cigarette butt on to the wooden floor and stamped on it.

McTaggart ignored the gesture. Smoothly he said, 'I'm sure the police will catch the culprits for each of these murders. I only hope the courts manage to get them to the gallows.'

His hands on McTaggart's desk and leaning forward until his face was close to the inspector's, Hector spoke levelly. 'Given your blinkered, unimaginative approach to investigation, thank God the courts are there to make sure that innocent men don't hang.' He turned and strode out of the room, leaving the door swinging on its hinges.

*   *   *

'Cup of tea before you go home, my lord?' Forbes asked as Hector removed his wing collar, trying not to drop ash down the front of his waistcoat. 'Not an easy day,' he added.

'Mostly my own fault,' Hector said. 'And yes, please, but not too strong.' While he waited for his tea, which Forbes tended to make using half the leaves in the caddy, Hector reflected on a bad day. He should not have responded to McTaggart's provocation and he should not have given everyone in court the sharp end of his tongue.

A knock on the door signalled the arrival of his tea. Having put it on the table, Forbes stood back. 'We may have an interesting time tomorrow, my lord.'

'How so?'

'The body in the bunker. There have been arrests.'

'Do you know who?'

'An old friend in the police told me just now that Wullie Kay and his cousin, Martin Kay, have been charged.'

'Good lord!'

'The dead man owed Wullie wages as a caddie. Wullie went to the Criterion Bar in St Andrews on Tuesday evening, very angry and threatened to kill Mr Murnian. Martin was there. Last night, the two of them were back in the Criterion spending money like water. Today, Martin had more than twenty pounds on him. He said he got it from Mr Murnian's wallet, and he led Inspector McTaggart to where he'd thrown the wallet into bushes. And that was close to where the murder took place.'

'Really?' One thing Hector could say about McTaggart was he knew how to make a quick arrest. No doubt an unsolved crime offended his obsessively tidy nature.

'I'm told they will appear tomorrow on a petition charging them both with murder and robbery.'

'I see. Do you know what Martin Kay does?'

'He's a greenkeeper, my lord. He claims he didn't know about the murder and just happened to find the wallet.' Forbes's tone of voice showed what he thought of that story.

'Thank you very much for telling me, Forbes. Did your informant say if anyone believes they did it?'

'Inspector McTaggart's very pleased, my lord, and so is everyone else. It reflects well on the police.'

'Provided they've got the right man,' Hector muttered.

*   *   *

'Frankly, O.B., I'm embarrassed. McTaggart is going for the most obvious targets without really asking himself what has been going on.'

Hector had left a message at the Grand Hotel inviting O.B. to the Royal and Ancient for an evening drink. They were sitting together in the bay window of the Big Room, overlooking the first and eighteenth fairways. Simply furnished, with comfortable leather chairs and round wooden tables, eminent golfers of the past frowned down from high walls. Beneath these paintings, lockers of the senior members of the club stood like sentry boxes, guarding the heritage and traditions of the game. Thousands of golfers had been disconcerted by the thought of driving off the first tee under the scrutiny of tweed-clad old gentlemen sitting in that bay window.

They paused to watch the elegant swing of Percy Alliss as he played his approach to the eighteenth through a steady drizzle. 'I don't know what evidence the police will get against either Madsen or Varvell for Jim's murder,' Hector said. 'But whether they're put on trial or not, in St Andrews these two homosexuals will be marked down as child killers. If they get off, people will say the police couldn't prove it.

'On the other hand, I think they will have enough evidence to put the Kays on trial for killing Murnian. Did you hear about the dust-up over the ball in the rough?'

'You bet. Across the road in the Grand, everyone's talking about the murders.'

'Wullie Kay's a rough diamond. He might kill someone with a hay-maker of a punch, but he wouldn't murder a man deliberately, as Murnian was killed.'

'They say he was shot through the head with his own gun.'

'He was certainly shot. I saw the body. I don't know about the gun.' Hector winced as the image flashed through his mind. 'Is it possible that Murnian was the child killer and someone took the law into their own hands?'

'If that's what happened, I guess the caddie and his cousin would like it to become known. You hang murderers in this country, don't you?'

'That's right. I've been in court only twice when someone's been sentenced to death. There's an elaborate ritual. They hold a black cap, which is really just a bit of black cloth, over the judge's wig. Then there's a set form of words about taking the man to a "place of execution where you will be hanged by the neck until you are dead". You can cut the atmosphere with a knife. Both times it made my spine tingle. And I saw a lot of death during the War.' He shuddered. 'Manage another?'

'Thank you.'

As Hector signalled to a waiter, O.B. said, 'I wired a friend in the States who tells me that hobo, name of Harris, is due to go to the electric chair for the Scioto murder.' He paused. 'On July nineteenth, the Tuesday after the Open.'

Hector's stomach tightened. He lit another cigarette, briefly ashamed of the shake of his hand, and forced himself to think. 'Have you heard what Murnian's family plan to do?

Will they leave town before the end of the championship?' he asked.

'I'm told they intend to leave after the Open, as planned. Some say Ralf would have wanted Paul to play. Others say it was too difficult to change their arrangements and have Enid travel in the style to which she is accustomed.'

'How are they taking it?'

'Hard to say. They haven't been seen much about the hotel, though Paul played a practice round on the New this morning.'

'Do you have the list of those here who were also at Scioto? There's no point in giving it to McTaggart, for now at least.'

O.B. handed over two sheets of paper at the same time as the waiter put whiskies down on the table. 'The draw for the qualifying rounds was in *The Times* yesterday. I hear Tommy Armour isn't going to show, which is too bad. I guess winning our Open at Oakmont last month made him change his mind about coming.'

'I can't think why. He might at least have had a shot at doing what Bobby achieved last year.'

'He must feel he won't give a good account of himself. A lot of men lose form after a really big win. There's a rumour that he played in the Shawnee Open the week after Oakmont and took a twenty-three on one hole, so he may have hung up his clubs for a time.'

'Twenty-three? I don't think I've ever done that.'

'Well, that's the story I heard. The hole was a par five. If it's true, it's impressive that he kept counting. I believe his elder brother, Sandy, is making the trip, although I haven't seen him. Maybe we can ask him.' O.B. sipped his whisky before returning to the main business. 'Counting Sandy but not Tommy, there are twelve Americans entered for next week and I think that all but two were at Scioto. Bob and his father helped me

with their recollections, but it's tough to be sure. Only Bill Melhorn finished high up. Paul Murnian was doing well after two
rounds, but he fell away on the last day. For what it's worth,
the young boy was murdered on the Saturday night, July tenth,
after the final round finished. He'd watched Bob, hung around,
then cycled home. Only he never got there.'

Hector scanned the first sheet. Listed alphabetically, in a
neat hand, the names were:

Sandy Armour
Jim Barnes
Lord Terry Coates-Moulton
Bobby Jones
Joe Kirkwood
Charlie Mayo
Bill Melhorn
Paul Murnian
Larry Nabholtz
Kenny Nolan
Dick Robinson

'You've listed eleven players, all bar one American.'

'Lord Terry was the only Brit in the field. Remember, it was
just after your General Strike, and there was hardly any time
between your championship and ours. Yours finished June
twenty-fifth and ours started July eighth. Within three weeks,
Bob won your Open at Lytham, crossed the Atlantic, travelled
to Ohio and won our Open at Scioto. I remember Lord Terry
on *The Aquitania*. A real, reserved British gent. He couldn't
believe the welcome New York gave Bob, with a grand tick-
er-tape parade down Broadway.'

'He probably thought it was vulgar,' Hector snorted.

O.B. raised an eyebrow. 'You don't care for him?'

'He's a cold fish. I played with him in a medal, and the blighter totally ignored me. When we holed out on the eighteenth, he just said, "tough luck, old man". I'd finished in eighty-one and didn't think it was too bad.'

'Well, Lord Terry sure found Scioto difficult. The USGA had let the rough grow real high. Jock Hutchison claimed he lost his caddie in it. Then the wind blew. Did you hear that on the fifteenth in the second round, Bob called a penalty on himself? His ball moved half a turn on the green after he had addressed it.'

'That happened before didn't it?'

'The previous year, only then it was in the rough and no one else could have seen it. His honesty cost him that championship, but when he was congratulated, he said you might as well praise a man for not robbing a bank. Last year, in the final round, he was four shots behind Joe Turnesa with seven to play and overtook him to win by one.' Shaking his head, he sipped his whisky. 'Competing at his level puts a terrible strain on Bob. When you see Tommy Armour pulling out after winning our Open, it sure puts a perspective on Bob's achievement.'

Hector nodded.

'Did you know Bob's the only man to have won the British Open and the US Open in the same year?' O.B. asked.

'I did, actually. He's a remarkable player. I notice you always call him Bob.'

'That's how he's known to family and friends, yet to the world at large he's Bobby.' He pointed to the second sheet. 'Now, this lists all the camp followers I can remember. Males only, for obvious reasons. It includes Murnian, Sabbatini, Big Bob, and me of course.' He grinned. 'Before that week, Big Bob used to think he was Bob's hoodoo, and he stayed away from championships for a time. Scioto cured him of that nonsense.'

'Can you remember if Enda Murnian was there?'

'I don't remember seeing him, but then he and his wife don't stand out in a crowd.'

'They looked miserable, even before the killings. Have you any idea why they follow Paul about?'

'Ralf kept them all on a tight rein. But they say Enda is bright and wanted to steer the business along legitimate lines.' O.B. shrugged.

'What about Mrs Van Dyke? I was surprised she didn't follow Paul in his big match.'

'Trouble in Paradise. The last I heard, she was trying to make Paul jealous by flirting with Lord Terry. Is he going to become a duke or something?'

'Just an earl, actually. That's a couple of notches down from a duke. And his father, the Earl of Silloth and Solway, is in pretty robust health, as far as I'm aware, apart from the fact that he's recently had some valuable emeralds stolen. They say the earl's violently anti-golf and can't understand how Terry can spend all his waking hours improving his game when he should be hunting, shooting, fishing and breeding heirs. Terry's mother, the countess, is a dragon who eats debutantes for breakfast, so maybe it's no wonder so few of them go to the castle. I wouldn't mind being a fly on the wall if he took Mrs Van Dyke back to met Mummy.' He chuckled. 'But, to get back to your lists, it would be interesting to know what they were all doing on Monday just after five, then on Tuesday evening from dinner time onwards.'

'We saw all the Murnians at dinner on Tuesday. Something sure was eating Ralf. He sat and scowled, and no one said much.'

'Do you think that if I went round asking the people on

these lists what they were doing at the relevant times they would tell me?'

'It depends what they were doing, and with whom. Don't worry, you'll get cooperation, Hector. You're the sheriff. You may just have to be a little sensitive to certain situations.' Seeing Hector's frown, he added, 'Bob and his father know your role, but they know how important it is for golf that this guy is caught before he kills again. They'd be happy to be questioned, and be seen to be questioned.'

'That would be very helpful. I should be able to see most of them either tomorrow or at the weekend.'

O.B. looked at his watch and got to his feet. 'I must go, Hector. Dinner calls. Do you still dress for dinner at home?'

'Not unless it's a special occasion. A lot of people still do.'

'At the Grand you get a better table in a tux. When in Rome...Thank you for your excellent whisky.'

Hector shook his hand then slumped back in his chair. He lit a cigarette and stared out of the window. Rain was falling hard and puddles were forming, making golf all but impossible. A solitary, bedraggled player made his way up the eighteenth. His caddie, hunched and miserable, staggered in his wake.

*   *   *

'He's self-satisfied, supercilious and downright insolent.'

'Do you think one of his family, or Sabbatini, killed Murnian?' Lavender asked, weary of Hector's diatribe against the inspector.

'There are probably a lot of people who will be happy to see the last of Ralf Murnian, for a variety of reasons, but I suppose we have to start by looking at his family, and Sabbatini. Unlike the inspector, we must keep open minds.' He gulped his whisky and lit a cigarette. He saw Lavender watching the shake of his hand. 'I shouldn't really be getting involved like this, darling, and it's not going to be easy to get McTaggart to listen.' He knew he sounded vulnerable, but didn't care.

'Well, if anyone can sort things out, it's you, my love. I'll do what I can, not that it's very much, and O.B. is a brick.'

'An all-round good egg.' Hector smiled. 'I just wish I didn't have to rely on O.B. and Forbes to tell me what's going on and what's being said.'

'If you want to find out what's really happening in a big house, ask the servants. You could do with someone who can tell you what's being said by the staff in the Grand, and by the caddies.'

'I can't go to the hotel kitchen or the caddie shed and just ask.'

'There must be someone you can approach without making a song and dance over it. A discreet chat with someone sensible and you'll learn a lot. Some of it will just be gossip, but someone must know something about these killings. Would the killer not have had blood on him?'

'McCann's killer might have. It would depend whether the awl held the blood in the wound till he got away. The poor man didn't die quickly. It was possibly his own struggling that caused the blood to flow as it did.' In a quieter voice he said, 'I haven't heard the details, but I imagine Jim's killer would have had blood on him.'

'It's just horrible. I can't bear to think about it.' She went over to him, took his drink, and put it on the sofa table. Then she sat on his knee and held his face between her hands. 'I believe in you, darling. Never forget that.'

'How could I?'

She kissed him then said, 'Dinner should be ready. Mrs Alves said something earlier about mince and dumplings. Comfort food.'

6

Friday 8 July

Hector got up determined to keep calm and to think logically. His favourite breakfast of kippers in front of him, he laughed indulgently as Marie and Charlotte ran round the table, holding their noses and shouting 'poo!' Lavender kept the window beside her open as she ate her poached egg, half-heartedly checking her daughters.

'I never mind kippers so much in the summer when we can get rid of the smell. It's in winter, with the windows shut all day, you can still get a whiff of them in the evening.' Inhaling the fresh morning air, she took Hector's arm and walked him round the garden before he left for Cupar. As they passed a border of fragrant tea roses she stooped to pick a red bloom that had just come out. 'Isn't it beautiful?' she asked. 'Just wait and I'll fetch a pin.'

Hector stood beside the rose bed, allowing himself to take in its colours and scents. 'We are so lucky, darling,' he said when she returned. 'We're alive, for a start. On top of that we have all this.'

'It's good to hear you say that,' she said, her voice catching. With studied concentration she secured the rose to his lapel.

He jutted out his chin. 'And privileges bring responsibilities.'

'I know, darling, I know.'

'Thank you for everything.' Not trusting himself to say more, he kissed her and climbed into the driver's seat of his Bullnose.

She stood out on the road, waving him goodbye till the back of his car disappeared from view.

'Do we have to walk today?' Marie demanded, standing in the front doorway, hand on hip.

*   *   *

When Hector arrived at court Forbes gave him the latest news. The procurator fiscal had told him that Murnian had died of asphyxia. Bruising at the back of his head and neck together with sand in his airways suggested he had been knocked out then, probably conscious, suffocated by the sand in the bunker; a horrible death, as Forbes reported ghoulishly. According to the professor who had examined him, he was already dead when he had been shot once in the temple. The time of death was estimated to be somewhere between eight in the evening and midnight. Everyone was delighted by the early arrests, Forbes said. The Kays would appear in private before Hector that morning and the judicial process would be under way.

Although Madsen and Varvell had appeared together, the fiscal decided that the Kays should appear separately. Wullie Kay was handcuffed when two policemen led him into Hector's chambers. Unshaven and dishevelled, in need of a wash and sporting a black eye, he looked round the room beetle-browed and distrustful. He perfectly fitted the popular image of a murderer. When asked to acknowledge his name, he did so with a noise that was something between a growl and a grunt, his eye fixed on the open window to Hector's right and the blue skies beyond. His solicitor, Hotchkiss, said that his client wished to emit a declaration.

Hector warned Wullie that he need say nothing, nor need he answer questions. Anything he did say might be used at his trial.

The caddie looked at him levelly. 'I understand,' he said.

After three years on the bench, this was the first time that Hector had encountered an accused who wished to give a declaration. After a whispered discussion with the clerk of court, he wrote a heading on the single foolscap sheet and looked at Wullie. 'What is it that you wish to say? Please do not speak too quickly, as I have to write down everything.'

His voice gruff, Wullie spoke deliberately, his eyes never leaving Hector's face. 'I had an argument with Mr Murnian because he accused another caddie of cheating when he hadnae. Murnian was the cheat and he owed me wages, but I didnae kill him and I ken fine my cousin didnae kill him. That's all.'

Relieved at his brevity, Hector read it back to Wullie and signed it. 'You must sign too,' he said.

'I cannae with these on.' He held his hands up in front of him.

'Take them off his right hand while he signs,' Hector ordered.

The police escorts exchanged glances before one produced a key and released Wullie's right wrist. He rubbed the red marks where the metal had chaffed, stretched his fingers, then took the pen Hotchkiss offered him and signed in a hand that was primitive but legible. As soon as he had put down the pen, the handcuff went back on, causing him to wince. He looked resigned when Hector told him that he would be remanded in custody until his next appearance in a week's time.

Martin Kay was next. His name had meant nothing to Hector, but he immediately recognized the simple, red-faced man he had seen working on the golf courses. In place of the inane grin he usually gave Hector, Martin's face bore the terrified puzzlement of a newly-captured animal. Hotchkiss represented him also and announced that he, too, wished to make a declaration.

Hoping that Hotchkiss knew what he was doing, Hector gave the appropriate caution and waited for Martin to speak.

'I found a wallet. It was behind the ninth green. After I took the money oot I threw it in the whins. There was lots of money notes. I'm sorry. I'm very bad.' He looked round desperately. 'Can I go home?'

Hotchkiss grimaced, but was not permitted to intervene. Hector knew there was something else Martin had to say. 'You need not answer this, but did you kill a man?' he asked, hoping that panic and confusion would not lead to the wrong answer.

'I didnae kill anyone.'

Suppressing a sigh of relief, Hector read it back to Martin then signed, the paper stirring in the draught from the window. He looked at Hotchkiss, his eyebrows raised.

'He can't write, so he'll make his mark, my lord.'

'Very well,' Hector said. He gestured to the escort to release his right hand. Deliberately, his tongue out, Martin put a cross at the foot of the page. Hector recorded that, as he was unable to write, the cross was his mark.

As Hector finished writing, the procurator fiscal moved to have the case continued for one week for further examination, Martin to be remanded in custody.

'Very well,' Hector said, and the examination would have ended had Martin not pulled his right wrist away from the unfastened handcuff. With a roar like a raging bull, he made a run for the double sash window and dived for the one on the right, which was wide open. Grabbing the central panel, he swung his lower body round and out. For a moment he hung on to the sill then, as the startled escorts reached out to grab him, he fell backwards into the fresh air. The next noise was a crack like a gunshot. From the street below a woman screamed. Everyone in Hector's room rushed to the window, twenty feet above the pavement where Martin lay spread-eagled on his back, his left leg forming a crazy angle. When he got his breath back he let out a howl that raised the hairs on Hector's neck.

'When a man tries to run, you know he's guilty,' Forbes said smugly to Hector after Martin had been taken away in an ambulance and the excitement had died down.

'And a wild bird will always try to fly out of its cage,' Hector replied, not caring when Forbes pursed his lips in disapproval.

*　*　*

It was with an apologetic air that the clerk informed Hector that the case down for proof that day had settled. Muttering about working on a written judgment, Hector handed a bundle of signed papers to Forbes and set off for St Andrews.

He was half way there when he realized he had left the papers for his judgment in Cupar. It did not matter. He had decided to visit Enid Murnian.

Resisting the temptation to visit the club for a spine-stiff-ening whisky, Hector parked on the Scores and entered the lobby of the Grand Hotel. He thought back to the letters of condolence he had written to widows during the war, with their permutations of 'brave', 'gallant' and 'sacrifice', his pen sticking at the words 'not died in vain'. He had tried to make each one different, if possible appropriate to the young man in question. But he had lied resolutely when necessary to conceal coward-ice. As he had sealed each envelope he could not escape the feeling that he, the man's commanding officer, had let him and his family down. The least he could do was to make that family proud. The widow he was about to visit, he suspected, would be unlike any of those to whom he had written.

A bellboy showed him up to her third floor suite. The main feature of the sitting room was the semi-circular area forming the corner of the hotel. The windows gave spectacular views round three quarters of a circle from St Andrews Bay and the links to the hotchpotch of buildings running up the side of the eighteenth fairway.

'So good of you to come calling, Sheriff.' Sheathed in black, a handkerchief in one hand, her cigarette holder in the other, Enid Murnian reclined on a chaise longue. A magazine lay open on the floor in front of her, a wine glass beside it. Reading upside-down, Hector saw that the magazine was *The New Yorker*, cover side up to keep her place. The hot, smoky atmosphere caught the back of his throat. He felt his eyes watering.

'I just wanted to express my condolences on your sad loss, Mrs Murnian. Is there anything I might be able to do to help?'

'You might give me a little more of that Chablis sitting in the bucket over there.' Dropping her handkerchief, she picked up the glass and held it out for Hector to take. Her fingers boasted more rings than British taste would allow, each ring holding at least one large precious stone. In pride of place, beside her wedding ring, was a huge emerald.

'Of course,' he said, his eyes moving to observe the heavy application of white powder on her cheeks. He drew the bottle from the ice bucket on the sideboard and poured a generous measure.

'Do help yourself to something,' she urged as he brought her drink over.

He poured a whisky and soda, placed it on an occasional table and sat in an armchair. Enid Murnian said nothing but half smiled at him. He brought out his cigarette case. After vigorously tapping the loose leaf from the end of his cigarette, he flicked his lighter. For once it started first time.

'Bravo for your friend's lighter,' she said.

Hector sipped his drink. 'This must have been a terrible shock for you,' he said.

She nodded.

'Particularly as it happened so far from home.'

'That hasn't helped,' she agreed.

'May I ask what your plans are?'

'I'm staying with our schedule. We sail out of Glasgow a week Monday, straight home to New York. Ralf never said, but I know he would want to be buried in the Bronx. Washington Heights, you know, where his parents were laid to rest. And he wouldn't want Paul to miss out on the British Open.'

'Have you been away long?'

'Too long, now, Sheriff, and a tough trip. When the German economy crashed, Enda saw that as a great opportunity. He wanted Ralf to buy some engineering company that makes automobile parts. Ralf didn't much care for the idea, but he respected Enda's intelligence. As soon as the National Open was finished in mid-June we all sailed for Bremerhaven, Germany. From there we went to Berlin, where Ralf and Enda met with some people. Then it was back to Bremerhaven, and from there to Southampton. We made our way through England to St Andrews. We've been here a week. I'll be mighty glad to be home.'

'Your husband was obviously keen on following Paul's golf.'

'He'd have loved to see his son win something real big. Paul won the State Championship and was one of the early leaders in the National Open last year. I've never seen Ralf so excited. Now it's something he'll never see.' She fixed a cigarette in her holder. Hector stood up and flicked his lighter several times. 'Wow,' she said as the flame subsided. 'Coming to St Andrews was a big deal for him. He was happy till that goddam match.'

'He was a strong character, interesting company.' Hector avoided mention of the qualities that had made him dislike Murnian.

Enid Murnian pursed her lips and her expression hardened. She gulped her wine. 'Frankly, Sheriff, he was an immoral bully. He loved to keep people hanging on the end of a string, dancing to his tune. Oh, there'll be a huge funeral for him back home, but I wonder how many will really miss him.'

Hector shifted in his seat. She had swung round like a weather-vane from sepia-tinted wistfulness to disconcerting honesty. Unable to think of a suitable response, he shrugged.

She said, 'I apologise for being so frank. It's the American way.'

'Please don't concern yourself.' He sensed she might need to talk, and there were some things that were easier said to a stranger.

'Sheriff, you're very polite, but you're not a fool. I saw your expression at that party. Ralf and I had a modern sort of marriage. Ralf was incapable of being faithful, and I have had my admirers. But our children, Enda and Paul, mattered to both of us. "Blood's thicker than water," Ralf often said. He liked to have his family round him. And so do I. But he kept us all right where he wanted us. Sheriff, I stopped loving him years back, but I never stopped loving our sons or his money.' She stole a glance at Hector, who kept his face impassive. 'I had a long-running affair that ended three years ago. Ralf knew about it, he got the evidence and could prove it any time he wanted. If I had left, he'd have painted me as the loose-living marriage wrecker. My name would have been dragged through the mud, he'd have tried to turn the boys against me and I couldn't have lived on what the courts would have awarded.' Suddenly she looked very vulnerable. She carried on in a soft voice: 'I'm not going to give you some baloney about my life being shattered, but you can't live with someone for twenty-six years and not feel turned upside down when they get murdered.' She sniffed and put her handkerchief to her eyes. 'Could you please pour me another?' She indicated her empty glass. 'I've probably had too much, but I don't know what to feel or think.'

'Tuesday night must have been terrible for you,' Hector probed.

'Tuesday was terrible, period. First, Paul lost that match. Then there was a message waiting here for Ralf that made him mad.'

'Do you know what it was about, from whom it came?'

She looked up sharply and he cursed himself for over-eagerness. 'No,' she said. 'I know nothing about it.'

'Go on,' he said. 'Sorry to have interrupted.'

'Then there was a row about Paul and Mrs Van Dyke. Neither Ralf nor I would have anything to do with her. She's nothing but a common gold-digger and she had no business appearing here out of the blue. I'm sure Paul was less keen on her than he had been, but he didn't like us telling him. I believe she wanted him to sit at dinner with her, but Ralf made it clear that he expected Paul to sit with us as we were here to support him. And Paul knows who pays the bills.' She took another cigarette and lit it before Hector could produce his lighter. 'Mainly to get away from Ralf laying down the law to Paul, I had a good, long soak in the tub. Ralf had to use the bathroom along the corridor and that made him real mad. At dinner, Ralf wouldn't speak to anyone, specially Paul. Mrs Van Dyke wasn't at her table and Paul was upset. He left the meal early. Ralf just glared at him.

Ralf went out of the hotel afterwards. He liked to go walking during your long Scotch evenings. "Roamin' in the gloamin'," he used to say. I hoped he would come back calmer. And that night the weather was fine. I went out too, along there. Alone, thinking.' With a languid wave she indicated the West Sands. 'The tide was in and the water was shallow, so I paddled. But the water was cold as ice, so I didn't paddle long.'

'Did you not miss your husband later that night?'

'Sheriff, I take something to let me sleep. I was in my bed, through there.' She nodded towards a door to her left. 'I didn't notice his bed was empty till morning. It wasn't unheard of for him to be out all night.' She raised an eyebrow. 'I do remember hearing him talking on the telephone in this room after I'd put the light out, but I was half asleep then.'

'Do you know to whom he was speaking?'

'I heard him say "Molasses" so I guess he was speaking to Mo Evans.'

'Mo Evans?'

'His attorney. They've been friends since childhood. As a kid, Mo was a slow runner, "as slow as molasses in winter" some coach bellowed at him. The other kids called him Molasses and over the years that got shortened to Mo, but Ralf still called him Molasses.'

'So he must have made the call then gone out again?'

'I guess so.'

Hector thought he saw a way to ask about Jim's murder. 'Your husband enjoyed going for walks?'

'Why do you ask?'

'Someone told me he often went out, even Monday afternoon when it was foggy.'

She frowned. 'You ask more questions than the police. I thought they had the guys who killed that poor kid.'

'I do have an examining role. Maybe Ralf saw something when he was out. We certainly don't want it to be said by the defence that the law enforcement agencies had too narrow a view.' Hector hoped she would be reassured by transatlantic terminology.

'So this is an official visit?'

'Partly.' He could say nothing else.

She put down her glass and looked at him steadily. 'And I thought you were just being friendly.' Carefully, she stubbed out her cigarette, fitted another into her holder, shook her head at Hector's lighter and flicked her own. 'Well, Sheriff, I remember my husband saying on Monday afternoon he was running out of cigars. I believe he visited a nearby tobacconist.' She blew smoke straight at him.

'Do you know what Paul and Enda did before the party?'

'I don't know that's any of your damn business. You can ask them.'

Hector could see that he had outstayed his welcome. 'Thank you for your time, Mrs Murnian. If there's anything I can do, please don't hesitate to contact me.' He placed his card on the table beside his empty glass and got up.

'Sheriff, I understand the two men accused of my husband's murder were in court this morning?'

'They appeared before me, yes.'

'Could you please tell me what sort of men killed Ralf?'

'The men who appeared before me were very ordinary, a caddie and a greenkeeper, and the law presumes them to be innocent until they are proved guilty, whatever the police might say.' Feeling pleased with this response, Hector bowed. 'Good day, Mrs Murnian,' he said.

Saying nothing, she stared out of the window.

7

Ill at ease, Hector crossed Golf Place. He made his way through the crowded hall of the Royal and Ancient and found solitude in the North Room. He noted down the information Enid Murnian had given him, reflected for a while, then went for lunch.

After lunch he went to the Road Hole. Perched on his shooting stick beside the wall on the far side of the road, his broad-brimmed tweed cap shading his vulnerable eyes from the sun, Hector watched Percy Alliss, Herbert Jolly and two of the Whitcombe brothers, Charles and Ernest, putt out.

A group attracting a bigger crowd came round the corner of the railway sheds. As the players reached their balls, Hector peered to try and identify them. Two men hit woods, both balls running too far and coming to rest among the stones, weeds and dirt of the road. Next to play was Bobby Jones, whose modest shot finished short and right of the green. The last of the four was tall and thin. After some discussion with his caddie, he hit a shot with a wooden club that climbed on to the green, turned away from the road at the last moment, and ran to within fifteen feet of the hole, winning some applause. Hector recognized the elegant swing of Dick Robinson.

Soon the crowd surrounded him. Standing to see, he watched Jones' deft pitch. The two players on the road, Joe Kirkwood, the Australian ex-ranch boy now based in America, and Larry Nabholtz of St Louis, made heavy weather of their recoveries. When it came to Dick's turn to putt he overhit the first then jabbed at the second, his head moving noticeably. Jones scored the only four on the hole.

As he followed the players up the last fairway, Hector noticed that Tommy, talking animatedly with Jones' caddie, was limping.

O.B. Keeler came up beside him, took his arm, and spoke confidentially. 'If you were to ask him at the end of this round, Bob would be happy to answer questions, perhaps in the lounge of the Grand, later this afternoon.'

'To encourage others, you mean?'

'Exactly.'

'I could offer to see him and buy him a drink in the club if he would prefer.'

'He's a member, anyway. He took his father and me in for a drink, but he couldn't take Kiltie Maiden as they don't allow professionals in. I doubt if it would be smart to question the amateurs in the R and A, and the professionals somewhere else.'

'No. Of course not.' Hector felt foolish. In the past, Walter Hagen had showed his disdain for this snobbishness by changing his shoes in a Rolls Royce parked ostentatiously beside the clubhouse. Hector scanned round and spotted a glum-faced Sabbatini. 'Benny looks subdued,' he said to O.B.. In a cream coloured suit, he made his way painfully up the fairway, appearing older and more bent than the last time Hector had seen him.

'He misses having someone to fight with.'

'What do you make of young Robinson?'

'As a person, don't know him. As a golfer, Kiltie rates him. But he can't putt. His young caddie has been telling him to keep his head still but it swings about like a lantern in a hurricane.'

Their rounds finished, the players came off the eighteenth green and walked over to where O.B. and Hector were standing at the foot of the steps up to the Royal and Ancient clubhouse.

'I like the way you play the seventeenth,' Hector told Jones.

'I don't reckon it's a place to show courage. Jack, here, has instructions to wrestle me to the ground if I try to take wood during the championship.'

Feeling pompous and deceitful, and hating it, Hector said, 'Bobby, you know there have been some tragic happenings over the last few days. As an officer of court there are some inquiries I should make. Would it be convenient for me to talk briefly with you to see if you know anything that would assist the course of justice?'

Jones' face showed no emotion. 'Of course, Sheriff. We must see justice done.'

'Might I visit you in the Grand later this afternoon?'

'Of course, Sheriff. Would half past four in the lounge suit you?'

'That would be admirable. Thank you very much.'

'If you like, I could have a word with the fellows I've been playing with, and you might speak with them as well.'

'Thank you, that would be most helpful,' Hector said gratefully.

'Not at all. I look forward to seeing you then.' Jones smiled politely and left them.

'Would that suit you, Dick?' Hector asked, aware that his exchange with Jones had astonished those who had heard it, other than O.B..

'I guess so. Can't see why not.'

Hector thought he detected a look of alarm flash across Dick's open face. He changed the subject. 'It was a fine second you hit at the seventeenth. Pity it went unrewarded.'

'Tommy wanted me to play safe, but the way I'm putting I've got to get close to the hole or I've no chance. I holed a few at Oakmont, but these greens are as big as oceans and they kinda spook me.' He grinned ruefully at Tommy, who was standing a little way off, avoiding Hector's eye. 'I'm going to spend the next hour practising my putts,' he added.

As Tommy got balls from the pouch in the bag Hector saw blue bruising round his mouth. It looked as if he had been fighting, probably a couple of days earlier. He remembered what Lavender had said about an informant from the ranks of the caddies.

On impulse he said to Dick, 'Do you mind if I borrow your caddie for an hour? I want to go and practise with my mashie and I'd like help with picking up the balls.'

'Go right ahead, Sheriff. I know what I've got to do on the greens. It's just a question of doing it. I'll see you about half past four.'

Ten minutes later, Dick and Tommy had made arrangements for the next day and Hector had fetched his mashie and a canvas bag full of old balls and re-paints from his locker in the Royal and Ancient. Together, sheriff and housebreaker set off towards the bridge over the Swilken Burn, an awkward silence between them.

Hector looked sideways at the sullen face. He decided to break the ice. 'You look as if you've been fighting.'

'It wis just a scrap.'

'Do you want to tell me what it was about?'

'No, sir.'

'Do you want to tell me why you're limping?'

'No, sir.'

'Have you got back that silver you stole?'

'No sir, no' yet.'

'Are you going to?'

'When I've got the money they want, I'll get it. As long as I dinnae tell the police on them.'

'How do you feel about Murnian's death?'

Tommy stiffened. 'He wasn't a nice man. I cannae say I'm sorry.'

Hector stopped and faced him. 'Do you know anything about his murder?'

The colour rose up Tommy's neck. A look of disgust on his face, he spat out, 'So this is what this is about, sir? To accuse me of murder?'

Hector cursed himself. 'No, but I have to ask. To be frank, I'm far from sure the Kays had anything to do with it.'

'So you think you'll pin it on me?'

'Not if you didn't do it.'

'Well I didnae, and you can fetch your own bloody balls.' Tommy threw down the club and the canvas bag and started to walk back.

'Wait!' It was an order. Tommy took two more steps then stopped. 'Do you want to help Wullie Kay?'

The lad stood still then faced Hector. He remembered this was the man who had given him a chance. His voice hesitant, he said, 'Yes.'

'That's what I want to do, but I need help.'

'What do you mean?'

'Tell me truthfully, do the caddies and greenkeepers think the Kays are guilty?'

'No one thinks they did it.'

'Well who did do it?'

'No one knows.' Tommy moved nearer, trying to read the sheriff's face.

'Are you prepared to talk to me about it?'

'If it'll help Wullie and Marty, yes, sir.'

'Well, pick these things up and we can start.'

Feeling foolish, Tommy bent to pick up the mashie. A few balls had spilled from the bag and rolled away. Wishing he was somewhere else, he gathered them up then asked directly: 'What do you want to know?'

'What's being said, gossip or fact, anything unusual that's happened, anything you think might help. Shall we walk?'

Tommy fell into step, thinking. He knew not to say much to the authorities, but he respected the sheriff. 'They say that on Tuesday he went to the Criterion. Wullie, I mean. He had nae money but he's a good customer so he got drink on tick. He was raging about Murnian, saying he'd kill him and that. Everyone knew it was just the drink talking. Marty was in the pub too and he took him away about seven. Marty doesn't drink but he sits in the corner of the bar for the company and has a ginger beer. On Wednesday, Marty was out early switching the greens on the Old. Someone said when he came in he was acting kinda sleekit, as if he had a secret. Wullie found a bag for the day. Auld Deadwood had a hangover. Later he was in the Criterion with Marty, paying off his debt to the barman. Marty bought drinks for everyone. Wullie tried to stop him. One of the notes he handed over was American. Yesterday morning the polis got Marty when he finished his work and they got Wullie in the caddie shed, but he landed a couple of punches before they had him.' He glanced at Hector and was surprised to see a smile.

'Does anyone know what Wullie and Marty did on Tuesday after they left the pub?'

'No' that I've heard. Usually when Wullie gets drunk Marty takes him for a turn round the old part of town till he's fit to go home.'

They had reached an area of rough links land sometimes used for practice. Hector began to hit mashie shots.

'Not as good as Dick Robinson, I'm afraid,' he said.

'No' bad for...'

'An old man? Cheeky beggar. I'm not forty yet.'

'I didnae mean that, sir, I'm sorry.'

'Oh yes you did, but don't worry. When I was your age I thought anyone over thirty had one foot in the grave.' He grinned.

Tommy grinned back. 'Right enough,' he said.

As they set off to pick up the balls, Hector asked if he had seen or heard anything unusual.

'No' that I can think of now.'

'Have you seen much of Mr Sabbatini?'

'He's always around, except if we're too far out on the course for him.'

'What do you make of him?'

'He's been good to me. He knows I help Dick, Mr Robinson.'

'But?'

Tommy looked surprised. 'I wouldnae like to get on the wrong side of him.'

'How's he been since the murders?'

Tommy shrugged. 'Hard to say. Quieter, maybe. I don't think he's as interested in the golf as he was. I'd shown Dick how most folk play run-ups here, what Americans call the St Andrews shot, and when Dick told him he just kinda nodded. That was yesterday.'

'He's pretty crippled, isn't he?'

'Yes, but I've seen him move quite fast sometimes.'

'That's very interesting. What about Hamish McCann's murder? Does anyone know anything about that?'

Tommy was astonished Hector knew so little. 'They say

the polis are looking into money-lending. He was a lad, was Hamish. Nae sense wi' siller.'

'Have you heard of any connection between these two murders, or anything at all about Jim Tindall?'

'No. I didnae know Jim that well.'

Hector held the canvas bag open for Tommy to put in a handful of balls. 'You've been very helpful, Tommy. I'd appreciate more help, if you were prepared to give it. But I have to warn you that it might be dangerous for you.'

'You mean the real murderer might go for me?'

'Possibly. And one more thing. If the police were to be satisfied that Wullie and Marty didn't do it, they might well look to someone short of money, who had been wrongly accused of something by Murnian, and who had marks of violence on him after the murder.'

'Me?'

'Yes, you.'

'But you don't think I did it?'

'No, Tommy, I don't.'

'Why no'?'

'I'm not telling you.'

Looking puzzled, Tommy shook his head. He picked up the rest of the balls and they walked in. Hector asked about Dick's golf and whom the caddies were tipping to win the Open. Jones was the near-unanimous choice. As they neared the caddie shed, Hector returned to the subject on both their minds.

'Look, I would really appreciate your help in this, but you have to be aware of the possible consequences for you.'

'Mr Drummond, Wullie didnae need to speak up for me when Murnian accused me of kicking that ball. I'm going to help him if I can. I'll no' see a man like that go to the gallows.'

'Good lad, Tommy. Don't tell anyone about this chat we've

just had. Keep your eyes and ears open and find out anything you can about any of the killings, fact or gossip. I'll make contact with you tomorrow. I can find out when Dick's playing. We can talk later. All right?'

'Yes, sir. I think he's due to tee off about ten. And sir.'

'Yes?'

'I reckon you'd be more consistent with your mashie if you had a fuller shoulder turn on the backswing. I didn't like to say earlier.'

Hector seized the club and tried some swings. 'You could have a point,' he said. He fished in his pocket and handed over a half crown. 'Maybe we can do the same tomorrow,' he said, satisfied with progress on more than one count.

*   *   *

'Will you take some tea, Bobby?' Hector got to his feet to greet Jones. He had selected a table in the corner of the lounge, in a place that would challenge the most determined eavesdropper. A short distance away, Larry Nabholtz and Dick Robinson sat together. When he saw Hector turn towards him, Nabholtz looked pointedly at his watch.

'No, thank you, Sheriff. I'd just as soon get down to business.' Jones sat in the chair opposite Hector, leaning forward. Without the tweed cap he wore on the course, and with little pomade to darken it, his hair was fairer than Hector had assumed.

'Do you mind if I ask you some direct questions? I want to eliminate you as soon as I can.' Nervous in his unfamiliar role of investigator, he knew as soon as the words were out of his mouth that he should not have given any reassurance.

Jones raised his eyebrows. 'Just like everyone else, I hope,

Sheriff. I would be disappointed if you were to give me special treatment.'

'Quite so. Well, I think O.B. may have talked to you about our concerns involving the boy killed on Monday and the possibility that whoever did that also murdered a lad last year at Scioto?'

'It seems likely.'

'And, of course, we've had two more murders on Tuesday night. They may all be connected.' Jones shrugged. 'Can you tell me what you did between arriving at this hotel on Monday afternoon and the Independence Day party?'

'I unpacked, I checked my clubs were undamaged after the journey, I wrote a letter to Mary, my wife, and then I lay in a tub drinking a Scotch and smoking some cigarettes. Then I dressed for dinner. I am sharing a room with my father and he should back me up. And O.B. came to my room to greet me after his honeymoon. I was dressing at the time. I did not go out in the fog. I'd seen enough of that during the crossing.'

'Thank you. What about Tuesday evening?'

'I had dinner with my father, O.B. and Eleanor, and Stewart Maiden. I went to bed quite early, just after nine. My father was a bit later, but not much. I didn't leave the hotel after dinner.'

'Did you notice anything unusual about the Murnians that evening?'

'I had my back to their table, but when we came in to dinner I noticed they looked gloomy. Ralf normally said good evening, but he didn't lift his eyes from his soup. We all observed that Mrs Van Dyke was not at her table.' He smiled.

'Did you register anything strange or out of the ordinary that might conceivably have a bearing on these killings?'

'Sorry, Sheriff. I've been thinking about that since O.B. mentioned the matter to me. I'm afraid I can't help you.'

'Thank you, Bobby. I appreciate you doing this so openly.'

A steely gleam showed in Jones' eyes. He leaned over and spoke earnestly. 'We need you to get this guy, Sheriff, alive or dead. We all need that to happen. But when I spoke to the boys, I didn't mention the possible tie-up with what happened at Scioto.

'Joe Kirkwood sends his apologies. He's staying with a land-lady, Mrs Macfarlane, in South Street who has his tea on the table at five sharp. She'd promised him haggis tonight. If he survives that, he could see you tomorrow, but, if it helps, he told me that Mrs Macfarlane, with her bacon and eggs, gives him an alibi for early Monday evening. I gather he spent Tuesday night in a bar called the Criterion and only just made it back to Mrs Macfarlane's. He says she was real mad and he doesn't want to tangle with her again. Shall I send one of these boys over?' He nodded towards Nabholtz and Robinson.

'Thank you. It doesn't matter who's first.' Hector jotted down some notes as Jones got up to go.

Larry Nabholtz came across, sat down and folded his arms. Short and sturdy like Jones, but built on a slightly larger scale, he showed little emotion as Hector thanked him for talking to him. For some years Nabholtz, who had worked his way up from being a boy caddie in Pennsylvania, had been regarded as a promising young professional. Now, despite being one of the longest hitters in the game, he was in danger of becoming a man with a glittering future behind him.

'On Monday a bunch of us went to the movies,' he said. 'The fog made golf impossible. We went to the little white movie house in North Street. It was real quaint, with musicians playing while the film ran.'

'Was the film good?'

'When it worked it was great, but the reel kept slipping.

There were a lot of breaks, but we didn't mind. It passed the time.'

'What was the film?'

'*The General*, with Buster Keaton. He got his girl in the end.'

'Can you remember who else was there?'

Nabholtz unfolded his arms and scratched his head then put his huge hands on his knees. 'I went with Kenny Nolan. I saw both the Murnian boys. The one who doesn't golf was there with his wife. Paul didn't sit with them, as I recall. He talked to different people during the breaks. Most of us did.'

'Was Paul there all the time?'

'I guess so, but I wasn't checking on anyone.'

'When did the film finish?'

'I don't know. Maybe quarter, half past five.'

'Can you remember anyone else who was there?'

Nabholtz frowned. 'Jim Barnes, Charlie Mayo.'

'Did you see anyone leave before the end?'

'With all the breaks, people were moving about, so someone could have left early, but I can't say. Kenny was there at the end. I can tell you that.' He pointed his finger to add emphasis.

'What about Tuesday evening?'

'Kenny and I were about to have dinner in Rusacks, where we're rooming together, when some expensive broad came looking for him. I ended up eating alone and going to bed early. Kenny woke me when he came in, but I don't know when that was. He'd had a few drinks.'

Hector beamed at him. 'Thank you very much, Mr Nabholtz. That's been most helpful. One thing, maybe you can jog my memory. How did you get on in the American Open last year?'

'Last year, you mean at Scioto? Oakmont was last month.' His face wrinkled with astonishment.

'It was Scioto I was interested in.'

'I didn't do much. The rough was horrible. I don't see why you're interested in that.'

Unwilling to explain, Hector fell back on pomposity. 'I am grateful for your time, Mr Nabholtz, but there is a point to all my questions.'

Nabholtz got up. 'Sheriff, I get seasick, but I came across the Atlantic to play the most famous golf course in the world, and it is still one of the best anywhere. I did not come to kill anyone, specially not some kid. And I'm sure the same goes for the rest of the Americans who have made the crossing. I'm not sure why you're doing this, as I understand the police have made arrests. I've answered your questions because Bob asked me to, but I can't say I like this.'

As Nabholtz strode out of the room, his head high, a wave of self-doubt assailed Hector. If he did not improve on McTaggart's efforts, he knew that he would look very foolish.

He put this thought to the back of his mind as Dick Robinson came over. Moving from one leg to the other, the young man hovered respectfully. He perched rather than sat on the edge of an armchair when Hector invited him to take a seat.

'Don't worry, Dick. There are just one or two questions I would like to ask you. I hope that's all right?'

'Of course, Sheriff Drummond.' His mouth twitched into a stupid-looking grin.

Patiently, Hector gave an explanation why he wanted to ask questions, without mentioning the boy murdered at Scioto. Dick nodded vigorously as he spoke. On being asked about Monday evening, Dick said, 'Sheriff, don't take this the wrong way. Mr Sabbatini, Benny, has given me this wonderful opportunity, but I kind of need to get away from him from time to time. We'd shared a cabin on *The Transylvania*, and his room's next to mine here in the Grand. As soon as we arrived I had to go out, even in that fog. I tried to find a bar where I could relax for a half hour. Benny doesn't like me to drink, and all through the crossing I'd watched him drink and I listened to the same stories. I'm sorry that sounds ungrateful, and I am real grateful to him, but I just needed to get away. That evening I walked about for a while before I found a bar in a basement. I had a beer and left so I could get ready for the Independence Day party.' As the words tumbled out, jerky hand movements betrayed his agitation.

'Do you know the name of the bar?'

'Sorry, Sheriff. And I couldn't lead you there now. I had to ask my way back here.'

'Could you describe it?'

'Kinda rough. Dark wood. A mirror behind the bar.'

'What about Tuesday evening, after dinner?'

'It was a fine evening. I took a walk. I figured I should have a look at the New, as it's one of the qualifying courses. So I took a mashie and some balls and walked the course. I tried to play your St Andrews shot, but it wasn't working for me. Yesterday Tommy showed me how to do it.'

'Did you see anything odd or suspicious?'

'No. I wasn't looking, of course.'

'Did you see many people on the links?'

'A few. Mostly walking, apart from those finishing their rounds. One or two had clubs for practice. Some had dogs.'

'Do you remember what you were wearing?'

'Oh, slacks and a sweater. I changed out of that dinner suit as soon as we left the dining room. I still can't tie the bow tie.' He grinned ruefully.

'What time did you get in?'

'Maybe a quarter after ten. I said goodnight to Benny and went to bed.'

'Did you see Ralf Murnian that evening?'

'I don't recall seeing him after he paid Benny. When the match finished, he kinda stormed off the course, but he was waiting in the hotel lobby. He came up to Benny. I thought he might hit him, but he had a pile of pound bills, mostly with big numbers on them. He counted them out and handed them over. Just like that. And he said something to him. I didn't hear what it was.' He paused, looking thoughtful. 'Oh, I do believe we may have passed him on the way in to dinner. But our table wasn't near his.'

'Thank you, Dick. Is there anything else you could tell me that might have a bearing on any of the murders?'

'I don't believe so.' Hector could see the tension in his shoulders easing as he sat back in his chair.

'Did you know Hamish McCann, the clubmaker?'

Dick looked momentarily startled. 'No. No sir, I did not know him.'

'Oh, one other thing. How did you get on at the US Open last year?'

Dick swallowed. 'At Scioto?'

'Yes.'

'I had a good first round then the wind got up and my putting let me down. I made the last day, by one shot. Saturday, my putting was even worse. I four-putted one green.' He scowled at the painful memory.

Hector grimaced sympathetically, then changed the subject to Dick's golf and how he liked the Old Course.

'I think it's great. I've seen nothing like it. Playing with Bobby today was a real honour. He really thinks his way round, and Tommy's a great caddie. I'm surprised he was still available when I arrived.'

'Funny how things work out,' Hector said, smiling.

*   *   *

The moment Hector got home, Lavender pressed a whisky into his hand and sat him down in his favourite chair. 'Come on, spill the beans,' she demanded.

Hector rubbed his forehead and summarised his meeting with Dick Robinson. 'He had obviously decided to make a clean breast of things, hoping that I would believe him, even though he was out and about when Jim was killed, and only that late phone call to Molasses, which Dick probably doesn't know about, puts Murnian's murder later than his return to the hotel.'

'Do you think he was rehearsed?'

'Not exactly rehearsed,' he replied. 'But he'd pre-planned a lot of what he said. And I have to say, I think I believe him. There's a sort of guilelessness about him. When I brought up McCann and Scioto out of the blue, he looked startled. Innocent people often seem taken aback when they are asked to account for themselves and crime is involved. I'd have expected a guilty person to act in a more controlled way. And I understand why he wanted to get out. Can you imagine being cooped up with Sabbatini for a week with him talking non-stop and Atlantic rollers making you lose your breakfast?'

'Anyone would need to get away from him.'

'Benny would try the patience of a saint. Particularly if he kept the lad from his grog.' Hector sipped his whisky. 'Dick's a queer chap,' he mused. 'On the course, he's assured and confident. Off it, he's immature and doesn't seem to have much personality.'

'He is young, and this style of living only came to him when Benny took him under his wing.'

'I suppose so. He's certainly not the first person to change dramatically on the sports field. I must have told you about

Guy Mountcastle at Glenalmond. Always praying and reading his Bible, but the dirtiest player on the rugger pitch. Last I heard they'd made him a bishop.'

'Many times, darling. What about the Murnian boys? With all these breaks in that film, someone could have left early without their absence being noticed.'

'And there's that narrow lane, Butt's Wynd, leading past St Salvator's to the Scores practically opposite the cinema.'

Lavender stroked her chin reflectively. 'Someone could have got fed up with the film and wandered off to the Scores just in time to bump into Jim?'

'I think I should concentrate on the Murnians, and I should certainly have a chat with Sabbatini.'

'That might take all day, darling.'

'I don't regard Bobby as a suspect, and I think we can discount Nabholtz, and Nolan too. Joe Kirkwood's ferocious landlady almost certainly puts him in the clear.'

'But whoever is our murderer will probably have engineered an alibi for himself.'

'I know, but we've got to narrow down our search. And frankly, darling, I'm keen to avoid upsetting too many of the world's top golfers.'

'That would never do,' she said, deadpan. He looked at her sharply to see if she meant it. 'So, what will you do tomorrow?' she asked.

'I'll carry on asking questions and I'll make a particular effort to see Paul Murnian.'

'Do you think Wullie Kay might be able to tell us something important?'

'He might, but he's remanded in Perth Prison, and I couldn't possibly visit him there.' He shook his head emphatically.

'Someone else could.'

'Who? No, not you. Under no circumstances.'

Putting on her most demure expression, she suggested that the girls might like it if he were to read them a story.

8

Saturday 9 July

'Hello?' Hector called out. He had stepped into Auchterlonie's shop and the bell above the door had failed to bring anyone.

'Just a minute,' Laurie's voice came from the workshop.

Hector looked round the clubs on display and tried a few strokes with an old-fashioned, wooden-headed putter.

'That's for Mrs Doig of the Ladies' Putting Club, sir,' Laurie said, emerging from the workshop. He wiped his hands on a rag.

'Is it new or have you just spruced it up?'

'It's new. Not many people like to putt with this style these days. It's all blades, like Mr Jones and his Calamity Jane.'

'But Mrs Doig doesn't follow the fashion?'

'Pity there weren't more like her. This has balance and beauty.' He took the club from Hector and caressed its head in his strong hands. With his large nose, he looked like a huge crow fussing over an egg. 'Sorry I was busy, sir. I was pouring lead into the back of a driver and that's not a job you can leave.'

'I don't imagine so. How are you, Laurie? You must have got a helluva shock the other morning.'

'I'm fine, thank you, sir. But it's given my dad a terrible jolt. He was really looking forward to the Open. It's thirty-four years now since he won. This business has taken all the shine off it for him. He hasn't come to the shop the last two days. I've replaced the top of the workbench. Didn't even try to get the blood off.' He swallowed and turned his head away. 'Hamish had his faults, but he was a real craftsman. We'll miss him.' He blew his nose loudly.

Embarrassed by the young man's distress, Hector picked up a club and waggled it. When he judged that Laurie had recovered his composure, he asked, 'Have you heard any word of an arrest?'

Laurie's eyebrows went up. 'I'd have thought you might tell me, but I heard the police took Peter Nugent in for interview last night.'

'I don't think I know him.'

'He's one of the chefs at Rusacks. They say he came up the road to meet Hamish by arrangement about quarter past ten. He left an assistant to do some crepes Suzette, whatever they are. The story is Hamish owed Nugent money.'

'Do the people you've spoken to think Nugent's the killer?'

'Well, sir, they say he was acting strangely on Tuesday. A few of his dishes were sent back by the diners yet he's supposed to be a good chef.'

'Very interesting. I don't suppose you knew Mr Murnian?'

'I don't believe so. There was an American gentleman in the shop last Saturday. Shortish, dark haired. Could have been Mr Murnian. He was inquiring about a repair. He spoke to Hamish. I didn't pay attention, and I don't remember a club coming in.'

'I don't suppose you knew of any connection between Hamish McCann and young Jim Tindall?'

Laurie shook his head. 'I never knew of one.'

Hector changed the subject to British prospects in the championship. After dissecting the games of the three Whitcombe brothers, Archie Compston and George Duncan, and bemoaning the absence through illness of Abe Mitchell, Hector took his leave.

'But what were you in for, sir?' Laurie asked.

'Oh, golf balls. Give me half a dozen Silver Kings.'

*   *   *

Hector carried his unnecessary purchase down Golf Place and put the balls in his locker in the Royal and Ancient. He ordered a coffee and repaired to the North Room, where he could watch players driving off the first tee. One he recognized as Bob Jones (senior). Never better than a club player, he was with three friends no more skilful than himself, yet a small crowd followed them down the first fairway. Dick Robinson and three other young professionals, including the former public schoolboy, Henry Cotton, had preceded them taking no spectators with them. Shaking his head in amazement, Hector drained his cup and checked his watch. It was time to go out and try to catch Paul Murnian at the end of his round.

Sitting on his shooting stick at his favourite spot behind the seventeenth green, Hector wondered at the compliant nature of some people. Earlier, Mary, the receptionist at the Grand, had blushed, become flustered, and called him 'my lord' when he had announced himself and told her that he wanted to ask a few questions. Not only had she been happy to tell him that Paul Murnian had left for an early round shortly before eight, but she had given him far more detail about Ralf Murnian's telephone call to New York than he had asked for. About half past six on Tuesday evening, Mr Murnian had phoned from his suite and asked her to book a call to Mr Mo Evans of Evans McGrady and Rubenstein, Attorneys at Law, of Park Avenue, New York City. Mr Murnian had already spoken to Mr Evans on a number of occasions and, with the charges set by the Postmaster-General running at fifteen pounds for the first three minutes and five pounds for each additional minute, he had run up a considerable bill, without taking account of the ten per cent extra that Mr Tomkins had decided to charge. Mary and the St Andrews operator had become quite familiar with the American Service operators based in London. She now knew that New York, for some reason, ran five hours behind Britain. It had not proved a problem to book a person to person call between Mr Murnian and Mr Evans for quarter to eleven at night, British time. In a hushed voice, Mary had confided that, without eavesdropping of course, she had gathered they were planning some big business deal involving a company with a German-sounding name. It sounded like 'hoots mon', although that couldn't be right. She was also able to give Hector a note of the New York number.

At quarter to eleven the call had come through and Mary had personally telephoned Mr Murnian's suite, from where he had spoken. This had not been a very long conversation. It had come within the three minute bracket. But fifteen pounds for a three minute chat! It would take her a couple of months' wages to pay for that, even without Mr Tomkins' ten per cent on top. Mr Murnian had sounded quite as usual, calling Mr Evans the funny name he gave him. She was sure it had been Mr Ralf Murnian who had taken the call. He had always been very short and direct with her, and his accent was very New York, sometimes difficult to understand, and, although she didn't want to speak ill of the dead, he could get quite impatient. The hotel had been hectic all week, like Piccadilly Circus, Mr Tomkins had said, and he had worked in London. Mary had been far too busy to notice when Mr Murnian, or anyone else, had gone in or out that night, and Rab the porter had not been able to help the police when they had asked him. It was a terrible business, quite distressing when any guest in the hotel was cruelly murdered. Mary had paused to use her handkerchief, giving Hector an opening to thank her very much and depart.

His thoughts were interrupted when the next group of players came round the sheds from the seventeenth tee, a few spectators with them. One of the golfers was extraordinarily tall and, after a huge drive, was the last to play his second, a running shot that found the front edge of the green. As he drew closer, Hector recognized 'Long Jim' Barnes, the champion in 1925 and US Open winner of 1921. Born in Cornwall, he had emigrated to the States aged twenty. He had lived there for a further twenty years and had become a US citizen. He was one of those Hector wanted to see, and, although Barnes had a reputation for being amiable, he did not look forward to approaching him.

As Long Jim stooped to read the line of his putt, Paul Murnian, who was also in the group, climbed into the Road Bunker. Peering over the steep face, he spotted Hector on his shooting stick across on the other side of the green. His face creased in either concentration or irritation, he played his recovery too strongly. Having over-shot the green, his ball bounced and rolled about on the rough surface of the road before coming to rest a few feet from Hector. Paul banged his club into the sand, swung again without a ball, and, leaving his elderly, red-faced caddie to smooth over the marks he had made, walked across the green and down the steep bank to the road, his niblick in his hand. Hector thought it prudent to draw back from the ball but that did not save him from a glare before Paul assessed his shot.

The shot from the road can be played in two ways. Either the player lofts the ball into the air so that it carries on to the green and stops before the Road Bunker claims it, or he bumbles it along the ground, hoping for the best. Most St Andreans, scarred by experience, favour the latter, less glamorous, option. Behind Paul's ball there was a small stone which made the crisp, clean impact necessary for the lofted shot all but impossible. As Paul addressed his ball, the face of his niblick open so as to give the shot as much height as possible, Hector knew exactly what was about to happen.

Paul swung confidently but in vain. The small stone caused the ball to fly off the road low and hard. It bounced once before diving back into the Road Bunker, just as the caddie was clambering out of it.

'Pick it up,' Paul shouted, angry and embarrassed. Long Jim, who had stood watching, leaning on his putter and chewing some grass, smiled, shrugged, then crouched into a knock-kneed stance and laid his putt dead for an easy four. The other two in the group had played safe. One got a four and the other a five. As he followed them up the eighteenth, Hector hoped that Paul's mood might improve before he spoke to him about his father's death.

'Mr Murnian, could I have a word?' Hector said, claiming his attention as he came off the eighteenth green.

Paul wheeled round. 'My mother spoke to me about you, Sheriff Drummond. I will be in my parents' suite at half past twelve. I'm prepared to talk to you then, although I really don't see the point as the police have arrested my father's killers.' He turned abruptly to his caddie, giving him orders for the next day.

Trying to look unaffected by Paul's rudeness, Hector went over to Jim Barnes, who was closely examining one of his irons. His drive at the last hole, slightly miss-hit, had landed on Granny Clark's Wynd and he had played a stunningly fine shot off the rough surface of the roadway. The sole and leading edge of his mashie-niblick had been damaged.

'There are plenty of people in St Andrews who will file down these marks for you,' Hector said.

Barnes smiled. 'I guess they'll have had a lot of practice. Who do you recommend, sir?' A transatlantic drawl on top of a Cornish burr gave him a distinctive but mellifluous voice.

'Stewarts in Argyle Street will do repairs. Forgans are the nearest. Just there, overlooking the green. They'll do a good job. Auchterlonies specialise more in woods, but they'd do it too.'

'I guess I might go visit Tom Stewart's place. Bob Jones often talks about his pipe brand irons. Charlie, here, has been wanting to pay them a visit.' He nodded towards one of the other players. Hector realized this must be Charlie Mayo, another on his list. This was his opportunity. He took a deep breath.

'Before you do that, I wonder if I might have a quick word with you, and Mr Mayo as well, if possible. I'm Sheriff Hector Drummond and, as you will know, there have been three murders in St Andrews this week. I want to make sure the police have not missed something important, and I am asking a few questions of people who might know anything that might prove useful to the course of justice. Bobby Jones immediately agreed to answer my queries, and I hope that you and Mr Mayo might give me five minutes or so, perhaps now, if that would be convenient?'

Barnes' face wrinkled. For a moment Hector thought he was going to refuse, but he shrugged in resignation. 'Well, I could sure use a cup of tea. It's the main thing I miss about Britain. Charlie and I are staying in the Grand, and I was just about to head there.'

Hector took the hint. 'I'll order tea in the lounge. For two or for three?'

Mayo was discussing something with his caddie. Barnes went over and clapped him on the back. 'Charlie, this gentleman's the sheriff and he wants to talk to us. He's offered to buy us tea in the Grand. Are you coming?'

'I suppose so, sure.' Mayo sounded doubtful.

Ten minutes later, Hector was sitting by a window overlooking the course, giving the same explanation he had given to Nabholtz and Robinson. Mayo, another Englishman who had emigrated, frowned. Barnes, folded in his chair like a lethargic daddy long-legs, remained impassive.

'On Monday afternoon we went to the movies. Together. And we left together to change for the party here.' Barnes' tone remained friendly, but his eyes narrowed as he looked directly at Hector.

'I gather it was a Buster Keaton film they were showing?'

'It was, and at the end Keaton got his girl and his train back.'

Hector was mystified. 'His train?'

Barnes grinned. 'You tell him, Charlie. Maybe it's the sheriff who needs an alibi.'

As Hector stiffened, Charlie Mayo described the plot of *The General*. Set in the Civil War, Keaton played a Confederate engineer whose train and girl were taken by the North. 'So you can tell we waited through all the breaks till the end,' he concluded.

'And we were up most of Tuesday night playing cards with Reggie and Charlie Whitcombe,' Barnes added, draining his cup.

'Could we go back to the film, please?' Hector tried to establish some authority. 'I understand there were a few unscheduled breaks. Did either of you see anyone leaving early?'

The golfers exchanged glances. Barnes shook his head.

'I can't think of anyone who left for sure,' Mayo said cautiously.

'For sure?' Hector leaned forward.

'I don't want to get a fellow I like into trouble he doesn't deserve by telling you something that's wrong.'

'I understand you can't be sure, but it's very important to have all the information. I'll take it with a pinch of salt,' Hector added.

Mayo was silent for a while then said, 'Jim, do you recall Paul Murnian saying during one of the breaks that he'd already seen the film on Broadway?'

Barnes put a strong, brown hand to his chin and thought. 'Now that you mention it, yes. He came over to talk to us after the manager came to the front, wringing his hands and apologising, and these kids threw things at him from the balcony.' Barnes grinned.

'Did you see Paul at the end?'

Barnes said, 'Can't say I did. He moved away from us, I thought to the back of the stalls to make sure he didn't get hit by these pesky kids. I wondered about moving myself, but we heard some noise as the kids were put out, so we stayed where we were. At the end of the film, we all stood for *God Save the King* and left. The fog was as thick as ever. I didn't see Paul then, but I wasn't looking for him.'

Mayo nodded. 'Same goes for me,' he said.

Hector tried to picture the scene. 'Did either of you see Larry Nabholtz or Kenny Nolan?'

Barnes spoke again. 'We walked down the road with them. I guess they must have been sitting behind us in the stalls.'

'What about Paul Murnian's brother, Enda?'

'I barely know him and I don't remember seeing him there. What about you, Charlie?'

'I don't remember seeing him.'

'Do either of you know Enda's wife, Vera, I believe she's called?'

Both men shook their heads.

'Can you remember the time when you left the cinema?'

'About twenty past five, I think. It was supposed to finish half an hour earlier. We didn't have time for tea before the Independence Day party.' The elder of the two, Barnes spoke for both again.

Hector beamed at them. 'Thank you both very much, gentlemen. That has been most informative.'

'Thanks for the tea, Sheriff,' Barnes said as he rose slowly to his feet, putting a shortbread biscuit in his mouth as he did so. Mayo got up as well. They left Hector, deep in thought, staring into space, his tea untouched.

'Did you learn anything?' Hector started when O.B. whispered to him.

'Where did you spring from?' Hector asked as O.B. slipped into the seat beside him.

'Behind that pillar. I didn't want to interrupt you.'

'I wouldn't have minded, but yes, I learned something. The film doesn't give Paul an alibi. The same might apply to Enda, too.' Hector told O.B. what had been said.

'Well, I have something for you. Sandy Armour spent Monday and Tuesday in Edinburgh, seeing family and friends, and Wild Bill Melhorn didn't arrive in St Andrews till Thursday. That's two of the Scioto eleven we can forget about.'

Hector beamed. He took out a piece of paper and made some jottings. 'I need to speak with Lord Terry, but I haven't seen him about,' he said.

'Terry's due to play an exhibition game at Gleneagles tomorrow. Bob's playing, too, but he's resting today. He likes to get a day without golf just before a championship. Like the Old Course, herself.'

Hector chuckled. 'Did you hear about the visitor to St

Andrews who asked Old Tom Morris why there was no play on
the Old on Sundays?'

'Can't say I have.'

'Old Tom said to the visitor: "You may no' need a rest, but
the course does." It's true enough.' A thought struck him. 'What
time are they playing tomorrow?'

'Early afternoon. Are you thinking of going there?'

'Lavender and I will be going to Glenalmond. It's not too far
away, and young Jake would love to see Bobby play. Are you
planning to go?'

'Eleanor adores your Scottish scenery. I hear Glendevon is
beautiful. We wouldn't miss it.'

'I'll probably see you there. Oh, and tell Bobby I hope he
beats Lord Terry hollow.'

O.B. smiled and shook his head. 'And I thought you two
were best pals.'

Hector looked at him sharply then saw the twinkle in his
eye. He said, 'I'd better go. I have an appointment with Paul
Murnian in their suite.'

*   *   *

'Come in!' Enid Murnian answered the bellboy's knock. When
Hector entered he found her in black, but looking much sharper
than at their previous meeting. She reclined on the chaise
longue, a newly-lit cigarette in her holder. To her right, also
smoking, was Paul, still in his golf clothes. He sat cross-legged
on an upright chair, showing well-muscled thighs under black
and white stockings that failed to go with the brown check of
his baggy tweed plus fours. At the foot of the chaise longue, on
adjacent upright chairs, sat Enda and Vera. Sharing their coun-
try-men's enthusiasm for tweed but without the flamboyance,

both had selected a subdued charcoal grey cloth. The two brothers wore black ties. Not one of their faces led Hector to think that his visit was welcome. A further upright chair had been placed on its own in the middle of the room. Hector sat on it before he could be asked, or not asked, to do so.

'I...'

'We know why you are here, Sheriff Drummond,' the widow cut in. 'Although the police have arrested my husband's killers with commendable speed, you have taken it into your head to pursue your own investigation. I find that distressing and impertinent, and so do my sons. Despite his grief, Paul is steeling himself to compete in the British Open, as his father would have wished, and Enda is getting to grips with my husband's business interests, which he will be taking over. I have been advised that we are under no obligation to humour you by answering questions, but to prove we have nothing to hide, we shall talk to you, on this occasion only. We will not be so co-operative in the future.'

Hector tried to appear unruffled. 'I'm sorry you look at it that way, Mrs Murnian. I assure you that I have no desire to cause additional distress, but, as I pointed out the last time we met, it would be most unfortunate if, at the trial, the defence could get away with saying that no thorough investigation took place. Craigie Aitchison KC and Macgregor Mitchell KC, our best criminal advocates, are ruthless when it comes to destroying a badly-prepared Crown case.'

Enid Murnian blew out a smoke ring. 'My husband would have found a word for that, but I'm not going to use it. You'd better ask your questions, Sheriff. It's nearly time for lunch.'

'All right.' Hector was determined not to be rushed. He took out his cigarette case, tapped out the loose tobacco with particular care, then, praying it would not let him down, flicked his lighter. The flame spurted on the third attempt. He lit the cigarette and inhaled deeply. Giving what he hoped was an encouraging smile, he asked, 'Paul, what did you do after dinner on Tuesday, the night your father died?'

Paul stared aggressively at Hector. 'The night he was murdered, you mean? I went out. I met Charlie Mayo and Jim Barnes, who were heading for Rusacks. They said they had a card game arranged. I left them and went a walk out the course.'

'Still dressed for dinner?'

'Yes.'

'Is your dinner jacket black?' Hector thought back to the night of the party and pictured Paul coming over to their table.

'Yes.'

'Did you see your father?'

'Yes.'

'Did you talk about your relationship with Mrs Van Dyke?'

A flicker told Hector he did not like the question. 'Yes.' He thought for a moment then added, his voice shaky: 'I'd been upset at dinner. Alone, out on the course, I sat on the grassy bank in the middle of the fourth fairway and got to thinking. Dad came walking out the course, too, and he saw me. We talked some, then walked a bit, I left him on the fifth green then came back. I never saw him again.' His voice caught.

'Did you quarrel?' Hector asked softly.

'We talked. There was no quarrel.'

'Sheriff Drummond, are you trying to upset us?' Enid hissed.

'But she had come here to be with you and your parents were against you seeing her. Did you not at least argue with your father?' Hector persisted.

'Are you accusing me of something?'

'Not at all. I just want to know all I can about your father's last hours.'

Paul inhaled deeply then blew smoke in Hector's direction. 'He was my dad. He gave me advice. I took it in. We were fine. His last words to me were: "I'll see you in the morning, son. Tomorrow's gonna be a new day."' He swallowed hard then looked defiantly at Hector.

'Where did you go after you left your father?'

Paul turned to his mother. 'Mom, I have to do this, show I have nothing to be ashamed of.' He gulped and looked out of the window. 'I can't remember how long it took, but I came back here. I did sit for some time on the lip of a bunker, kicking my heels. I went to my room then had a beer in the lounge about eleven.'

'Do you remember anyone who saw you then?'

Paul thought for a moment. 'It was the tall young fellow who served me. We had a discussion about light and heavy beers. Then I went to bed.'

'Did you try to find Mrs Van Dyke?'

Paul looked first to his mother and then his brother, but they retained poker faces. Picking his words, he said: 'I know she was interested in Terry Coates-Moulton. I asked around to find out where she was. I know he's staying in some grand house out of town, and I thought he might have picked her up in his Rolls Royce.'

'Do you not care for Lord Terry?'

'I'd shove a poker up his ass if he didn't have one there already. Sorry, Mom.' Enid glared at him but said nothing.

'You wouldn't be the first to want to do that,' Hector said, hoping to improve his stock with Paul. 'Did you go out after dinner because you wanted to find her?'

'Yes. Charlie Mayo said he thought he'd seen Gloria head

down the road to Rusacks. I assumed she was meeting Coates-Moulton there for dinner. I went with them, but they persuaded me not to go in and make a scene.'

'Did you see her at all that evening?'

'No.'

'Have you spoken to her since your father's death?'

Paul shook his head.

'Did you see anyone you knew during your walk on the golf course?'

'I didn't notice anyone in particular.'

'On Monday, I understand you went to see a film?'

'I did. So did Enda and Vera.'

'Did you stay till the end?'

'Yes. Of course.' He glanced towards his brother.

'Had you seen the film before?'

'No.' Hector thought he answered too quickly.

'When did you get back here?'

'I don't know. I had a tub and dressed for the party. I was dressing when I found the message from Gloria saying she was here. It came as a big surprise. I went to her room.'

'Were you late for the party?'

'I believe so.' Hector thought there was a suspicion of self-satisfaction about that reply.

Turning to Enda, Hector asked if he had stayed till the end of the film.

'Like my brother, yes. Do you want me to describe the plot?' Hector had not before spoken with Enda. There was a languid insolence about his reply that mirrored his posture. The clear, blue eyes he turned on Hector seemed intelligent but untrustworthy.

'That won't be necessary, thank you. Did you, your wife and your brother sit together?'

Enda shrugged and Vera seemed to tense. Enda said, 'I really can't remember.'

'I would appreciate it if you tried. I suppose you do want the truth to come out?'

The reply was steely. 'I can't remember.'

'Well may I jog your memory? I've been told you and your wife did not sit with your brother, and that he moved about during the breaks in the film. Am I wrong?'

Enda coloured slightly and stroked his wispy moustache. Paul interjected, 'I smoke and they don't. The smoke was getting in their eyes, so I moved. Some kids were throwing things from the balcony so I moved again and sat at the back of the stalls. I did stay till the end.'

'We all stood up for *God Save the King*. It was real quaint.' Vera spoke for the first time. Her voice was soft and coquettish, identifiably American, and lacking both the harshness of New York and the drawl of the South. Hector did not think her voice went with her appearance, which was mousy to the point of dowdiness.

'Did you all come back to the hotel together?'

In unison, Paul and Vera said, 'yes'. Enda nodded.

'Were any of you aware of the late Mr Murnian visiting Auchterlonies' shop at any time?'

All four appeared puzzled and shook their heads.

Hector asked Enda, 'May I ask about your movements on Tuesday night after dinner?'

Without hesitation, he replied, 'I took my wife for a drive down the coast to Crail. It was a beautiful evening. We talked a bit and came back to the hotel about ten. I did some work on a business deal. We didn't go out again.'

'And your room is?'

Vera's eyes narrowed. Enda replied with exaggerated

patience: 'Next door to this room. Then there's a bathroom, then my brother's room, so we have most of this corridor. My parents' room and their bathroom are the other rooms leading off the vestibule outside this room. They form a suite.'

'So apart from your parents' bedroom and bathroom you will all get a good view of the golf course?'

'Exactly,' Enda replied with an air of finality.

'Do you all have keys for this sitting room?'

'As a matter of fact we do.' Enda did not hide his growing irritation.

Hector said diffidently, 'Forgive me, but I heard that the late Mr Murnian received a message before dinner on Tuesday and it appeared to upset him. Do any of you know anything about that?'

'We do not.' Enid Murnian spoke quickly and forcefully. Her sons shook their heads.

Hector smiled at them. 'Thank you very much for your time. I am sorry to have intruded into your private grief, but I do believe it was necessary. You have been away from home for some time, I gather. Was your trip to Germany a success?' He looked at Enda.

'I believe so,' Enda said. 'I hope we will soon own the Hundsmann company. I'm not spilling a secret, Sheriff. It's been talked about in the papers and their stock is up fifty per cent this week, so on Monday you'll be too late to make a killing.'

Hector ignored the implied insult. 'Was your father well-disposed towards the deal?' he asked.

'He came round to it. In fact, during his last telephone call, he told our attorney, Mo Evans, to go right ahead.'

'Going to Berlin can't have been ideal preparation for this championship?' Hector turned to Paul.

'Not a bit of it. I played Wannsee with your Percy Alliss. He's the professional there.'

'That's a piece of luck. Well, good luck next week. I'm sorry there isn't more bounce in the fairways, and the greens will be awfully slow, but it should be a fine championship for all that.' Hector got up to go then swivelled round, as if with an after-thought. 'At least things will be easier for you than they were last year at Scioto. Did you watch your brother play there?' He smiled disarmingly at Enda, who started. Out of the corner of his eye he saw Paul shift on his chair.

Enda recovered quickly. 'After his first round, my father was convinced my younger brother would become National Open Champion. I travelled hundreds of miles to see him get blown away by the gales.' He twisted his lips, more sneering than smiling.

'Almost everyone else got blown away too,' Paul said sulkily.

'Well, thank you again. It has been most helpful.' Their faces registering varying degrees of suspicion and hostility, the Murnians sat silent and immobile as Hector left the room. He heard Enid's icy voice say 'Goodbye, Sheriff Drummond' before the door clicked behind him.

As he crossed the road to the club, Hector sensed that some-thing about her was different, aside from her alcohol consump-tion. He knew it would niggle him till he put his finger on it.

*   *   *

Hector looked out of the window of the Big Room, trying to make sense of the Murnians. He wanted to catch Tommy at the end of Dick Robinson's round and, when he spotted their game on the eighteenth tee, swallowed his drink and went to meet them.

The Valley of Sin was a dip in the ground with a near-vertical slope about four feet high leading up to the eighteenth green. Most players carried it with a high shot, which they hoped would stop before running far past the pin. A few ran their ball along the ground. Hector could see that Henry Cotton, about whom he had heard Cyril Tolley speak highly, was about to try the running shot. A look of intense concentration on his sharp features, he swung his mashie to and fro, feeling the shot. When he executed it, his hands and arms did all the work. The ball ran up the slope and seemed to stop, leaving Cotton with a good chance of a birdie three. As he replaced the club in his bag, the ball began to move again, slowly at first, then running back to finish in the deepest part of the dip. When he saw what had happened, Cotton pursed his lips and glared, but said nothing.

Hector was amused to see Tommy take the mashie out of Dick's bag, encouraging him to try the run-up as well, but Dick took his niblick, favouring the high shot that he knew best. A crisp strike left him a couple of yards past the pin, nearest of the four players.

After they had all holed out in par fours, Hector caught Tommy's eye as he left the green.

'Tomorrow's Sunday, and I plan to spend all day putting,' Dick said. 'That putt on eighteen didn't even look like it might drop. So I'll see you Monday for the first qualifying round. We're quite well down the list for the Old.'

After Tommy and Dick had made their arrangements, Tommy said he could meet Hector in a quarter of an hour, after he had rubbed up Dick's clubs, a vital part of the caddie's duties. That gave Hector time to visit the club for another whisky.

*   *   *

'Sir, no one thinks Wullie and Marty are guilty,' Tommy said as they walked towards the rough ground for more mashie practice. 'But a few say they'll hang anyway.'

'If I have anything to do with it, the only reason they'll hang is if they're guilty,' Hector said. 'I've been talking to the Murnians, and they're a strange lot. Have you heard anything interesting?'

'Please don't say I told you this, sir, because he's paying my wages, but Robbie Walker says he saw Mr Sabbatini on the thirteenth in the sma' hours of the morning the night Mr Murnian was killed.'

'Mr Sabbatini? Who's Robbie Walker? Why was he there?'

'A caddie, sir. He takes a drink, does Robbie, and at times he's no' welcome in his own hoose. If it's a fine night, he might go wandering. He says he's sure, sir.'

'I didn't think Mr Sabbatini could walk that far.'

'Robbie says he was moving real slow, and he needed a stick, but he's quite a character, sir, and people know him.'

'What was Mr Sabbatini doing? What was he wearing?'

'Robbie says he was looking down into the Coffin bunkers. He didna' say what he was wearing.'

'How near did Robbie get?'

'He said he'd had a wee sleep in a spot beside the fifth green of the New, so he was maybe a hundred yards away.'

'Has he not gone to the police?'

'Naw. He and Sergeant McNeill don't get on at all. Don't tell Dick, or anyone, I told you this, please, sir.'

'Don't worry. I'll protect my sources, as the journalists say, but thank you, Tommy. Oh, look there. That fellow's going to go far.' They were passing the eighteenth green of the New. About eighty yards down the fairway, Henry Cotton was practising run-ups with his mashie. About a dozen balls nestled near the pin, but there was a bigger number beside him. A dedicated young man, he appeared far from satisfied.

Hector's less intense mashie practice was soon over, his play benefiting from the fuller shoulder turn that Tommy had suggested the previous day. On the way back, Hector had a brainwave.

'If you aren't needed by Dick tomorrow, would you like to visit Wullie in Perth Prison and find out if he saw or heard anything at all unusual when he was working for Paul Murnian?'

'I'd do it, sir, but how would I get there?'

'I'll give you a lift. I'm going to Glenalmond to see my stepson and then on to Gleneagles, so I'll be passing the prison. It'll be quite an early start and you'll be kicking your heels a bit before we pick you up, but I'll take you door to door, and my housekeeper can make up sandwiches for you. Are you on?'

'Yes, but will they let me in?'

'Wullie's entitled to plenty visits as he's untried. I'll write a note you can show the warders if they're tricky.'

'But will they let me out?'

'I'm not so sure about that.' Hector put on a serious face.

Tommy looked at him then raised his eyebrows. 'You do like yer wee joke, sir. I hope.'

9

Sunday 10 July

'The ring!' Hector exclaimed, throwing the sheet off. 'Sorry, darling,' he added as Lavender stirred beside him.

'It's far too early for Wagner, darling. I couldn't bear it,' she muttered.

'Enid Murnian wasn't wearing her emerald ring. Yesterday, when I saw her.' Hector sat up in bed and poured himself a glass of water from his carafe.

Lavender opened her eyes. Daylight was filtering into the room and she knew there was little chance of more sleep. 'Why should she wear it?' she asked.

'When I visited her on Friday, her fingers were dripping with jewels, and beside her wedding ring there was this humdinger of an emerald. Yesterday, when she knew I was coming, her fingers were still dripping with precious stones, but there was no emerald.'

'It must have been a whopper for you to notice, my love. Could she not have been wearing it on some other finger?'

'I suppose so,' Hector conceded. 'I didn't specifically register it at the time. It was one of these subliminal things. I suppose it came to me as I was dreaming.'

She sat up and hugged him. 'Well, you're better dreaming

of emeralds than of corpses. I was having a nice dream then. And today we see Jake. I'm so excited. I just hope whatever he wants to talk to us about isn't too serious. Cup of tea?'

'Good idea. Is the shortbread finished yet?'

'Wait and see,' she said suggestively, putting on her dressing gown with a theatrical flourish.

'You know how the Earl of Silloth and Solway had his emeralds pinched recently and offered some huge reward?' Hector asked five minutes later as Lavender placed a tray of tea and shortbread on her bedside table.

'Yes. Could there be some tie-up with the Murnians, do you think?' Carefully, she passed a cup and saucer across the bed.

'It seems unlikely, but yes.'

'Not so unlikely, surely,' she said. 'The Eyes of the Fox are collectors' pieces. Broken up, they wouldn't be worth half of what they're worth intact and together. A bit like the shortbread. Please watch the crumbs, darling. Now that they're stolen, the only people who would touch them would be egocentric, very rich, totally unscrupulous and probably not British. Does that remind you of anyone?'

'De mortuis nihil nisi bonum. But for all that, Ralf Murnian. And by a coincidence, both he and the earl have sons competing in the Open.'

'Another unlikely coincidence,' she said. 'Do you think you'll get a chance to talk to Lord Terry today, about the murders, I mean.'

'I don't know. He's appallingly arrogant. I'll try, anyway. With Bobby around, he'll probably be on his best behaviour. That shortbread is lovely.'

'Remember to tell Mrs Alves. She's not the most adaptable, but at short notice she's made up a mountain of sandwiches for your young caddie friend. He'd better eat them all.'

'He looks as if he could do with a few square meals. Talking of which, I could manage an early breakfast.'

'I'm going to ca' canny. I don't want to spoil my appetite for a Gleneagles lunch.'

'So I suppose I might as well finish the shortbread?' Hector reached over to take the last piece from the plate.

* * *

'An old head on young shoulders,' Lavender commented as they drove away from Perth Prison, having dropped Tommy outside the forbidding gate of that large, dismal edifice. Solid, grey and menacing, it was the first significant building of the Fair City encountered by travellers approaching from the South. Beside the majestically meandering Tay and the ample grass swards of the Inch, the jail struck a sobering, discordant note.

Wearing his best suit, Tommy had been waiting outside his front door when Hector had driven down Bridge Street. After an awkward introduction to Lavender, and an exchange of optimistic remarks about the weather, the lad had tucked in to the parcel of sandwiches awaiting him on the back seat.

'Are you not going to leave some for later?' Lavender inquired as he drained the first of three bottles of ginger beer Mrs Alves had put with the sandwiches.

'Someone else might steal them, ma'am. Specially in a prison. Do you mind, sir?' He feared he should have asked earlier.

Hector laughed. 'Not at all. Have them when you want, but don't make a mess of my leather upholstery.'

'This is a Bullnose car, isn't it, sir?' Tommy asked, enabling Hector to talk happily about the Morris Oxford's four-cylinder engine and its Dynastart mechanism. The conversational ice broken, Lavender questioned Tommy about his mother and sister. She tried to conceal her shock at how much responsibility rested on him, and he barely told her half of it. The morning was beautiful and the roads were quiet. The journey passed quickly. With instructions to be waiting at the same place about seven, Tommy got out, a letter from Hector to facilitate his mission in his pocket. He was primed to squeeze as much information as possible out of Wullie Kay, without divulging the extent of Hector's interest in his case.

Taking the Crieff road out of Perth, Hector drove confidently over winding but familiar roads. He reached Glenalmond and steered slowly down Front Avenue, a host of memories, not all comfortable, flooding back. Perched on a high point beside the River Almond, against a background of gentle hills, the school, conceived by pious men and constructed of grey-red sandstone, was as picturesque as the jail was drab. In his day it had been a Spartan institution, rigorous, demanding and bone-chillingly cold during the long winters. Hector had left Glenalmond with a strong sense of belonging, based on a camaraderie forged by shared tribulations and successes. Moral worth had been as important as education. Suppressing the feeling that he should not have come down Front Avenue in the comfort of a motor car, he parked on the gravel beside the main entrance. He paused to inhale fresh, highland air and gaze over the green slopes and playing fields where, just over twenty years earlier, caked in cold mud and bleeding, he had, he thought, given his all. Beside him had been John Taylor-Smith. Now he was back at Glenalmond, doing his duty to his dead friend by acting as a father to his son. Trying to shut out bitter-sweet thoughts, he took Lavender's arm and escorted her through the arch and into Front Quad where other parents were waiting for Chapel to end.

They had not long to wait. A procession of stern-faced men of varying ages wearing black gowns with academic hoods strode out of the Chapel doorway. A horde of teenage boys followed, walking sedately from the building before re-grouping, chattering and laughing. They were all dressed in lovat green tweed jackets, but their kilts showed off the colourful diversity of Scottish tartans. A dark-haired boy with a round face, taller than the rest, his kilt predominantly red, broke away from a group of juniors.

'Mama, Uncle Hector,' he greeted them. With a self-conscious air, he kissed his mother on the cheek then shook hands with Hector.

Unable to stop seeing the father in the boy, Hector concentrated on the present. 'You're looking well, Jake. How would you like to have lunch at Gleneagles?'

'Smashing!'

'Then watch Bobby Jones play an exhibition match on the King's Course?'

'Better still!'

'Let's go, then.'

They lost no time in climbing into the car. Before they reached the top of Front Avenue, Jake asked about the St Andrews murders.

'The police have made some arrests,' Hector said, not wanting to be specific.

'But they have got the men for Jim's murder?'

'That'll be for the trial court to decide.'

'You don't sound very sure, Uncle Hector. Have you seen the men they've arrested?'

'Yes, I have.'

'What are they like?'

'A bit strange, frankly.'

'How, strange?'

Hector did not know how to respond. Lavender rescued him. 'Jake, the men they have arrested for Jim's murder are two homosexuals.' A grunt of disgust came from the back seat. Lavender continued, 'I'm concerned that's the only reason they've arrested them, but it will be up to the court to decide.'

'So Jim's killer may be free?'

'That's a possibility, I'm afraid,' Hector agreed.

'That's terrible,' Jake said in a soft voice. He sat, silent and brooding, until they passed the solid stone houses with their neat gardens on the outskirts of Crieff.

'How are things at Coll?' Hector asked, using the name Glenalmond people gave to the college.

'Fine, thanks.'

'Are you still getting on well with the other Probationers?'

'Oh yes, they're good chaps, but I'm really looking forward to going into Warden's next term. Most chaps reckon it's the best house.'

Hector remembered dissembling to his parents as to how much he was enjoying school, but Jake seemed genuinely happy. 'Things are certainly changing. They didn't have houses in my day. How are the lessons going?'

'Some are boring, most are all right. I hate Latin.'

'Well you'll just have to put up with it. Aequam memento rebus in arduis servare mentem, as Horace wrote.' Hector saw Lavender's frown. 'If you stick in, you'll be able to come out with tosh like that when you're older,' he added.

'Have you been getting into trouble?' Lavender asked, mystified as to what Jake wanted to talk about.

'No more than anyone else. I haven't been beaten for months.'

'You seem to be enjoying cricket?' Hector asked.

'You bet. Price, he's Captain of Cricket as well as Captain of Coll, says I'm very promising, and he helped me with my cover drive. He's going to Oxford next term.'

'Your father had a lovely cover drive,' Hector said as Jake launched into a description of his last two cricket matches. He reached the final ball of the second one as they pulled up beside the smooth lawns in front of Gleneagles Hotel.

A huge, grey building with a slate roof, created by the Caledonian Railway Company and looking more like a French chateau than a Scottish hotel, Gleneagles had opened its doors in 1924, to be hailed as a Riviera in the Highlands and, with even greater hyperbole, the Eighth Wonder of the World. In truth, the place owed its growing celebrity to the plain, dour Scot, James Braid, who, among sand and gravel ridges, designed two wonderful golf courses, the King's and the Queen's. The thirteenth on the King's, a long par four with a heather-edged fairway, dipping valleys and an undulating green, not to mention spectacular views, well justified its epithet, Braid's Brawest.

Hector, Lavender and Jake went straight in for lunch. The spacious dining room was already busy, and Hector was glad he had reserved a table.

'Is that Bobby Jones over there?' Jake asked in a stage whisper.

'Yes, it is,' Hector spoke normally.

'He waved at you just then!'

'I know. We've met a few times.'

'Wow. Do you think I could meet him later?'

'You never know.' In fact, Hector had hoped to introduce Jake to Bobby after the round.

Their order was taken and they sat back to wait. Lavender could contain her curiosity no longer. Speaking quietly, she said, 'Jake, darling, you wrote asking us to see you before the end of term. What is it?'

Looking very young, Jake shifted in his chair then took a deep breath. 'I don't want to be known as Taylor-Smith next term when I go into Warden's. I want to change my name,' he said. 'I want to be a Drummond like the rest of the family.' He turned to Hector. 'I want you to be my father. Officially.'

'What?' Hector said, louder than he intended. His sense of duty to his friend was roused. Jake flashed him a look that combined hurt and pleading. A stunned, awkward silence followed.

Hector sensed that his relationship with Jake might be ruined irretrievably, and he knew that would be the last thing that John would have wanted. He was the first to speak. 'I'm taken aback. That's probably the biggest compliment anyone has paid me in my entire life. Thank you, Jake.'

The boy's face lit up. 'Would that be all right, then?'

Hector rubbed his forehead. 'If it were to be just you and me, I would say yes right away. But it's not that simple.' Searching for the right words, he carried on. 'I am really very flattered that you should think that way, but you've got your grandfather's estate to consider. He left it to you, of course, but he attached a lot of conditions. I mean, you get no control till you're twenty-one. And I'm almost certain you have to retain the Taylor-Smith name.'

His voice catching, Jake replied: 'I remember when my family was just Mama and I. Then we became another family. Mama could become your wife. Why can't I become your son? Why can't I be properly in the same family as Mama? I don't feel as if I am a full member of this family. Marie and Charlotte are, but I'm not.' He began to cry.

Hector wished they were somewhere else. 'Jake, I'm talking about your birthright, Lammerstane. "Blood's thicker than water," as they say.' As soon as he said this, he knew it was a mistake.

'But there's more than water between us,' Jake sobbed. Hector looked despairingly at Lavender.

'You are absolutely part of this family, my love,' she said, reaching out to hold Jake's hand. Her other hand she placed on Hector's arm. 'Whatever name you have to go by, you will always be part of this family.' She bit her lip.

'What brought this on?' Hector asked gently.

Jake wiped his face then twisted his starched linen napkin in his hands. 'All my friends have a father, but I don't. Horwood, I'm very friendly with him, he had a first father, who's dead, killed in the War. He had a different name, but his mother married Dr Horwood, and he and his brothers are all Horwoods now.' He looked pleadingly at Lavender. 'Mama, you changed your name.'

'Lammerstane is important, my darling,' she said.

'I like living in St Andrews. I never want to live at Lammerstane. It's so, so...empty.'

'Your grandmother's still there,' Lavender pointed out.

The eloquence of Jake's silence was broken by the arrival of plates of roast beef and Yorkshire pudding. If the waiter sensed the tension round the table, he did not show it. Slowly at first, then with increasing appetites, the three of them ate their meal, grateful for the fact that they did not need to speak.

As Lavender, last to finish, used a potato to wipe up her gravy, Hector cleared his throat. 'We have to know exactly where we stand, but if, at the end of the day, that is what Jake really wants, I am enormously flattered, and, from my own point of view, I am happy to accede to his proposal. What about you, darling?'

'If that's what he really wants...Whatever happens, you might let him call you Papa?'

'Good idea. Is that all right with you, Jake?'

The boy nodded.

Hector continued, 'But, I don't think we can make a final decision until we know what your grandfather's trust deed says. The precise wording is vital. I know Rory McIlwham. He's a partner in J. & R.A. Robertson, who act for the trust. He used to brief me when I was at the bar. I'll write to him and explain the situation. When he replies, we will know where we stand. Then we can decide. I hope that is satisfactory.' The sheriff had given judgment. Lavender and Jake nodded.

'Right, what are we going to have for pud?' Hector demanded, scanning the card in front of him. 'I fancy bread and butter pudding.'

*   *   *

A few hundred spectators, full of anticipation, had gathered round the first tee of the King's Course by the time Hector, Lavender and Jake arrived. With a bit of jostling, Hector secured a view of the drives for Lavender. Spotting a gap, Jake darted round to the far side of the tee. Jones was first to play. For most of those present it was their first sight of his swing. Those who knew their golf noted his full pivot and the smooth, fluid application of exceptional power. There were gasps of awe as his ball sailed far and true down the broad, welcoming first fairway. Next to play was Gordon Lockhart, the Gleneagles professional. Unused to such scrutiny, he appeared nervous, but hit a creditable drive nearly as far as Jones. Their opponents, also amateur paired with professional, were Lord Terry Coates-Moulton and Joe Kirkwood. Neither of them seemed bothered by a gallery and they too hit decent drives. The game was on. For the spectators, the rush was on. Almost all of them had eyes only for Bobby Jones, to an extent that was discourteous to the other players. The stewards needed to exert themselves before enough people were moved to enable Coates-Moulton to play his second. His square-jawed face remained impassive, but Hector guessed that he was grossly affronted and seething inside.

By the time Hector and Lavender had climbed up to the plateau on which the first green sat, the crowd was too densely packed to allow her to see. They went behind the second tee to wait for the players.

'After they've driven, I think I'll go off and sit on a mound and see you later,' she said. 'You'll manage better without me holding you up. It'll give you and Jake some time together. Yes, that's what I want to do,' she added as he began to protest.

Movement among the crowd told them that the first hole was over. Hector and Lavender had a splendid vantage point from which to watch the drives. As the cavalcade moved on, Lavender stayed behind. She could see Jake, distinctive in his Cameron tartan kilt, striding out beside her husband, for all the world like father and son. That kilt had been John's when he was a boy. The Taylors claimed kinship with the Clan Cameron, and John enjoyed telling people that he was directly descended from a bloodthirsty sixteenth century Cameron known as Black Tailor of the Axe. Hector's lineage was not nearly as exotic.

For a while Lavender wandered among the heather and bracken, blind to the scenery, trying to come to terms with Jake's request. At length she selected a sunny slope above the seventeenth green where she sat down to think. How much did a blood relationship really matter? More to Hector than to Jake. Maybe, in general, it mattered more to fathers than to sons, 'fruit of my loins' and all that. Sons were probably more concerned with who actually fulfilled the paternal role. Sons needed fathers more than fathers needed sons, at least before the sons grew up. Hector had always respected John's memory, sometimes too much. The slain warrior had been like a household god, placed reverently in the hearth, who as the years passed had crept gradually away to a place behind a curtain. Now that curtain had been pulled aside and the god was back in their midst. What would John have wanted? Dormant memories of her first husband and the passion they had shared flashed through her mind. John had been a freer spirit than Hector, more of a scamp as a boy. He had dismissed an aunt's house as a mausoleum because it was full of pictures of people who were dead. Once, outwith Hector's hearing, he had been scathing because his best friend was so governed by duty. Hector had always been concerned with what was right. At the bar, he had never been comfortable presenting a case in which he did not totally believe. On the bench, he had been criticised on appeal a few times for preferring his own sense of justice to the letter of the law.

Hector had been good to Jake without showing the warmth he felt for the girls. She had sensed his disappointment when she had produced daughters, not sons. But his own father had been distant, cold and untactile, reluctant to show emotion. Perhaps he would have been like that, even with a son of his own blood.

While he kept an invisible barrier between himself and Jake, he seemed to really care about his inferiors, Alf and now Tommy. The social gulf was like a moat. Behind it, Hector felt secure enough to show his feelings. Lavender had heard one of Hector's fellow officers described as 'a father to his men, a commanding officer to his sons'. Hector was a bit like that. John had not suffered from absurd emotional blocks. On a brilliant summer day in beautiful surroundings, suddenly she missed him desperately.

Her thoughts flew to Lammerstane, a place that evoked so many memories, she soon felt uncomfortable thinking about it. By rights it, and the Taylor-Smith money, should go to Jake. Whatever he said, he was John's son not Hector's. Every day a word, a gesture or a look provided a reminder of his blood-line. Now it was a character trait of his natural father that led him to reject his name.

High above a buzzard hovered, circled and dipped its wing. Then it flew off, seeking prey elsewhere. Lavender picked two sprigs of bell heather, one for each of her men, and lay back on the soft grass. It had been a big lunch and she felt tired...

Dry-mouthed, she woke with a start, her solitude gone. The crowd had surged round the corner of the dog-leg, all bar a handful gathering round a particular ball. At the front was a dark-haired boy in a red kilt. A tall man with a tweed cap stood right behind him. He moved his hand up as if to lay it on the boy's shoulder, but all he did was to wipe his eye.

*   *   *

'Congratulations on that sixty-seven, Bobby,' Hector said, having pushed his way to the front of the crowd of well-wishers beside the eighteenth green, Jake with him.

'Sheriff Drummond, I saw you on the course. A day away from the ranch? Is this young man your son?'

'Er, yes, this is Jake.'

'How do you do, son?' Jones smiled and extended his hand.

'How do you do, sir,' Jake said, nervously yet proudly.

'Well, Jake, I have no further need of this.' Jones reached

into his pocket. He signed the ball with which he had just equalled the King's record and handed it to Jake. He smiled warmly as the boy stammered his gratitude.

As Jake showed his trophy to Lavender, Hector spotted Terry Coates-Moulton. He was standing beside his Rolls Royce while his caddie loaded the clubs into the boot. This was as good an opportunity as any.

'Terry, bad luck out there today. No doubt you're saving it for next week?'

Coates-Moulton's face was blank. 'You are...?'

'Hector Drummond. Sheriff Hector Drummond. We played together at St Andrews in the Autumn Medal.'

Coates-Moulton smiled with his lips only. 'Oh yes,' he said vaguely.

Sensing that it would be a mistake to go straight in with the questions he wanted to ask, Hector praised the young aristocrat's iron play and bemoaned the lack of manners of some spectators.

'Most of them, actually,' Coates-Moulton said acidly, his clipped voice betraying the degree to which he had taken offence.

'It may be the same at St Andrews. I believe they're expecting record crowds. They're painting white lines down the middle of the shared fairways and round the greens, so that should help,' Hector said.

There was no response other than raised eyebrows. Hector knew he had to get to the point. 'The thing is, Terry, there have been three murders in St Andrews over the last week, and I, as an officer of court, feel it's my duty to make sure the police don't miss anything and that no prosecution will fail because of lack of investigation or preparation. I've been asking people in town for the Open, including Bobby, I might say, some questions and I'd be grateful if you would give me five minutes of your time.'

Coates-Moulton looked blankly at him. 'Sheriff Drummond, I can't see how I could possibly help you, or the police. I'm aware of these murders, but I know nothing about any of them and, frankly, I'm not particularly interested.'

Hector kept his temper with difficulty. 'You were at the Independence Day party. I saw you. And my gardener's son was raped and killed just along the road shortly before it started. Did you see anything suspicious?'

'No.' The tone was glacial.

'What were you doing from about half past four until the party started?'

Coates-Moulton, some four inches shorter than Hector, leaned his head back so that he could look down the full length of his Roman nose. 'That's none of your business,' he said disdainfully.

'I can come along to Kirkleonard and ask the Hamiltons if they can help. They're good friends of mine.'

Cold, brown eyes stared at Hector. Coates-Moulton's face twitched as he calculated his response. 'Because of the *haar* I couldn't practise, so I spent the afternoon in the club, mostly reading the newspapers. I had brought my dinner clothes in, so bathed and changed in the club before going across to the Grand.'

'Did you see anything that might cast some light on the murder?'

'No.'

'On the Tuesday night, where did you have dinner?'

'At Kirkleonard, with the Hamiltons.'

'Not at Rusacks with Mrs Van Dyke?'

'No. Whatever gave you that idea?'

'I heard she was showing some interest in you.'

Coates-Moulton gave a hollow laugh. 'I met her at that party and my title obviously attracted her. The next day she bumped into me, on purpose I suspect, and insisted I had tea with her in the Grand. She and Murnian had fallen out and frankly she was crass, common and boring, pretty well what I would expect of Murnian. I made my excuses and left.' As he spoke, his gaze drifted to the crowd behind the eighteenth green. It fastened on someone and followed them as they moved about. Hector realized that the person was Jake.

'And Mrs Van Dyke didn't join you at the Hamiltons'?' Hector asked.

'Certainly not. Did Murnian tell you she did?'

Hector remembered that, according to Larry Nabholtz, Kenny Nolan had spent the evening with an 'expensive broad'. Gloria Van Dyke had been determined to make Paul jealous, or she had lost interest in him. 'No,' he replied. 'Do you and Paul Murnian not get on?'

'Not after our game in the Walker Cup last year. He was left with a short putt on the eighteenth to halve the match. He obviously thought I should have given it, but I didn't and he missed. He was upset with me, but that was nothing compared with his father.'

Coates-Moulton continued to stare past Hector at Jake. Slightly unnerved, Hector asked, 'Can I ask what you did after dinner on Tuesday?'

'That's a bit impertinent, isn't it, Sheriff? After all, I gather the police have done their job. But I've nothing to hide and I don't want the Hamiltons to be bothered. If you must know, they'd arranged a small dinner party, but I found the people they'd invited pretty stifling, so I made my excuses after coffee. I got in the car and drove to the Eden Course. I found a quiet green and practised my putting for an hour. It was a fine night.'

'Did you see anything suspicious?'

'No. There were a number out on the links, some with clubs, some with dogs, some with both.'

'Thank you very much. One last thing, has anyone approached you in connection with the emeralds stolen from your parents?'

Coates-Moulton's eyes lit up and he became suddenly alert. 'No. Do you know anything about them?'

'No, I don't know anything. I'm just looking at things very broadly.'

Coates-Moulton moved close and spoke with great urgency. 'If you hear anything about these jewels, anything, you must tell me immediately. They've been in my family for over a hundred years and my parents are devastated. We absolutely must get them back, do you understand?'

'I understand,' Hector said, then added, 'I trust that you will let me know if you learn anything relating to the murders?'

He smiled insincerely. 'Absolutely, er, Sheriff. Absolutely. Now I must be off.' He climbed into the driver's seat. The Rolls started first time and purred majestically down the drive towards the main road. Heads turned in admiration, but the driver, alone and aloof, his jaw set and his head tilted back, stared straight ahead down the full length of his Roman nose.

'You look as if you've just sucked on a lemon.' The male voice to Hector's right was American.

'O.B., Eleanor, hello! Your boy did very well this afternoon.' O.B. and Eleanor both looked as pleased as Punch.

Eleanor laughed. 'Did he not? We watched the start and the finish and betweentimes we took in some great scenery. Lord Terry seemed very unhappy at the end. Were you able to console him just then?' She put on a concerned face and held his arm.

'I didn't try very hard, but I did learn that he has no real alibi for Monday evening or Tuesday night.'

O.B. looked impressed. 'You're doing well, Hector. Tell me, if we proved he was the guilty party, as a lord, would you hang him or chop his head off as you did to Charles I and Mary, Queen of Scots?'

'We'd hang, draw and quarter him, as happened to William Wallace. No, we'd hang him as a common criminal.'

Eleanor pretended to be appalled. 'You Brits are losing your sense of romance,' she said in a shocked voice.

Before the conversation could become more macabre, Lavender and Jake came over.

'Look what Mr Jones gave me,' Jake burbled, fishing in his sporran for the ball.

'If he wins the Open next week, I'll try to persuade him to give your father one of the balls he used for that,' O.B. said, and engaged Jake in conversation, asking about school and sports.

As they talked, Lavender invited Eleanor to come, with O.B., for supper the following evening. 'You know that other things are casting a shadow over the championship,' she added. 'I think it might be a good idea to exchange notes.'

'I do agree,' Eleanor said enthusiastically. 'O.B. is very worried. And it would be a pleasure to visit a real Scotch home.'

As they finalised arrangements, O.B. put his arm round Jake's shoulders. 'I've enjoyed meeting Jake,' he said. 'Bob was about his age when I first laid eyes on him, and he had the same spark of determination. You should be mighty proud of him.'

'We are,' Hector and Lavender said in unison.

It was time to take the boy back to Glenalmond for Evening Chapel. Before he got out of the car in front of the school, he leaned forward and hugged both Lavender and Hector. Taken by surprise, Hector, whose own father had never embraced him, hoped Jake did not notice how his muscles tensed involuntarily.

*   *   *

'Lord Terry gives me the creeps,' Hector said as they turned on to the Crieff-Perth road. 'While I was speaking to him, he kept on looking at Jake. You know, it was the sort of look that a chap might aim at a pretty girl. And, he doesn't have an alibi for any of the killings; and he was at Scioto.'

Lavender was shocked. 'So he's a real suspect. Has there ever been any scandal about him?'

'Not that I'm aware of. I haven't heard his name being linked romantically with any particular girl, either. The talk I've heard is that his mother scares them all away, but maybe she gets the blame and he just isn't interested.'

'You may be right,' she said thoughtfully. 'But it doesn't necessarily mean he wants to rape and murder boys. He might just have been looking at Jake's kilt. He did stand out. Almost everyone else was wearing trousers. What else did Lord Terry say?'

When Hector finished telling her, she was silent. Then she spoke slowly. 'The more we look, the more links we find. Ralf Murnian blames Lord Terry's lack of sportsmanship for Paul losing his Walker Cup match. A year later, Lord Terry's family jewels are stolen and Enid Murnian wears a ring with a big emerald which she takes off when she knows you are coming.' She added, 'I imagine that Ralf Murnian was someone who bore a grudge, and if anyone was capable of having the Eyes of the Fox stolen to order it would have been him.'

Tommy was waiting outside the prison. He climbed eagerly

into the back seat and seemed disappointed when he realized that there was no food in the car.

'He swears he didnae do it, sir. He's real upset. But he was pleased tae see me.'

'Did he say anything useful?' Hector asked.

'No' really. We started tae speak about Murnian saying I'd cheated, and he said that minded him of Trapdoor.'

'Trapdoor?' Lavender was puzzled.

'Aye, ma'am. He wis a caddie, years ago. He made out that one leg was longer than the other when all the time one of his boots had a big, hollow sole. There wis a sort of trapdoor in the heel, and he'd kick balls he found in the rough through the door and intae the heel. It could hold six balls at once.'

Hector shook his head. 'For heaven's sake, Tommy. The man's life is at stake. Was there nothing he could tell you about the Murnians, however odd?'

'Well, sir, I dinnae see how it could help, but there was the funny driver.'

'Tell us anyway,' Hector said.

'You watched the match on Tuesday, sir, and you'll mind Mr Murnian kept hooking?'

'Of course.'

'Well, that morning he'd put in his bag a driver belonging to his faither. It had a face that sat open rather than square, and was supposed to help someone who hooked. He told Wullie his faither had a worse hook than he had. He didnae use this driver till the ninth, and then he hit the biggest hook of the day, into Mrs Kruger. So he didnae use it again. Wullie had a feel of the club, and he said it felt wrong, out of balance, he said, and when Mr Murnian hit his drive, it gave a kinda funny noise, no' a proper click. Wullie said the club had been really well rubbed up. "Like the back of an otter", he said, as if it had been at a clubmaker's. And it had a big brass sole-plate. It was a Walter Hagen club, made in America. After he hit the drive with it, Mr Murnian looked as if he was going to throw it in the bushes, but he handed it to Wullie and, with a bit of swearing, said he was going to give it back to his faither. That was the only odd thing Wullie could tell me about, sir. I'm sorry.'

Hector and Lavender exchanged glances.

'You may have done very well, Tommy. Have you any clue where that club might be now?'

'Probably in the Murnian's hotel, sir. I'm pretty sure it's no' in the caddie shed.'

'Is there any way at all we could get our hands on it?' Hector asked.

'You dinnae mean steal it, sir?'

'Strictly speaking, I suppose I do. But in a good cause.'

Tommy shifted in his seat. 'Er, what would happen if I got caught? I'm no' risking the borstal for this.'

'You'd appear before me and I'd go easy on you.'

'What do you mean easy?'

'I could fine you then give you the money to pay the fine. But you mustn't say I put you up to it, or I wouldn't be able to help you.'

Lavender turned round and faced Tommy. 'You can trust my husband,' she said. 'During the War he cared more about his men's welfare than he did about his own, and once nearly died because of it.'

Hector said hurriedly, 'But I'm sure you won't be caught, if we plan it right...'

Lavender had a point to get across. 'He gave his respirator to a wounded private who couldn't move, but didn't get away in time himself. He was mentioned in dispatches for that. He won't let you down.'

Glancing in his mirror, Hector saw surprised admiration on Tommy's face. Secretly he was pleased. Boastfulness having been hammered out of him as a child, he seldom spoke about what had been an instinctive act. 'Do you know anyone working at the Grand who could take it from the Murnians' rooms, assuming it's there?' he asked.

'I could speak to my pal Billy. But why, sir?'

'I think we owe you an explanation,' Hector agreed. The full account that he considered the lad entitled to occupied the remainder of the journey to St Andrews. As he pulled into his driveway, Hector impressed upon Tommy that he had to keep what he had learned to himself. Seeing that he was starving, Lavender insisted on making him a three-egg omelette with bread and cheddar, which he ate at the kitchen table, washed down by two large glasses of Hector's claret.

'I hope you can join us tomorrow evening for supper, here,' Hector said as Lavender slipped a parcel of cold ham into his pocket. 'We plan to have a council of war, and you're very much a member of the team. Now, I'll give you a lift home, but not one word about this to anyone, do you understand?'

As Hector drove him into town in the gathering dusk, Tommy pinched himself. When he woke up during the night, he could not believe what was happening, but the ham was real, and all three of his family would eat breakfast in the morning.

Hector was less happy. He had a letter to write and a eulogy to prepare. Jim's funeral had been set for three o'clock the next day.

10

Monday 11 July

'Oh, quite,' he said vaguely, not having listened to Lavender's question.

'You didn't, did you?' Her tone was sharp.

'Didn't what?'

'Sleep well. You tossed and turned. Were you composing that eulogy?'

'Yes. Sorry I wasn't listening there.'

Her exasperated expression melted. She shook her head. 'Poor darling. This should be such a nice time, but it's one problem after another.' She went behind his chair and gently kneaded the tight muscles at the base of his neck. 'At least you don't have to play golf today, even if the Open competitors do. Look at that rain.' Outside the sky was dark, and heavy rain was forming ever-expanding puddles down the sides of the garden path. She put her lips to his ear. 'Could you possibly give me a lift into town on your way to court? It's the committee of the 1920 Club at Molly Garfield's in South Street. Normally I'd take my bicycle, but it's just too drenching out there.'

'Of course. I was planning to take the girls. But please try to keep me out of the next production.' The 1920 Club was a St Andrews play-reading society, enthusiastically supported by the ladies of the town and surrounding area, and perpetually short of men willing to participate. A degree of ingenuity was required to avoid the readings. Hector feared his plea would not be sufficient. 'How will you get home?' he added.

'I'm sure Esme Hamilton will be happy to drop me off here. Her chauffeur will probably wait for her in town. I'll be able to ask her about her house guest.'

'Lord Terry?'

'Who else? Assuming that I get her to dry up about Harley Granville-Barker.'

'Do I know him?' Hector was shocked at the thought of the redoubtable Esme Hamilton looking beyond her long-suffering husband, Bean.

'He's the theatre man, you silly sausage. You should approve of him. He encourages Shakespearean actors to gabble their lines to get the play over quicker. Esme and he nearly clicked years ago, according to her anyway.'

Hector sighed. 'I remember now. I'd better stimulate my brain before I get to court. Is there more coffee?'

* * *

'We've another first appearance in a murder case, my lord,' Forbes told Hector when he arrived in Cupar, late for once after a journey slowed by the rain. 'One of the chefs at Rusacks, Peter Nugent. Charged with killing McCann, the clubmaker. Inspector McTaggart will be establishing some reputation for himself. Edinburgh will want him soon. We'll be lucky to keep him here, I think.'

Hector did not trust himself to reply.

The potentially time-consuming part of the day's business comprised a number of summary criminal cases, but Hector dealt expeditiously with the assortment of bleary-eyed drunks and petty criminals who had spent the weekend in the cells. He hoped to see the end of Jones' first qualifying round, although he was one of the early starters.

As Hector waited in his chambers, the windows securely shut, he anticipated a short, formal first appearance.

'My client wishes to emit a declaration, my lord,' Pirie, Nugent's solicitor said when the hearing began.

Hector was astonished. Pirie had a keen appreciation of the value of the right to remain silent. Nugent might tell them important things that the Crown could not otherwise prove at the trial and thus put a noose round his own neck.

The chef was a wiry, middle-aged man with receding, dark hair and a pasty complexion which accentuated the effect of being unshaven, but the overwhelming impression was one of anger. He stood before Hector, twitching and restless despite his handcuffs, glaring as he looked round the room. When he acknowledged his name he seemed to force the words through thin, tight lips with as much pride as the circumstances allowed.

Armed with pen and paper, Hector reminded Nugent that he was not obliged to say anything and asked him to speak slowly. But used to barking out orders and being in command, words flowed from the chef in a torrent. Hector found it hard to remain even-tempered and shouted at him to slow down after politer requests had been ignored. Seeing Hector as another enemy, Nugent became increasingly agitated and his account became disjointed. At last they reached the end of the declaration. As it had been difficult to follow, Hector had not taken down every word. Taking a deep breath he read it back very slowly, encouraging Nugent to make corrections.

'I am the head chef at Rusacks Hotel. I knew Hamish McCann. He told me he was short of money and I gave him a loan to tide him over. That was January. He did not pay it back, and when he died he owed me twenty-five pounds. I had asked him time and again for payment, and he kept promising, then letting me down. On Tuesday, at the start of dinner service, I found a note from McCann telling me to meet him at Auchterlonie's at ten that night and he would repay me.

'I left service early, but I was still late. I had to leave Frankie Rolland to finish. I didn't tell him why.' Hector put the first foolscap sheet to one side and picked up the second one.

'I went up the road. There was no light in Auchterlonie's. I tried the door and it wasn't locked. I went in. There was no one in the main shop. I said his name but there was no answer. Something made me check the workshop. The door was ajar. I pushed it. It was dark and I couldn't see at first. My foot hit something soft that moved, but like dead meat moves. I put my hand out. I'll never forget the feel of his shirt. His body was warm underneath it, but it was all wet. I felt him to see if he was alive but I swear he was dead. And there was this thing sticking out of his back. T-shaped. I think it pinned him to the bench.' Hector moved on to the third sheet. 'I felt round about, just to see if my money was there. It's daft what you do sometimes. And I thought, Hamish has been murdered, and I'll get the blame if people learn I've been here. So I crept out and shut the outer door just as I found it. I went back to the kitchen and I was washing my hands when Frankie saw me. He was all upset over his crepes Suzette. I didn't kill Hamish, I swear.'

As he read this final version, Hector was aware of Nugent's expression gradually melting. 'Thank you, sir,' he said.

This having been done, the declaration was duly signed on each page. Hector continued the case for further examination, Nugent to be remanded in custody. With a sly smile, Forbes advised that there was no further business and Hector set off for the golf course, his macintosh, gum boots and umbrella on the passenger seat, his notes for Jim's eulogy in his pocket.

*   *   *

'Delighted, my dear, delighted,' Esme Hamilton gave a snort as she watched Lavender struggle to pull her rubber galoshes over her shoes. 'Smart has the car at the door, so we'll have you back, dry as a bone, in no time.'

Lavender had found the meeting frustrating. The 1920 Club Committee were all women, and Lavender thought that, in their choice of plays, they should demonstrate that they were capable of thinking and holding sensible opinions about the main issues of the day. By no means a rebel by nature, she had been sickened by the callous lack of imagination of those running the war that had killed John, and so many more. When women got the vote in 1918, she considered it long overdue. It had been one of the few issues on which she and John had fundamentally disagreed. He saw no irony in the fact that she was far more interested in current affairs than he was. In the General Elections of the early twenties she had voted, proudly yet secretly, twice for the Liberal candidate and once for the Labour candidate, unable to comprehend why the franchise continued to be withheld from women under thirty. She sought intellectual stimulation in literature and liked plays that reflected the grim realities of life and the absurdities of the class system. Her suggestion that the 1920 Club should read *Pygmalion* or some other work by Shaw had gone down like a lead balloon, Esme deriding the suggestion with a snort like the one she had aimed at Lavender's galoshes. In many ways it would have been preferable to walk home.

Once settled in the back seat of the Bentley, Esme regaled

Lavender with the famous Shaw/Churchill exchange: 'Here are two tickets for my opening night. You may bring a friend, if you have one.' 'I regret I am unable to attend that night. I would like tickets for the second performance, if there is one.'

Before the equine laugh had subsided, Lavender, who did not care for Churchill, raised the question of Esme's eminent guest. 'Hector was saying that Lord Terry Coates-Moulton is staying with you. That must be interesting.'

Esme beamed. 'Oh yes. Plug and Letitia are old friends. Plug was at Eton with Bean.'

Previously unaware of the Earl of Silloth and Solway's nickname, Lavender persisted. 'Hector says Terry is very single-minded.'

In a contest between discretion and showing off there could be only one winner. Dropping her voice to a normal volume, and looking over her shoulder as if a spy might have slipped unobserved into the car, Esme said, 'Between ourselves, my dear, Plug set us a challenge, and we've rather failed him, so far. Terry's the heir, as I'm sure you know, and Plug wants to see him married. "I want him to match and then I want him to hatch. Then he can go off and play his confounded golf." That's what he said. So we've had all the decently-bred fillies in the county to dinner, some of them damn good-looking. I've had to tick Bean off a couple of times. But Terry's just not interested. He goes off in his Rolls to practise if the weather's good, and he goes to bed if it's raining. The boy's a dead loss. Doesn't talk much, hardly ever laughs. When I remember how dear Harley used to chase me over the fences...' She smiled wistfully. 'Sometimes, of course, I let him catch me.' She whinnied happily.

'Does Terry stay out late when he's practising? I remember Tuesday night was fine and dry.'

'Out till after dark. Don't know how he can see. No doubt

wanting the coast to be clear and the horses back in their stalls. I don't think he's like that,' she added quickly, emphasising the 'that'. 'He'll do his duty one day, but it would have been nice if we could have set the wheels in motion. You don't know any suitable fillies, do you?'

Finding a mate for Lord Terry was the last thing on Lavender's mind. 'I'm afraid not,' she said after pretending to think. 'You haven't heard him talk about meeting a clubmaker, or getting some special driver, by any chance? It's just something Hector was saying at breakfast, and I like to show that I was listening.'

'Don't listen to that sort of golf talk, I'm afraid, my dear. You just tell Hector he'll have me as a mother-in-law in Rookery Nook. That'll loosen his cough, I bet.'

Lavender could not help smiling, despite her apprehension. The committee preferred light comedy, and Ben Travers was their favourite playwright ('He served in the War, my dear.'). Esme had declared Hector to be perfect for the male lead, Gerald Popkiss. Lavender wondered how long she could delay breaking the news to him.

'Any word about the emeralds?' she asked.

'Not a cheep, worse luck. Letitia's sure one of the servants gave the thief information, but she feels she can't go round accusing them all. Have you ever seen the emeralds? They're beautiful.'

'I hear they're worth a fortune.'

'And they're worth an awful lot more than money to Plug. His grandfather brought them home from India. Killed a maharaja to get them, apparently, and got roundly cursed by some naked holy man: "The green eyes of the tiger will bathe in blood," or some such tosh. He gave Plug's ancestor the heebie-jeebies, anyway. So much so that he changed "Eyes of the

Tiger" to "Eyes of the Fox" when he presented them to his mem-sahib back home in Silloth. Plug says they were a peace offering. He'd caught something nasty off a native gel, but by that time he'd sired Plug's pa, so it didn't really matter.'

As this tale of the Empire concluded, the Bentley drew up outside the front door of Ballochmyle. The grey-uniformed chauffeur opened the door for Lavender. Her galoshes had indeed turned out to be superfluous. She was still wearing them when she sat down to think, a generous glass of sherry beside her.

＊ ＊ ＊

A thousand spectators had come to watch Jones in the first qualifying round. They came to admire his play and be able to say they had seen him. About the man himself the jury was still out. His sportsmanship had been well reported but what would he be like if events turned against him? Would success have made him arrogant? Gum-booted, sweating in their raincoats and armed with umbrellas, their pursuit of the champion had not been comfortable.

Having easily identified Jones' match, Hector drove the long way round the back of the Bruce Embankment to the West Sands car park and looked at the sky. Seeing patches of blue, he put on his raincoat and cap then, leaving gumboots and umbrella behind, set off to watch Jones play the eighteenth. He need not have hurried. Unable, despite his height, to see over those gathered round Jones' ball after the drive, he refused to join in the stampede after he had played his second. From the top of the steps leading up to the Royal and Ancient, Hector managed a glimpse of his birdie attempt, but that was all he could see. A man beside him said Jones had taken a seventy-six.

It was not good but acceptable in the weather and, barring disasters on the New the following day, would see him safely into the championship. It was only the qualifying test. When the championship proper began everyone would start level.

In the hall of the Royal and Ancient the depressing odour of damp tweed hung in the air. In the Big Room the happy, familiar fug of smoke and whisky was filled with excited talk about the morning's play. Carelessly, Tolley had taken four putts on the eighteenth, yet finished in seventy-three. Melhorn had putted wonderfully on the New for the same score. Also on the New, George Duncan, the champion in 1920 and one of Britain's best, had taken forty-two to the turn after repeated visits to the whins. Hector was savouring all this when he felt a tap on his shoulder.

'Could I have a word, Hector?' Norman Boase's tone was peremptory.

'Norman, of course. What is it?'

'I'd rather discuss it somewhere quieter. Henry Gullen's office is free just now. Would you mind? Bring your drink.'

Feeling like a schoolboy in trouble, Hector followed Boase along the corridor. Boase entered without knocking and took a seat on one of the long sides of the big table in the middle of the room. Hector took a chair at one of the short sides and sat back, his eyebrows raised.

In his late fifties, his distinguished career of business success and public service at its zenith, Provost Boase, CBE, Chairman of the Championship Committee, was no fool and certainly no push-over. His confident, erect bearing and forbidding facial expression gave him a considerable physical presence. But as he looked across the corner of the table at Hector, his dark, bushy moustache moved from side to side as he chose his words. Hector did not see why he should help him.

'Hector, this is a delicate matter,' Boase began, his voice uncharacteristically hesitant. 'I know that the unfortunate, no, tragic murders last week have cast a shadow over the championship, but the police have done an admirable job in arresting the men they believe are responsible, and I have had complaints that you have used your position to pry into matters that are not the concern of a sheriff-substitute.' Hector remained poker-faced.

Swallowing, Boase continued. 'That would be no concern of mine, and I understand your superior sheriff has been informed, but I am worried that your meddling may deter Americans in particular from coming to play in our championship in future years. For some reason you appear to have concentrated on them.'

'Who has complained?' Hector asked coldly.

'Mrs Murnian has been particularly distressed, and Paul complained on her behalf as well as his own.'

'Paul's not exactly the cream of the Americans.'

'I have also heard directly from Larry Nabholtz that he resented being questioned and I understand that Barnes and Mayo were less than pleased.'

'But you haven't spoken about this to either of them?'

'No.'

'And I bet you haven't spoken to Bobby Jones either.'

'I trust you haven't been treating him as a murder suspect?'

Hector felt his temper rising, but knew he must keep calm. 'Bobby Jones insisted on being treated the same as everyone else. He was happy to answer my questions fully.'

'Jones is a very remarkable young man. But Hector, I think you are exceeding your authority for no good reason, and that could have a disastrous effect on this championship in future years. I take that very, very seriously. Almost all the best players in the world are American these days. Since 1921 we've had only one British winner, Havers. If the Americans stop coming, the Open will become something quaint and old-fashioned but not truly the golf championship of the world, as I believe it should be. We've got only twelve Americans starting this week. Where's Hagen? Where's Saracen? What about Armour, Cooper, Diegel, Turnesa, Farrell? If you love this great game, you must see that.'

Hector remained silent then decided to be frank. Boase worked tirelessly and effectively for golf without any financial reward. 'Norman, were you at Scioto last year?'

'For the US Open? No. Why?'

'Then you probably don't know about the boy who was murdered there, like Jim Tindall a week ago.'

'No.' Boase looked apprehensive, as if his quick brain had guessed what was to come.

'Then I have something important to tell you.' Patiently, Hector explained his reasons for investigating the three murders, stressing Jones' appreciation of the importance for golf, if nothing else.

When he finished, Boase sat back and puffed on his cigarette. Hector lit one of his own. The two men sat smoking, each with their own thoughts.

At length Boase carefully stubbed out his cigarette then spoke. 'I should have known there would be a sound reason behind what you're doing, Hector. I owe you an apology. Have you any idea who might be responsible?'

'Not yet, I'm afraid. Now, if you'll excuse me, I'd better have some lunch. I'm due to deliver the eulogy for my gardener's son at three o'clock.'

'Of course, my dear chap, on you go. And thank you.' Boase lit another cigarette and slumped in his chair, stunned, deflated and, intangibly, rebuked.

11

Following the loss of his wife and daughters, Alf Tindall had lost faith in God and belonged to no church. Though baptised as an infant, when his father had been devout, Jim had not attended Sunday School, and it had taken a request from Hector to persuade his own minister to bury the boy after a full church service. He brought Alf round to the idea by telling him it would make him feel better, in the long term at least. A service would honour the boy and give him a dignified departure. Hector also had his own reason. If he was to do a eulogy, he wanted to do it in church. Secretly, he did not trust his emotions if he were to speak beside the damp clay of an open grave. In the matter of a lair, matters were easier. Alf's wife's employer, a Mr McCready, had purchased space for the decimated family in the Western Cemetery, and Jim would lie there.

St Leonard's Parish Church, a solid, grey stone building with a square tower, was situated among solid, grey stone houses, a ten minute walk from Ballochmyle. The interior of the church was simple and stark. Twenty minutes before the service mourners began to arrive. In all about two hundred people showing varying degrees of distress shuffled into the fine, Austrian oak pews. They included a party from Jim's school. Gentle music from the organ played. Hector and Lavender sat in the front left pew. Looking behind him, Hector saw that as usual the rows near the front remained unoccupied. The main body of the congregation liked to keep the principal mourners at a distance. Supported by a man Hector took to be his brother, Alf came in, gaunt and drained, and sat on the right beside a bird-like lady with white hair. Hector assumed she was Jim's granny.

Shortly after three o'clock, four solemn, black-clad pall-bearers carried the small pine coffin down the aisle and placed it reverently before the altar. Grasping Lavender's hand, Hector tried to stop himself from imagining the state of the body inside. The minister, a whey-faced, portly man, started the proceedings with a short prayer then invited the congregation to sing the twenty-third psalm, to the tune Crimond. Hector knew the words by heart, having sung them on many occasions, few of them happy. As the congregation took their seats, Hector got out his speech. The minister introduced him and he walked forward. Standing at the open Bible, composing himself, he looked round the sad faces and was surprised to see, at the back, Bob Jones (Senior) and O.B. Keeler. Just in front of them Inspector McTaggart sat, stone-faced.

'"Man's inhumanity to man" is a phrase coined by Robert Burns,' Hector began. 'It expresses completely the circumstances of Jim Tindall's death. But let us remember that the quality of a life is not measured by its length. Though it was far too short, Jim led a good life. He was lively and fond of fun. He was a loving and dutiful son and grandson. All those who knew him have been devastated by his death.' He glanced sideways at the coffin. On it sat a bunch of flowers, roses from his garden, lovingly grown by the boy's father, tied together with twine. Only the other morning he had inhaled the perfume of these very blooms. A single, blood-red petal had become detached.

Insignificant in itself, that sight destroyed Hector's emotional reserve. He pulled the silk handkerchief from his breast pocket and blew his nose vigorously, hoping no one would notice him dabbing his eyes. But the tears would not stop. He felt foolish and unmanned. But he had to finish properly. He looked down at his notes. Words, mere words. He had selected and arranged them the previous night; futile, empty sounds conveying half-believed hopes of a better hereafter. But the roses were real, the coffin was real, and the abused body inside it was real. Hector pointed at the coffin. 'May the fiend responsible rot in hell,' he cried, his voice shaking. 'And I will not rest till he is brought to justice.'

He returned to his seat, quivering, then held his head in his hands. 'I've made a complete fool of myself,' he muttered.

Lavender put a hand on his knee. She whispered, 'I'm so proud of you.' Behind, one person clapped. A few joined in. Others murmured approving noises.

The rest of the service passed in a blur. At the church door, Alf took Hector's hand in an iron grip. Neither man trusted himself to speak. On withdrawing his hand, Hector found that the card for cord number three had been placed in it. He would have to keep his emotions in check as he helped lower Jim into his grave. As he and Lavender stood on the lawn near the door, McTaggart strode past, heading for his car where a young constable on chauffeur duty stood waiting. The undisguised fury in his expression perversely lifted Hector's spirits. At last, he had got under the policeman's skin.

When Hector and Lavender made their way to their unchauffeured car, a poorly-dressed man with a rough, stubbly face stepped in front of them, blocking the pavement. Hector's immediate reaction was one of alarm. 'You spoke for us all in there, sir,' the man said, then moved out of the way, bowing as they passed.

The sun peeped out from behind a cloud, but lightened no one's heart as Jim was lowered into the wet earth. Once it was over, in the car, Hector squeezed Lavender's thigh. 'We've been invited back to the house,' he said. 'I think I'd better go. Do you mind? I could drop you off at home.'

'I'm coming,' she said.

Jim's granny, Alf's mother-in-law, had busied herself. The little flat was cleaner and tidier than it had been for many years. Plates of scones spread with butter and strawberry jam were on the table beside an assortment of glasses and cups for whisky or tea. When Alf saw Hector and Lavender enter the over-crowded room, he reached into a cupboard to get his best two glasses for the guests of honour. He poured them both drams, then came up close to Hector, a perplexed look on his face, whisky on his breath.

'I thought they had arrested the men who...did it?' he asked.

'Alf, I hate to say this, but I think they may have arrested the wrong men.' After his outburst in church, Hector had to come clean.

The gardener's face fell. 'Who, then?'

'I don't know, but Alf, I'm trying to find out. I really am.'

'It's wrong, Sheriff. It's unfair and it's wrong.'

Hector looked into the wrinkled, brown face in which all joy and hope had been crushed. 'I'll do my best, Alf. I will,' was all he could say.

He and Lavender did not stay long at the wake. They walked the short distance to Market Street, where Hector had parked.

'Feeling better?' he asked.

She nodded. 'Thank God that's over.'

'I agree. Do you fancy a cup of tea in the Grand?' he asked, forcing himself to sound bright. 'I need to see Sabbatini.'

'Good idea,' Lavender said. 'There's Gloria Van Dyke as well.'

'I'm sure Benny would talk to both of us, but I fancy Gloria might respond better to a man.'

'There's no doubt about that,' Lavender said, smiling for the first time that afternoon.

＊　　＊　　＊

Although the weather had improved, several spectators had drifted off home after Jones and most of the other prominent players finished their rounds. Hector found a parking place surprisingly near the course and, feeling calmer every minute, went to see what story the chalk markings on the big, black scoreboard behind the eighteenth green would have to tell.

'Who is Golias?' he asked a man standing beside him.

'They say he's a Frenchman from Paris,' the man replied.

'He must be some golfer, anyway,' Hector said, marvelling at the seventy-one which Golias had returned, the best of the day on the Old.

Noting which match was on the eighteenth, Hector consulted the copy of the draw he had cut from The Times and calculated that Dick Robinson would not finish for another half hour. It would be at least that long before Sabbatini returned to the Grand. Lavender had gone ahead to wait for him there. Hector found her in the lounge and explained the situation. 'I suppose I should see if Mrs Van Dyke is willing to have a chat,' he said.

'Well get me a couple of newspapers from the rack, darling, and I'll sit here ready to intervene if she's too much for you.'

Hector grinned and went to the rack where the papers hung, clamped length-ways into wooden holders. He selected

The Times and *The Scotsman* and carried them across. Then he went to the reception desk, where Mary was on duty.

'How are your inquiries going, my lord?' she asked, louder than Hector would have liked.

'Very well, thank you, Mary, but I'm trying to keep everything quiet.' He tapped the side of his nose. 'Tell me, is Mrs Van Dyke in by any chance?'

Mary's lips pursed in disapproval. 'I think so, my lord. Do you want to see her?'

'I do rather. Could you get word to her?'

'I'll try, my lord.' She sat at her telephone desk and dialled. At first it appeared that Mrs Van Dyke was not going to answer. Mary rolled her eyes then suddenly straightened her back and said primly, 'There's a gentleman to see you in the front lobby, Mrs Van Dyke.' After turning to Hector she said, 'I hope you don't mind, my lord, but if I had said it was you she might not have come down. Gentlemen do come in all shapes and sizes these days.'

Sure that a compliment was intended, Hector waited behind the door in the lounge, ready to pounce as soon as the 'expensive broad', to use Nabholtz's descriptive phrase, entered. He might want to cut off her escape.

He did not have long to wait. The door swung open and Gloria Van Dyke made a languid but eye-catching entrance, swaying her hips and smoking. She wore a figure-hugging black skirt with a silky sheen, partially concealed under a Flapper pink wool cardigan. Her neck was adorned with a long string of pearls, while vivid red lipstick and precariously high heels accentuated the vampish effect. She walked straight to the middle of the room where she stopped and looked round, one eyebrow raised.

'Mrs Van Dyke, how nice to see you,' Hector said.

She turned in a stately manner. A look of disappointment flashed across her face when she saw Hector behind her. 'I'm sorry?' she said.

'Hector Drummond. Sheriff Hector Drummond. I wonder if I might have a quick word with you?'

'About what, Sheriff?' She made it sound like an invitation.

'It concerns the tragic murders here last week.'

She opened her eyes wide. 'I'm not a suspect, am I? That would be just too exciting.' Her accent sounded like New York with an extra twang.

Hector swallowed. He looked at her inquisitively and she fluttered her eyelashes. 'Do you mind if we sit down, and we can discuss it?' he asked, gesturing towards a seat.

'I don't have long and I don't know much, but I don't want to get on the wrong side of the law.' She perched elegantly on the edge of the chair Hector held for her. He sat down so that he faced her.

'I understand that you came over by yourself and that you are, or were, very good friends with Mr Paul Murnian?'

'That is correct.' She sounded condescending.

'When you arrived last Monday, did Paul Murnian expect you?'

'It was always going to be a surprise.'

'I believe you arrived here about four?'

'I wasn't concerned with the time.'

'Did you leave a message for Paul?'

'I asked the hotel staff to inform him of my arrival. I don't know how they did it.'

'When did you first see Paul that day?'

'After a while. He said he'd been out, then had a tub before he got my message.'

'Did he come to your room?'

'What sort of a question is that to ask a lady, Sheriff?'

'I've been told he did go to you.'

She shrugged. 'Maybe he did.'

'Was there anything unusual about his behaviour?'

'Well, he was definitely pleased to see me.' Suggestively, she put her hands together in her lap as if she was gripping something.

Hector found himself blushing. He decided to be more direct. 'So you both needed a wash and brush-up before coming along to the Independence Day party?'

Her eyes twinkled. 'My, my. And I thought you Brits never talked about sex.'

'Was I?' Hector was glad that Lavender was at the other side of the room.

'Touche, sir.' She smiled, for once using her eyes and her lips. 'Yes, we made love then came along to the party. I take it you reckon he couldn't make love to me if he'd just raped a boy. I wouldn't know about that.'

'What do you mean?'

'What I say, Sheriff. I don't know. He's a stallion, if you get my meaning. And he did mention he'd had to wash out his knickers in the tub. He didn't say any more, before you ask.'

Hector thought back to the match the day after Jim's murder. Paul had worn American-style slacks that day. He had worn tweed plus fours, called "knickers" by Americans, on Saturday.

'The night Ralf Murnian was killed, you didn't dine here?'

'I don't want to talk about that night.'

'I can't force you, but two men have been arrested for his murder. If they're guilty or innocent, we still need to know as much as possible so justice is done. Whatever sensibilities are involved.'

For a moment she looked at him searchingly. Then she

spoke deliberately: 'Sheriff, I suspect you'll know the story. Mr and Mrs Murnian disapproved of me. I was not good enough for their Paul.' She leaned forward, causing Hector to move back as the holder carried her cigarette perilously close to his face. Her voice became little more than a whisper. 'He was a two-bit crook who's gotten lucky. She's a dried-up snob with a magnetic pull for big rocks and booze. I come from a good Boston family. I've had my adventures, sure, but I have more class in my little finger than a room full of damn Murnians. And Paul! He was happy to go to bed with me, but not prepared to stand up to his parents. On Monday they told him I couldn't join them for dinner. Tuesday morning, he said he wasn't allowed – allowed – to eat at my table. Boy, I let him have it. I even took tea with your stuffed Lord Terry to shake him up. Luckily, Kenny Nolan is an old friend. He's staying at Rusacks. Well, he was...' Her voice tailed off. 'Tuesday evening, Kenny and I had a few drinks at Rusacks. We ate dinner late. Too late. Have you ever tasted crepes Suzette with no orange juice, Sheriff?'

'Fortunately, no,' he said, reflecting that underneath the façade of worldliness, she was as wounded by rejection as anyone. He asked if she had heard anyone speaking about emeralds, or an odd sort of driver, or visits to a clubmaker. Drained by the effort of being herself, she shook her head listlessly. Feeling sorry for her, Hector held the lounge door as she made her exit, her customary swagger absent.

Coming the other way, Bob Jones (senior) ignored her and greeted Hector. 'I was in church this afternoon, Sheriff. You did well, very well.' In a gesture that was entirely natural he put an arm round Hector's shoulder.

Gratified, Hector asked him if he wanted to join Lavender and have some tea.

'I can begin to understand what your poor gardener is going

through,' Jones said as he sat back in an armchair. 'Bob was real sickly when he was little. There were times we thought we might lose him. We moved out of Atlanta to East Lake for his health. Fortunately he knew how to eat...'

'When did he start golf?' Hector asked.

'He started swinging a club at five. You know, it was the darndest thing, he had the gift of imitating golf swings. We'd have friends round for drinks on the veranda and Bob would go out on the lawn right in front of them and swing his little club just like they did. He made us laugh, I can tell you. Fortunately, Kiltie Maiden came to East Lake, so Bob had someone real good to copy.' He smiled. 'Golf became his life. What do you say to a six-year-old who asks: "Dad, what do people do on Sundays who don't play golf?"'

'Was he always promising?' Lavender asked.

'I guess so. I'll always remember the day I was on the fourteenth green and he came up to me with this card in his hand. Eighty. He was only eleven. I put my arms round him and hugged him hard.'

'It must have been difficult in a way, bringing up a boy with an exceptional talent,' Lavender said.

'Ma'am, we gave him love and we taught him right from wrong, just like any boy. He wasn't troublesome. Oh, he threw a few clubs when he was younger, but we talked about that. Now, if you'll excuse me? Thank you for the "cuppa char" as someone called it.'

As Hector and Lavender were leaving, in the lobby they encountered Sabbatini. He was describing to Frank Moran, the golf correspondent of *The Scotsman*, a putt that had gone in. To Hector's surprise, it was one of Dick Robinson's. Hector went over to them, smiled at Dick, and asked him how he had got on.

'A seventy-five, Sheriff Drummond. One better than Bobby

Jones,' Sabbatini crowed before Dick could open his mouth. 'That young caddie, Tommy, finally sorted his putting.'

As Sabbatini drew breath, Dick interjected, 'He told me to watch the hole, not the ball, on short putts. I missed only one, at the eleventh, but it was real tricky because of the slope.'

Smiling, Hector said, 'Be careful not to be too generous with that advice. If Mr Moran publishes it tomorrow everyone will be trying it, and maybe putting better.'

'I think I'll keep it for my reflections at the end of the championship,' Moran said solemnly. He had heard too many claiming they had found the secret of putting.

When Moran left them, Hector asked Sabbatini if he might have a quiet word with him.

The pleasure drained from his face. 'Of course, Sheriff. I've been expecting a visit from you.' He turned to Dick. 'On you go, Dick and have a good, long soak in a tub. You deserve it.'

Hector led the way back to the lounge. Without mentioning Scioto, he gave his usual explanation for his inquiries, adding that Lavender was helping him. Silent for once, Sabbatini sat back, the wrinkles in his face deepening, shaking his head sadly.

After ordering more tea, Hector started by asking about his relationship with Murnian.

'Sheriff, I know nothing about his death, but I'll tell you the full story as you'll get a version of it from someone else anyway. We were friends once, in the late 1890s. He was Irish, I'm Italian, and business-wise we were in competition, but we laughed at the same things, liked a few drinks, and we chased broads as if there was no tomorrow. Then we both fell for the same dame. You can guess who won...I've always been a sore loser, Sheriff. I did some things to hurt his business, then he did other things to hurt mine. Our businesses weren't your regular grocery stores, if you get my meaning, and we fought over an area of Brooklyn. Then he did something real disreputable. A lot of Irish joined the police, and he told one of them stuff about me.' His lips twisting, he spoke quietly. 'I served four whole years in Sing Sing, Sheriff. To this day, I can't bring myself to wear a shirt or a sweater with horizontal stripes.' A distant look came into his eyes and he shuddered. He carried on, 'I needed help to deal with the Irish, and I knew some of the families from Castellammare, Sicily. What followed was bloody, and it didn't do either side any good, so the heads of the families met the Irish and called a truce. But Ralf Murnian and I never made it up.' Suddenly he smiled. 'Tell the truth, I miss the S.O.B.. For the first time in years, there's no living human that I hate. It sure feels strange.

'Anyway, Sheriff, I've turned over a new leaf. I'm getting to be too old. Prison would kill me. There's a young guy just come back to Brooklyn, "Joe Bananas" they call him. He's smart and well-organized, in tune with the modern world. He's better at running the business than I am now. And I have to get ready to meet the big guy upstairs. I guess he'll be frying Murnian right as we speak.' He smiled wistfully. 'You know his son, Enda? He's a bright kid. Once you've made your money you don't need our sort of business. I'm told Enda was trying to get his dad to see that. But I knew Ralf. He wouldn't listen. It wouldn't surprise me if he had been behind that big emerald theft. He had a fabulous collection of rocks, but he couldn't show them off. What's the point of that?' He held his knarled hands out for emphasis.

'How did you spend the night Murnian was killed?' Hector asked.

'I went to bed early. I was nearly asleep when Dick knocked on my door to say goodnight. Some time later, I woke. The Scotch I'd drunk earlier had worn off and my hip was sore. I have to keep moving through the pain, Sheriff, so I got up. It was a fine night. Dawn was already breaking. I figured it was my best chance to see the course, walking at my own pace. So I went right out to the Eden Estuary and back. It was wonderful, to see this great golf course waking up. And Sheriff, I had no idea that Murnian was lying dead in one of these bunkers.'

'Did anyone see you leave the hotel?' Hector asked.

'That old guy, Rab, was behind the desk. He has arthritis, too. We've compared notes. But he was asleep in his chair. I let myself out without waking him. The tall young guy was on the desk when I got in.'

'Can you remember what you did when you arrived last Monday, before the Independence Day party?'

'I did go out, Sheriff. I went to Dick's room and he wasn't there. I thought he might have gone for a walk and I tried to follow him. I nearly got lost in that fog, a "pea-souper" I believe you call it, so I came back to the hotel.'

Lavender said, 'Why did you feel the need to supervise Dick?'

Sabbatini shot her an appraising look. 'Dick's not good with drink,' he said carefully.

'He seemed fine after he'd had wine with his dinner that night,' Hector said, puzzled.

'No one crossed him. I've seen him get into fights. It's best he doesn't touch it.'

'You're very good to him,' Lavender said. 'He's a lucky young man.'

'If someone who lost both parents when he was just a little kid can be lucky. It's our great game that's lifted him. The supervisor at the orphanage, Father Clement, was a real good golfer. He told me he had this kid who showed a lot of promise and I checked him out. Last year, at the National Open, I met him again and liked him. So I offered to sponsor him. I guess he

thinks I'm just an old guy with more dollars than sense, but...'
As he spoke, he crumpled the lace antimacassar on the right
arm of his chair into a shapeless ball.

Hector asked, 'So, having failed to find Dick in the fog,
when did you next see him?'

'At the party. He was in his room and I shouted through the
door that I was going down for the start. He followed soon after.
I guess his inexperience in a tuxedo showed.'

'It did a bit.' Hector recalled Dick's shambolic appearance
at dinner. 'When you did see him at the party, did you think he
had been drinking?'

'I guessed he might have, but he wasn't showing it, and I
didn't smell it on him. But then, I'd had a couple of Scotches
and some cigarettes.'

Lavender said, 'I gather Murnian paid you in cash after Dick
had beaten Paul. A thousand pounds is an awful lot of money to
carry about. Did that surprise you?'

'No, ma'am. Murnian and I have gotten used to carrying
cash a long time ago. We guard it real carefully.' He reached
into an inside pocket of his jacket and pulled out a tiny, curved
pistol with two barrels. 'My faithful Remington Derringer. Had
it before I went to Sing Sing. Once you're used to carrying a
shooter, you value the security it gives you. Murnian had one
just like this. Was it still on the body?'

'I don't know,' Hector admitted. A puzzled look passed
across Sabbatini's face but he said nothing as he replaced his
gun.

'On Tuesday night, did you see Murnian and his family at
dinner, Benny?' Lavender asked.

'Oh, yeh. They were real miserable, all of them. Ralf couldn't
bring himself to look at me, but he went up to Dick and said
something to him. Dick didn't like whatever it was, something

about cheating, he told me.' Sitting forward, he asked, 'Do you think the police have arrested the wrong guys?'

'Perhaps,' Hector said cautiously.

'Cops are the same everywhere. They're happy so long as they can pin a crime on someone. A lot of guys in my business have served time for things they haven't done.'

There was no answer to that. Lavender poured more tea and they all relaxed. 'Is there a Mrs Sabbatini?' she asked.

His face clouded and his hand clenched the left antimacassar. 'There was, but she died,' he said shortly. For whatever reason, it was clearly a subject he liked to avoid. As they finished their tea, he described Dick's round, and soon regained his usual ebullience.

On their way out through the lobby, they saw the wiry figure of Stewart Maiden.

'Kiltie, Kiltie,' Sabbatini hailed him, but Maiden paid no attention.

'Stewart,' he tried. Slowly, Maiden turned and gave him the sort of look he might have given a bad lie in a bunker.

Undeterred, Sabbatini pressed on. 'I've got a great new putting tip. Watch the hole, not the ball, on short putts. It's turned Dick's game round.'

Maiden shook his head. 'There's nothing new under the sun, sir,' he said, then turned and walked away.

'They call him "Kiltie the Kingmaker" back home, but he acts more aristocratic than Lord Terry,' Sabbatini complained.

'He doesn't say much. It's just his way,' Hector said.

After Sabbatini had returned to his room, Hector asked Mary if the Keelers were in. He would offer them a lift to Ballochmyle for their council of war.

12

When they got back to Ballochmyle, they found Tommy, again in his best suit, sitting at the oak kitchen table, stained and scarred by years of cooking and eating. An old, chipped blue plate with white dots, empty apart from some crumbs, lay in front of him.

'We meant you to eat with us,' Hector said, frowning.

'I bet he's got room for more,' Lavender said, eliciting a shy grin from Tommy and a stifled exclamation from Mrs Alves.

'I told the young man he should eat in the kitchen. It's not proper he should eat in the dining room,' she said stiffly.

'We're going to suspend the usual rules this evening, Mrs Alves,' Hector said firmly. 'Young Tommy's an important member of our team and the whole team eats together.'

'I've only set for four and I'll have to prepare more potatoes,' she responded huffily.

'I'll set the extra place,' Tommy said.

'You wouldn't know how,' she snapped. Tommy winced.

'Mrs Alves, I know this seems all wrong to you,' Lavender said in her most soothing voice. 'The thing is, the people here tonight are trying to make sure Jim's killer is caught, because we think the police may well have arrested the wrong men. Tonight we're going to compare notes and discuss what we should do next. We need Tommy to be with us, and we can't have him sitting watching us eat, so we want him to have his place in the dining room. The alternative is we all come through and sit round the kitchen table, but I'm sure you don't want that.'

Mrs Alves hung her head. 'I'm sorry if I spoke out of turn, Mrs Drummond.'

'Not at all, don't concern yourself. By giving us a good meal you're really helping. Now, why don't we let Tommy clean some potatoes while you set an extra place and I'll see to Marie and Charlotte.'

'They're bathed and waiting for their story, Mrs Drummond. Marie will want to show you the drawings she did today. She's quite the little artist. You'd better admire Charlotte's as well, but, well, oh dear...' The smile returned to her face.

'Thank you, Mrs Alves. We'd be lost without you,' Hector said. 'Now I'd better see to Mr and Mrs Keeler. I left them in the drawing room without a drink. Come through and join us once you've done your spuds, Tommy.' He failed to notice Mrs Alves' frown.

Hector need not have worried about his guests. While Eleanor admired the shelves holding Bristol Blue and dimpled cranberry glass Lavender had inherited from her parents, O.B. was examining a small water colour which depicted a group of golfers and caddies from a bygone era. With the unmistakable, jagged grey skyline of St Andrews in the background they were assessing a putt. The clubs were carried loose under the arms of the caddies, two of whom were young boys. The two grandest of the players wore lum hats that looked like chimney pots. One of these sported a red jacket, plainly superior to those worn by the rest. The painting was called 'A Stymie'. One white ball lay close to the hole, but with another ball on its line.

'See, the stymie has been part of golf since its inception,'

O.B. said when Hector entered the room. 'A lot of people want to abolish it, but Bob says it's absolutely part of match play.'

Although he loved the painting, Hector was one of those who wanted the stymie consigned to the golfing dustbin. He believed that you ought to be able to make your opponent mark his ball when it lay on your line, but this was not the occasion for such a debate. He poured whisky for O.B. and himself, with a dry sherry for Eleanor. With glasses charged, they sat and discussed the day's play while they waited for Lavender and Tommy. Apart from Jones' round, most of the talk concerned the disasters: Percy Alliss had driven out of bounds twice at the sixteenth and run up a nine, finishing on eighty; George Duncan had recovered from a crippling outward nine to finish on the same score over the New; another former champion, Arthur Havers, had an eighty-one; Roger Wethered, the British amateur, took eighty-two. Of the suspects, Dick Robinson's seventy-five was the best, while Lord Terry had a seventy-seven. Paul Murnian had taken seventy-nine on the New, where his hook was always liable to get him into trouble. It appeared that the qualifying score was likely to be about one hundred and sixty for two rounds, so the only suspect in danger of making an early exit was Murnian. O.B. was expressing admiration for the seventy-five scored by J.H. Taylor, Open Champion five times between 1894 and 1913, when Lavender led a hesitant Tommy into the room.

Hector poured Lavender a sherry then turned to Tommy. 'Sherry? Whisky?' he asked.

Blushing, the lad stammered, 'I'd like what Mrs Drummond is having, please, sir.'

Hector thrust a full glass into his hand and told him to draw up a chair. Obviously anxious, Tommy set down his drink on a table and carried a wooden upright chair in from the wall. He was about to sit when Hector introduced him to the Keelers. The others suppressed grins as he wiped his right hand on his trousers before shaking theirs. Perched on the edge of his chair, with great care he gripped the delicate glass with his fingers as Lavender had done and swallowed a mouthful of the sweet, brown liquid.

Hector cleared his throat and raised his own glass. 'Jim Tindall. May he rest in peace,' he said.

They stood and drank in respectful silence. As they sat down, O.B. noted Tommy's empty glass. 'Easy, cowboy,' he whispered, then winked reassuringly.

Hector fumbled with miscellaneous sheets of paper, most covered in a barely legible scrawl.

'I'm going to buy you a notebook for your birthday, darling,' Lavender said. 'Every sleuth should have one.'

'I know where I can find things,' Hector replied. Briefly, he described the state of the investigation as he saw it. He turned to O.B.. 'Have you anything to report, O.B.?'

'I have exchanged wires with the hobo's attorney. He knows about young Jim, but that's not enough for a stay of execution. The hobo's name is Art Harris and his appointment with Old Sparky is a week tomorrow, so we're going to have to come up with something solid before that. The good news is I can wire the attorney direct.'

'What about you, Tommy?' Hector asked.

The sherry had surged to his brain, bringing much-needed confidence. Tommy said, 'I've spoken to my pal, Billy. He's a bellboy at the Grand. He'll lend me his uniform so I could take that driver from the Murnian's rooms. Billy's going with Jean, one of the chambermaids, and maybe she'll help. I told him it would be worth his while, sir. I hope you dinnae mind.'

'When could you do this?' Hector asked.

'Tomorrow or Wednesday. Mrs Murnian has stayed in her rooms, even for meals, so it's no' going to be easy.'

'Well done, but the sooner the better,' Hector said. 'I bet our murderer is sitting back, thinking he's in the clear. We have to find a way of rattling his cage, and getting our hands on that club might do it. Is there anything else, Tommy?'

'Billy told me he served Paul Murnian some beer late on Tuesday night. Billy said he'd been drinking and asked a lot of questions about beer.'

'Could he give a time?' Lavender asked.

'No, Mrs Drummond. He said almost everyone had gone to bed. He shouldnae have been on then, but he was told to work a double shift. He was due on again at six in the morning.'

'It sounds as if Billy...' Lavender said, but was interrupted by a knock at the door.

'Dinner is served,' Mrs Alves announced primly. Lavender thought she detected a sniff as she returned to the kitchen. The loyal servant was easily the most conservative person in the house. She would need extensive mollifying once Tommy had gone.

A selection of cold meats with boiled new potatoes and salad awaited them. Mrs Alves had also made a pot of rich-tasting mayonnaise. Hector directed them to their places and poured claret into all the wine glasses.

'Tindall grew this salad,' he said as he sat down. Guarding against another show of emotion, he shuffled his notes then cleared his throat. 'I'm proceeding on the basis that Jim's killer also murdered the boy at Scioto. Excluding those who were at Scioto but have alibis for early Monday evening, our suspects are Paul Murnian, Enda and Vera Murnian, who could all have slipped out of the cinema, Ralf Murnian, Dick Robinson, Benny Sabbatini and Lord Terry Coates-Moulton. Paul Murnian went to Gloria Van Dyke's room when he got back to the hotel. I met her today and she says he had a bath and, curiously, washed his plus fours before going to her. They went to bed. She also...' He struggled to find appropriate words. 'She says he is a young man of vigour and stamina.' He cleared his throat. When the penny dropped, Tommy nearly choked on a potato. Seeing this, Lavender, her shoulders shaking, put the back of her hand to her mouth.

While Eleanor smiled, O.B. laughed out loud and said, 'Then I suppose their love-making doesn't exonerate him. But why on earth should he wash his knickers?'

'That has to be very suspicious,' Hector said.

Lavender said, 'Hector, as far as Enda and Vera are concerned, I cannot believe that a woman would combine with a man to do what was done to Jim. It would be just too unnatural.'

'My dear, I don't think we can ever say that something is too vile for some human beings to do.' O.B. spoke sadly.

Hector said, 'You're right, O.B., but it's the least likely scenario. I think the murders of Murnian and McCann must be linked. Not necessarily the same killer, of course. If we find out who killed either one of them, and why, we'll be well on our way.'

O.B. said, 'The phone call to Molasses plus the doctor's opinion puts Ralf's death at about the time Billy was giving Paul beer in the Grand. Sabbatini is the only suspect we know was out on the course very late at night.'

Hector said, 'Murnian and Sabbatini hated each other. They were striving for respectability in their old age, but they were still basically gangsters. They even boasted to me about the guns they carried.'

'Which were?' O.B. asked.

'Sabbatini's always been a Derringer man. At the party last

Monday, Murnian told me that for a year or two he's carried one too. It's lighter and harder to spot than the 1908 Colt he used to have.'

'The Colt was the weapon of choice of gangsters,' O.B. commented.

'What's a Derringer?' Tommy asked.

O.B. smiled. 'The smallest gun you get. It's curved, like an old-fashioned pistol, or a banana, only much smaller. A Derringer killed Lincoln. The Colt, on the other hand, has straight lines. It's more powerful and can fire more bullets. In the States we reckon the right to carry arms is important in a way you Brits don't.'

Lavender said, 'There may be no connection between the murders of Murnian and McCann and the two young boys. Didn't Ralf Murnian get some message before dinner on Tuesday that made him angry? Why did he give the go-ahead for the German deal, having been sceptical about it, and why did he go out on the course again to get murdered at the far end of the links?'

O.B. said, 'Maybe he had arranged to meet Sabbatini.'

Tommy asked, 'Do you think Mr Murnian meant to kill Mr Sabbatini?'

Hector said, 'It's quite possible. Or the other way round.'

O.B. said, 'The timing of events on Tuesday evening is getting to look more and more important.'

Hector said, 'It would be worthwhile to talk directly with Molassses. Why don't I try to book a call for later this evening?'

O.B. said, 'That's a good idea, but it's mighty expensive and there's a terrible rigmarole to go through.'

Hector got up. 'I'm going to book a person to person call now. Mary, the receptionist at the Grand, told me how it's done. Is New York five hours behind us?'

Eleanor looked at her watch. 'You're right, Hector. It'll be just past three in the afternoon there.'

While Hector was out of the room, the rest applied themselves to the meal. Briefly coached on table manners by Mrs Alves before going to the drawing room, Tommy had been amazed to observe O.B. and Eleanor cutting up all their food before using only a fork to eat. The thinly sliced meat was delicious and he had never tasted anything smoother than the claret. Hector had poured it from a delicately engraved glass jug with a silver spout and handle, shaped like the Open trophy. It was now sitting on the table in front of Tommy. He wondered if he might help himself, as O.B. had just done.

'Allow me, son,' O.B. came to his rescue and re-filled his glass. Tommy sipped the ruby-red liquid, swilling it about in his mouth. Last Monday he had been sentenced to borstal. Now he was in the judge's dining room, using his silver and drinking his wine. To hell with the tally-man, never mind if he didn't manage to get the knives and forks back, this was a great moment.

'Dick Robinson doesn't know you're helping us, does he, Tommy?' O.B. asked.

'No, sir, I dinnae think he can. He knows I've picked up practice balls for the sheriff, but I havenae told him anything else.'

'Well, best you don't. He seems to be a nice young man, but he is a suspect, and so is Sabbatini. Whoever's been killing these kids is hiding a horribly mean streak, and hiding it well.'

'I cannae believe Dick, Mr Robinson, would do such things, sir.'

O.B. smiled. 'I sure hope you're right, son.'

'Half past nine, our time, person to person with Mr Mo Evans.' Hector beamed as he re-entered the room, grabbed the claret jug and topped up the glasses.

Over the comforting splash of wine into crystal, Eleanor spoke firmly. 'You know, someone guilty of these dreadful crimes against young boys would certainly kill to protect himself.'

'And if Ralf Murnian was killed because he was the child-murderer, the clubmaker's death makes no sense,' Lavender added.

'Murnian's killer was cruel, deliberate and smart,' Hector said. 'Look at the way he left the wallet, with money in it, lying around so that someone like Marty Kay would pick it up.'

'Is there any way we can find out what the official investigation has come up with?' O.B. asked. 'Maybe there are fingerprints or something that would help us.'

'I'll try to have a word with PC Gemmell tomorrow,' Hector said. 'I've taken the rest of the week off, and, if I can catch him away from McNeill, he'll probably tell me if there's anything interesting.'

Mrs Alves entered, carrying a steamed syrup sponge. The chorus of praise for the main course, particularly the mayonnaise, made her beam with pride. After the feather-light sponge with its hot, golden covering had been devoured in near silence, they all went through to the drawing room for coffee. The talk soon turned to golf, and Tommy was demonstrating the St Andrews shot, without a club, for O.B. when the telephone rang.

'A bit early,' Hector said, consulting his watch.

Mrs Alves knocked then came in. After a discreet cough she inquired, 'Sheriff Drummond, would you be able to speak with the sheriff principal now?'

Hector's face fell. There could be only one reason for Crichton Fairweather KC to telephone, and he was not a man who could be hurried; long words flowed majestically from his full lips; no expression of opinion was complete without a sprinkling of Latin; he said 'Good morning' as if he was bestowing a favour.

'Does he know I'm in?' Hector whispered.

Puzzled disapproval clouded Mrs Alves' brow. 'Yes, Sheriff,' she said primly.

'Why now?' Hector muttered as he rose, his dislike of the telephone festering.

'Drummond, my dear chap, how are you?' The rich tones burbled out of the earpiece.

After Hector had assured the great man that he was well, and received similar reassurance in turn, a clearing of the throat warned Hector that Fairweather was about to get to the point.

'Fama nihil est celerius,' he began. 'Word has reached me that you have been adopting an unconventional approach to your duties as my sheriff-substitute.'

'Indeed?'

'Indeed, what I heard caused my brow to furrow with consternation. I heard that you were intent on adopting an investigative role in relation to certain cases of homicide, representing to persons, including the bereaved, that our procedure of continuing cases for examination bestowed on you a power to question material witnesses. I hear further that, by implication at least, you have suggested that the efforts of the constabulary were inadequate. I would be obliged if you would enlighten me on the matter.'

'Well, Fairweather, it's true.' Hector adhered to the bar convention of taking the senior man's lead in the manner of address. 'Inspector McTaggart has gone for the obvious suspects. I am afraid there is someone connected to the major golf championships who is a deviant and a child murderer. He needs to be stopped in his tracks, and as all the suspects will leave St Andrews at the end of this week after the Open finishes, I have been trying to repair the deficiencies in the police investigation. It was not so long ago that the Fifeshire Constabulary worked under the direction of the sheriff, so I do not believe what I am doing is objectionable.'

'Investigation of crime, or any case, is no part of a judge's role, Drummond, and I'm surprised, nay troubled, to hear what you have told me. Non omnia possumus omnes, as Virgil pointed out. You cannot do everything and it is folly to attempt to do so. Our system is refined and robust. The constabulary investigates, the Crown prosecutes in the public interest, appropriately qualified lawyers defend, and judges at all levels judge, and that is all they do. If the police have made a mistake, that will surely be rectified by operation of law at trial. Look at the Merrett case a few months ago. Sed quis custodiet ipsos custodes? I hear you ask. In so far as lawyers do so at all, they do it at trial. It is quite inappropriate that you should live up to your heroic name in this manner. The walls of St Andrews are not the walls of Ilium, but you will doubtless recall the unhappy fate of your classical namesake.' He paused to let that sink in. 'However, errare humanum est. You are generally well-regarded, and you will be forgiven, so long as you abandon this emulation of Sherlock Holmes.'

As the monologue carried on, it became clear to Hector that the matter held some importance for Fairweather. While the role of sheriff-substitute was full-time, the sheriffs principal came from the ranks of senior counsel, men still in practice at the bar who were dipping their toes in judicial water in the hope of securing appointment to the bench of Scotland's highest court. Fairweather's ambition was legendary and should one of his sheriff-substitutes blot his copy-book that might reflect on the sheriff principal, dashing his expectation of preferment. He would never forgive the errant sheriff-substitute. Hector was also aware of the time. Half past nine was fast approaching and he was determined to speak to Mo Evans. Red-faced and fidgeting, his eye fell upon a porcelain vase, hand-painted with more enthusiasm than skill by Lavender's Aunt Marigold. It sat beside the telephone on the hall table for want of anywhere better to put it. On an impulse he picked it up and threw it to the polished wooden floor, where it smashed with a satisfactory crash.

'Oh dear, Fairweather, Lavender's just had a fall,' Hector cried. 'I must go.'

'Indeed, my good chap, you must assist. Please remember what I have said...'

'Naturally, now I must go. Goodbye.'

'And I trust there will be more damnum than injuria...' the vocal equivalent of Mrs Alves' mayonnaise flowed on until the click of the telephone cut it off.

'What on earth has happened?' Lavender demanded, coming out of the drawing room. Simultaneously, Mrs Alves rushed from the kitchen.

'It was the only way I could get him to dry up,' Hector confessed. As Lavender wondered how to respond, the telephone rang again.

Desperation in his voice, Hector said, 'Mrs Alves, could you please answer? If it's the sheriff principal again, please say I am with Mrs Drummond, who has injured herself, then say you are needed too. Sorry to ask you to do this, but it's very, very important.'

Shaking her head, Mrs Alves nervously picked up the receiver. 'Sheriff Drummond's residence,' she said. 'Oh, Joyce, it's you...a Mr Mo Evans...did you say New York?...Yes, he's just here.' She handed the instrument to Hector and returned, flabbergasted, to the kitchen.

'Sheriff Drummond, I believe? How may I help you?' The

voice had an identifiable New York accent. To Hector's surprise, it sounded as clear as Fairweather's.

'Mr Evans, good of you to speak. I am the sheriff of St Andrews, where your client, Mr Ralf Murnian was tragically killed last week. I understand you were his attorney. There are a number of matters I would like to clarify now, before the body leaves the country, so that there will be no unpleasant surprises at trial.'

'I'm happy to help, Sheriff, but I understood you'd gotten the men responsible?'

'We don't want the defence to be able to say that there has not been a thorough investigation.' Conscious of the cost, Hector pressed on. 'I understand Mr Murnian spoke to you a very short time before he was killed. How did he sound?'

The silence at the other end of the line made him wonder if he had gone too quickly, then he remembered how far the soundwaves had to travel along the underwater cable.

'To be frank, Sheriff, he sounded as if he might have had a few drinks, which wasn't unusual.'

'I understand he had been sceptical about the Hundsmann deal, but had changed his mind?'

'You are well-informed, Sheriff. Enda was pushing that deal, but Ralf thought up one objection after another. When I saw he'd booked the call, I expected him to tell me to pull out, but I remember his words. "Molasses", that's what he called me, "I'm persuaded. Gotta move with the times, trust the next generation." Then he told me to wire our acceptance of the terms on offer. I gather someone else was interested in acquiring the company, so if we wanted the deal we had to move fast. I wired acceptance as soon as the call was over.'

'Mr Evans, if Mr Murnian did not make that call, but was already dead, what would happen to the deal?'

The silence that followed was caused by more than the sub-ocean cable.

'It would be very awkward. Although I had wired accept-ance, there were, and are, papers to sign, specially as it's a for-eign deal. The executors, who have to sign, have been happy to go along with Ralf's last wishes, but...What are you saying? I spoke to an imposter?'

'Could you have?'

'I don't believe so. But...' Another long, expensive, silence followed. 'I've heard Paul imitate his dad pretty good. I can't swear it was Ralf I spoke to, but I thought it was him at the time.'

'Of course you did, Mr Evans. It probably was him, but I felt I had to check.'

'Naturally, naturally. Well, if that's all?'

'It is indeed. Thank you very much, Mr Evans.'

'Do keep me informed, Sheriff. Things round here could get mighty tricky.'

'I will, Mr Evans. Oh, by the way, please don't say anything to the family yet.'

Hector replaced the receiver and uttered a low whistle. 'It could have been Paul,' he said. The others, who had crept into the hall to hear what they could, returned to the drawing room to digest the latest development.

'If Paul spoke to Molasses, he could have killed his father,' Hector said. 'Why else should he pretend to be him on the telephone?'

'Perhaps he wanted the Hundsmann deal as much as Enda did,' O.B. said, 'but what would Ralf have done when he found out?'

Hector said, 'Maybe it would have been too late, or too embarrassing, to stop it.'

'What about Enid?' Lavender asked. 'Remember, she went paddling along the West Sands.'

'I thought we were trying to cut down the list of suspects,' Tommy said quietly, but everyone heard.

Half an hour later, Hector gave the Keelers and Tommy a lift into town. As they dropped Tommy, O.B. offered to help take the Hagen driver from the Murnian rooms. 'The more I think about it, the more important it is to get a hold of that thing and have a look at it,' he said. This delighted Tommy, who was not looking forward to trying his hand again at theft.

＊　　＊　　＊

'Was Fairweather proving awkward, darling?' Lavender asked as she and Hector prepared for bed.

'Very. He told me to stop sleuthing immediately or I might share the fate of my classical namesake.'

'Didn't he get dragged round the walls of Troy?'

'Yes. Achilles tied his body to his chariot. I got ragged about it at school.' The unhappy memory of being dragged naked round the changing room as an eleven-year-old came back to him.

'That's a bit rich, even from Fairweather.'

'He's so ridiculous, it's easy to forget how venal and clever he is. He's desperate to be made a judge, and if this business goes wrong, it'll reflect on him.'

'And his wife, Clarinda, makes Lady Macbeth seem as benign as Mrs Alves. I met her once. She's terrifying. What are you going to do?'

'I'm going to carry on. I didn't spend all that time in the trenches to be intimidated by Fatty Fairweather. If we get to the bottom of this, you can be sure he'll claim the credit. If we don't...' he looked at her seriously, 'I'll be looking for a job.'

13

Tuesday 12 July

'If it weren't for that uniform, I'd have you over my knee, sonny.'

'Having some difficulty, Officer?' Hector asked. A few yards from the first tee of the Old Course, a blushing PC Gemmell was standing eyeball to eyeball with a burly, red-faced man of about forty whose ample frame strained the buttons of his brown waistcoat. Above his dirty white collar wobbly, half-shaved dewlaps supported a face twitching with anger. His accent was North of England. The board beside him gave his name, Harold Threlwall, and the odds he was offering. His left hand grasped a bundle of tickets.

'This gentleman and his colleagues have been told book-makers can't trade near the first tee, Sheriff,' Gemmell replied, drawing himself to his full height. Two other men with similar boards stood behind Threlwall. They looked no less rough but significantly less menacing.

In army officer mode, Hector stepped up to Threlwall and stared him down, his extra couple of inches giving him an advantage. 'I am the sheriff here, and there are more police officers nearby. If you don't leave the course this minute, I'll offer ten to one on you and your colleagues spending a night in the cells, then appearing in my court tomorrow morning.'

The dewlaps shook impotently. 'Nought wrong with what we're doing. Just helping people enjoy themselves a bit. Come on, lads. We know when we're not wanted.' With practised hands, he dismantled his board and carried it away, the other two in his wake.

Gemmell watched them go. 'Thank you, Sheriff. That was beginning to look awkward. Jimmy Alexander, the starter, told them off, but they paid no attention.'

'We may have done them a favour in the long run,' Hector observed. 'Offering ten to one against Bobby Jones and thirty to one against Jim Barnes is remarkably generous. I suppose they are confused by the size of the field and think that anyone might win, a bit like the Grand National. They'd better stick to horses in future.'

Gemmell's blush was receding. Hector saw that an opportunity had landed in his lap. 'I wonder if I could ask a favour of you,' he said.

'Of course, Sheriff,' he said hesitantly.

Hector led the way to a quiet spot immediately behind the new starter's box. 'You may have heard that I have been taking a wider view of the recent murders than your superiors. I do believe we should all be trying to get to the truth, and I'd appreciate it if you could tell me a bit about the official investigation. I'll not say where I got the information,' he added.

'What do you want to know?' Gemmell asked.

'Have any new eye-witnesses come forward?'

'No, sir.'

'Has anyone been seen acting suspiciously?'

'No, sir.'

'Have the scientists come up with anything interesting, whether it supports the case against the accused or not?'

'Well, the clubmaker, McCann, was killed by the awl, and

it was covered in Nugent's fingerprints. There was one of his fingerprints, in blood, on the door of the shop. Mr Murnian was asphyxiated by the sand in the bunker. Then he was shot by a bullet fired from a Remington Derringer. He always carried one, but it wasn't on his body. We've been looking for it. Inspector McTaggart says if Martin Kay threw it in the whins, anyone might find it.'

'Were Murnian's hotel keys found on his body?'

'Yes, sir. There were three keys, one for his bedroom, one for his bathroom, and one for the sitting room all the Murnians used. Martin Kay's fingerprints were on Mr Murnian's wallet.'

'What about Jim Tindall?'

'Jim's blood group was O. Group A semen was found on him and that's the same as Madsen's, the older man with the beard. Varvell is group O.'

Hector frowned. 'O and A are the commonest groups, aren't they?'

'Yes, sir, roughly four out of ten are O and four out of ten are A. It doesn't tell us much. That's about it, sir.'

'Well, thank you, that's been very helpful.'

'Oh, there is one other thing, sir. There were traces of strawberry jam on Madsen's shoes and on the carpet of their sitting room. Jim's granny had given him a pot and it smashed.'

'Oh. That is interesting.'

'Thank you, sir. And you won't mention...'

'Of course not.' Hector smiled reassuringly then went off to try to see some golf. It was a dreich morning, more like November than July. The ground was damp and a light *haar* reduced visibility. The east wind was not much more than a zephyr. Although uncomfortable for spectators, the conditions were ideal for low scoring.

The order of play for the second qualifying round was an

exact reversal of the first. Barnes, one of the last to finish on the New on Monday, was one of the early starters on the Old on Tuesday. Hector decided to walk out to catch him playing the last few holes. On the second, he caught up with Larry Nabholtz and was immediately impressed by his leisurely swing and the rude shock he gave his golf ball, an awe-inspiring brassie to six feet giving him a three at the long fifth. Hector followed him until the sixth, when he crossed over to watch Barnes on the thirteenth. Hector noted that, while Nabholtz had pointedly ignored him, Barnes gave him a lop-sided smile and touched his cap. On the thirteenth, Barnes sliced into whins and lost his ball, taking six, but he continued to strike the ball crisply and, after a seventy-four the previous day, could afford a few mishaps and still qualify with ease.

Hector consulted his draw sheet. A handful of games behind Barnes, the great Harry Vardon was playing. Two games after him, and three in front of Nabholtz, came Paul Murnian. After watching Barnes negotiate the seventeenth in safety, Hector walked back till he found Vardon, a plan forming in his mind.

A good crowd was gathered round the fifteenth green in support of the old champion, and he delighted them by holing a long putt. Full of admiration, Hector watched him play the last three holes. At the age of fifty-seven, his ball-striking was as precise as ever, but his short-range putting was distressingly fallible. With his seventy-five on the New, a seventy-nine on the Old saw him easily through the qualifying test.

After willing in the great man's putt on the eighteenth, Hector walked back to the tee, where Paul Murnian was waiting to drive. No spectators were with him. It seemed that Enda and Vera no longer felt obliged to come out in support. He ignored Hector, as Nabholtz had done, and struck a ferocious drive down the left of the broad fairway.

As Paul strode purposefully to play his second, Hector walked beside his slow-moving caddie. There was no black-headed driver in his bag. Hector quickened his pace until he was at Paul's shoulder.

'I know about the telephone call to Evans,' he said.

Paul could not hide the look of horror as he turned round. 'What call?' he blurted out.

'You know perfectly well. I have some questions for you, and it would probably be in your best interests to give me five minutes of your time after you've finished.' He fell back, giving the young man time to think.

Played with a mashie-niblick, Paul's second was supposed to travel through the air. Badly topped, it skipped and bumped along, ran through the Valley of Sin, and finished a few feet short of the hole. Paul turned to Hector and glared. Hector responded with a smile and a shrug. He was not surprised when Paul missed the putt, and required a few deep breaths before dealing with the resulting tiddler.

Hector lingered nearby as Paul checked his card before handing it in. After speaking to his red-faced caddie he came over to Hector, a scowl on his face.

As Paul opened his mouth Hector got in first. His voice low, he said, 'Inspector McTaggart does not like being lied to, and I haven't told him – yet. I suggest we go round to the other side of the Royal and Ancient and have a quiet word that the police and your family don't need to know about.'

'Come on,' Paul replied, his eyes blazing. Hector followed him in front of the big window towards the north side of the clubhouse where they could not be seen from his family's suite in the Grand.

'I don't know what you're talking about,' Paul blustered once they were round the corner of the building.

Hector looked pained. 'Oh, don't be silly, please. I've spoken to Molasses and I know you do a good imitation of your father. He didn't change his mind about the Hundsmann deal. He was never going to. As I say, McTaggart does not like being lied to, and once he gets an idea in his head, it's hard to shift it. Do you want to be arrested and charged with an attempt to pervert the course of justice? I couldn't care less about that German deal, but I care very much about these murders. The evidence against you is mounting, you know. Imitating your father on the telephone would look bad before a jury. If you didn't kill him, it would definitely be in your best interests to come clean to me now.'

The façade of bravado crumbled. Paul rested his forehead against the cold, grey stone of the clubhouse. 'I did it to get back at him,' he whispered. 'He had a real mean streak, my dad, and boy did it come out that night.'

'You can tell me,' Hector said. 'I won't use it unless I have to. But I do need to know everything.' As wisps of *haar* swirled around them, Hector suppressed a shiver.

'I was real mad at the way he'd made me snub Gloria. We had to do as he said all the time, like when we were kids.' He turned and leaned his back against the wall. His eyes staring blankly ahead, he carried on. '"He who pays the piper calls the tune" he used to say. Mom, Enda, Vera, me, we all lived as he wanted. In return, he gave what was most important to each of us. I got my golf career, not needing to worry about money. Enda got to see some of Dad's business, and that business was going to be his one day. That suited Vera, too, so she went along with it. And Mom, well, she got to keep us, her family.' He paused. 'It's terrible, but each one of us is better off now he's dead. We all know it. I'm the only one who says it, and I miss him most.'

Hector remained silent as the young man collected himself.

'Gloria had crossed the Atlantic to be with me, but Dad wouldn't have her at our table. She told me I was pathetic, and she was right, but I couldn't...She said a bunch of other things. Tuesday was a terrible day. There was my row with Gloria, then I lost that match. Dad was real, real mad at dinner. I had more Scotch than I usually have. I saw Jim and Charlie, as you know, and then I went out on the course. I saw Dad. He was kinda hunched up, walking fast, his hands in his pockets. I decided I was going to have it out with him, man to man. And I did, I had my say.' He paused. 'Then he had his. Gloria was a gold-digging tart. I was crazy to even look at her. She'd bring nothing but trouble. And so on. Then he turned on me. I'd let him down by losing that match, made him look a fool. I had only one thing to do, and that was to play golf, and I couldn't even make myself a winner at that.' Lowering his voice, he said sadly, 'I'd never realized he thought so little of me. I nearly hit him. I did. I came that close.' He held up his thumb and index finger, a tiny gap between them. 'But I didn't. I walked a bit, sat on the edge of a bunker.

'When I'd calmed myself, I got back to the hotel, went up to the sitting room and poured myself another Scotch. I was alone. The telephone rang. I answered. When I heard it was a person to person with Mo Evans, then and there I decided I'd get back at Dad for what he'd said to me. Enda wanted to buy that Hundsmann company in Germany. It seemed like a smart move to me, but Dad was dead against it. He kept on finding reasons for not going ahead, and Enda was scared we'd lose the deal. They'd argued about it before dinner. So I used the name Molasses, which only Dad used for Mo, made my voice a little deeper, a little more New York, and told Mo to go ahead and buy the company. When I came off the telephone I thought of what I had done, how Dad would react, but I couldn't speak to

Mo without booking a call, and I reckoned that when he cooled down, Dad would know he'd pushed me too far and he wouldn't ever speak to me like that again. So I went downstairs and had a beer. I know Dad didn't mean all he said to me out there, but it was the last time we spoke.' He looked at Hector, as if seeking a morsel of reassurance.

'You and your golf made him very happy. I could see him swelling with pride when he spoke about you. It's always a tragedy when people who have been close are parted by death after a quarrel. But, I have to ask this, does anyone else know you took the call?'

'If they do, they haven't said. The next morning, when we heard about Dad, I felt terrible. Enda, he's older, made the telephone calls. One of the first was to Mo. When Mo told him about Hundsmann, Enda couldn't believe what he was hearing, and he gave me a funny look. We haven't talked much about it, Sheriff. None of us wants to rock the boat. None of us wants to say much of what we feel. I don't know all that I feel. Thank goodness for golf. Out on the course, I concentrate all I can. On some shots, I sense him at my shoulder, willing me to make a good swing. A couple of times, I swear, he steered putts into the hole. But it's mighty tough going down the fourth, where we quarrelled, and, of course, the ninth.'

'Are you going to qualify?' Hector asked, his tone sympathetic. He had imagined his own father, during the weeks following his death, as a cold but supportive ghost on the links.

'I'm on a hundred and fifty-eight, which they say will be in comfortably.'

'Well done,' Hector said, meaning it. A question about the emeralds was on the tip of his tongue, but something stopped him from asking it. There was another matter requiring explanation, and he had to raise it.

'I've been told you washed your plus fours after you came back from the cinema last Monday. Would you like to tell me why?'

Paul's expression instantly became antagonistic. 'Washing blood off, do you mean?' He shook his head and a rueful smile spread across his face. 'At the movie house there were kids up in the balcony. They were throwing things at the folks down-stairs. I guess I may have done that myself once in a while. One emptied the end of his drink and there was this sticky stain on my tweed knickers. I washed it off in the tub, but my knickers took a while to dry. I couldn't wear them the next day. And before you ask, I didn't kill that boy.'

Casually, Hector asked, 'When did you first hear about Jim Tindall's murder?'

There was no hesitation. 'When I got back to the hotel after losing that match.'

'What about your father?'

'The same. When he heard, he went all quiet. I remember him saying to himself, "the S.O.B.".'

Hector said, 'Thank you for your time, Paul. I'll respect your confidence as much as I can.'

'Do you think the police have the wrong men for my dad's murder, Sheriff?' Paul asked intently.

'I'm afraid I do. But what you've told me is most helpful.'

'Well get the S.O.B., Sheriff. But don't let me near him, or I'll blow his rotten brains out.' Wiping his face and drawing himself up, Paul nodded to Hector then strode round the cor-ner of the clubhouse and past the big window, the arrogance in his bearing skin deep.

Slowly, wondering how much he should believe, Hector made his way to the front door of the club, where he found Tommy loitering.

'Go across the road to the scoreboard,' Hector said. 'I'll follow in a minute.' The scoreboard, behind the eighteenth green the previous day, had been moved to a better position across the road from the club. Hector did not want Tommy's cooperation in the investigation to be obvious.

Five minutes later, Hector stood behind Tommy, having run his eye over the others in front of the large blackboard. 'How did Dick get on?' he asked.

Tommy did not look round. 'Seventy-eight, sir. He'll be in comfortably.'

'Good. Are you going to manage the other thing?'

'Tomorrow, sir. Today's Rab's afternoon off, so Billy will be too busy. Mr Keeler's going to help.'

'Good.' Hector was disappointed they could not get the driver that day, but it was more important that the job should be done safely. 'It would be better if we could keep in touch and make plans through him rather than talking directly. He'll be out on the New this afternoon, watching Bobby Jones. I thought I might watch him as well.'

'I was hoping to see Mr Jones too, sir.'

'That would be fine. We won't acknowledge each other but we can both talk to O.B.. Sorry about the penny-dreadful, cloak and dagger stuff.'

'It's alright, sir.' Tommy casually strolled away, trying not to smirk. After genuinely checking the scores, Hector went back to the club, reckoning he had earned a stiff whisky and soda.

*   *   *

Inspector McTaggart sat on the sturdier of the two wooden chairs in the small interview room. He made to rest his elbows on the table in front of him, saw the stains and folded his arms

instead. He wrinkled his nose as the all-pervasive prison odours
of unwashed bodies and fear sank to his lungs.

A guard knocked then roughly pushed Jocelyn Varvell into
the room. His blond hair filthy and untended, buttons torn
from his shirt and a swollen, purple bruise under his left eye,
he straightened himself then walked, stiff-legged, to the second
chair and stood irresolutely behind it.

'Sit down, Varvell,' the inspector said.

Gingerly, Varvell sat opposite the inspector and looked
pleadingly at him. The inspector responded with a contemptu-
ous twist of his lips. Neither touched the table between them.

Varvell broke the silence. 'I have to get out of here,' he said,
his voice catching.

*   *   *

The gallery following Jones out on the New was, once more,
the biggest of the day. Lacking Hector's height and Tommy's
fleetness, O.B. required to anticipate where the best viewing
spots might be then get there ahead of the crowd. Hector joined
him on a mound to the left of the long third as Jones prepared
to play his second.

'That's a huge shot,' Hector exclaimed, as Jones' ball
bounced over the distant green. 'There's hardly any run, and
the contours short of the green make it hard to get home even
if the fairways are firm.'

'Is it bad where he is?' O.B. asked anxiously.

'There's heather and quite tough grass. He'll find it easily
enough, but it'll be tricky.' Hector was amazed by the nervous
tension O.B. showed when watching Jones. The champion, by
contrast, appeared unperturbed when he took five on the hole.
The strain was not yet telling on him.

The crowd following Jones was drawn from all ages and strata of society. It contained more men than women, but the ladies were well represented. Wearing bucket-style hats or berets, with sensible skirts and shoes, most had a good turn of speed and did not rely on courtesy to secure a view. Many of the men wore plus fours, the more fashion-conscious sporting flat caps in matching tweed. Suits and Trilbys suggested that a number of offices would be short-staffed that afternoon. Small boys and girls darted about, holding their caps and bonnets, squeezing and crawling past adult legs until they reached the front row. The crowd gave off a curious smell, an infusion of cigarette smoke, damp tweed and cheap perfume. There was noise, too: unnecessary raincoats that flapped, lighters and cameras that clicked, change jangled in pockets, whispers of protest or gratitude. Each shot Jones hit was aimed down the middle of a human funnel that Hector would have found terrifyingly narrow. Jack, his caddie, frequently moved or cautioned members of the mob, but Jones himself remained polite and patient, not allowing the potential distractions to divert him from his purpose and touching his cap to acknowledge applause.

After Jones reached the turn in thirty-four, O.B. visibly relaxed. Hector saw him talking seriously with Tommy high on a mound to the left of the tenth green.

After a near-flawless display, including some truly wonderful shots that burned themselves on Hector's consciousness, Jones finished in seventy-one. As he patiently signed autographs for young collectors, a grim-faced local turned to his companion.

'He's no' bad,' he pronounced.

'Aye, no' bad,' came the reply.

There were few left on the course, and Hector invited O.B.

into the club for a drink while they waited to see what the qualifying score would be.

Settled in deep leather armchairs away from other men, O.B. described the plan he and Tommy had devised for the following day, although the timings would depend on the draw. Hector agreed to meet them later. In turn, he repeated what Paul had told him.

'I have a strategy,' Hector confided. 'But we have to get our hands on that club, then we might jolt our man into breaking cover.'

Their drinks finished, they joined the throng in front of the scoreboard. One hundred and eight players, with scores of one hundred and sixty or better, had qualified to play in the championship proper. Cyril Tolley, the English amateur, had the best aggregate, a hundred and forty-four. The most notable casualty was George Duncan, champion in 1920. None of the suspects had failed. However, it was the performance of the champions of the distant past that impressed Hector the most; boasting a total of sixteen Opens and one US Open, and with a combined age of one hundred and seventy, the Great Triumvirate of James Braid, Harry Vardon and J.H. Taylor had all qualified with aggregates of, respectively, one hundred and fifty, one hundred and fifty-four and one hundred and fifty-five.

Hector went home, aware that O.B. and Tommy had arranged to meet later once the draw for the first round had been published. O.B.'s parting words resonated in his head: 'Let the Games begin!'

14

Wednesday 13 July

Although he had arranged to take the time off, Hector wanted to attend to the full committal hearing of Madsen and Varvell, when the case would be continued for trial. He drove to Cupar at his usual time, the court staff aware that he would want away early.

As he drove past slowly ripening grain fields, flattened in places by too much rain, he anticipated the complaints from farmers, men who never seemed to be happy. We all have problems in our lives, he reflected. Look at Tommy. His wretched father had left him to support his mother and sister. He was now comfortable with Hector, talking easily and looking up to him, almost like a son. Consciously or not, did he crave a good paternal influence in his life?

Like Jake, perhaps, in a way. Hector had always seen him as John's son. He had played with him, treated him as family, smacked him when necessary, but it had been Lavender who had taken the decisions about him, and Hector had been punctilious about not usurping John's place. Out of deference to his friend's memory, had he neglected his son? What had happened over the last few days was disconcerting; here were two boys, so different in age and background, yet similar in character and needs.

The cases were not ready when Hector arrived at court. He paced up and down his chambers, impatient to begin. To pass the time, he practised his putting on the worn rug, using the old putter and balls he kept for the purpose. There was a smooth area round one leg of his table, perfect for three-footers. After missing five in a row, he tried Dick Robinson's trick of looking at the target as he hit the putt. The next five struck the table leg squarely. He decided to stop before the magic wore off and went over to the window. The sky was grey and the little wind there was came from the east. It was another perfect day for scoring.

Forbes' knock on the door told him his court was at last ready. After a brief time on the bench dealing with overnight custody cases, he sat in chambers ready to take the full committal. If there was no charge of murder the question of bail would arise. Hector was minded to grant bail with a condition that the two accused left Fife immediately and returned only for court appearances. Their pantomime dame solicitor would be sure to find somewhere for them in Edinburgh. In a few months they would probably have to return to prison but, if Jim's killer had been found, they would serve their sentences as mere deviants, not as unconvicted child-killers.

An expression of insincere apology on his face, Forbes came to tell Hector there would be another delay. Madsen had been charged with murder and repeated instances of sodomy. The previous day, Varvell had turned King's evidence. He had already been released and would go Scot free.

Appalled, Hector gathered his thoughts. Had Madsen really killed Jim? He hated to imagine McTaggart having the last laugh.

When, at last, Madsen was led in, the arrogance of the previous week's martyrdom was gone. His eyes were dark and hollow. His beard was matted. He barely picked up his feet as he walked.

Beyond desperation, he had sunk to a condition of near-cata-
tonic hopelessness. Wilson, his solicitor, appeared to be nearly
as shattered as his client. The hearing was quickly over. Madsen left, fully committed for trial, with only capitulation by the
Crown or the verdict of a jury between him and the noose.

'I have set my life upon a cast

And I will stand the hazard of the die.'

Hector repeated the Shakespearean quote as he drove to St
Andrews. He hoped that he would fare better than Richard III
at Bosworth. He had committed himself and there must be no
going back now.

He parked beside the Eden Course and crossed the wooden
railway bridge leading to the whins and rough grass on the right
of the fifteenth on the Old. His timing was impeccable. From
the fourteenth green, a collective sigh indicated a missed putt.
A minute later the crowd was on the move. Hector had never
before seen so many people trying to watch one golf match.
Soon they parted like the Red Sea, giving Bobby Jones an avenue down which he might drive at the fifteenth. Wishing he
could see as clearly as he used to, Hector was startled by a dull
thud barely twenty feet away. He found Jones' ball, ankle deep
in long, clingy grass among hillocks. He was lucky not to have
ended up a whin, but it was an unappetising spot.

Standing almost on top of the ball, Hector guarded it from
the horde as people struggled and squirmed to see the next
shot. When Jones arrived his face was set and grim with concentration. He seemed not to see Hector and did not respond
to his smile. With no fuss he pulled an iron from his narrow,
leather bag. He checked that the crowd had given him enough
room then stepped up to the ball and, without removing the
cigarette from his lips, delivered a mighty wallop. The crowd
rushed forward so Hector could not see where the ball went

but, to his amazement, Jones' next shot was a putt from the left
side of the green and he got his par four with ease. An excited
man in the crowd told Hector that Jones was four under fours.
Three more fours and he would equal the course record.

The third and sixteenth holes of the Old shared a wide fairway. Unfortunately, bunkers encouraged players on both tees
to aim left, so they frequently met in the middle. Half-running
over the undulating fairway in order to get a view of Jones'
second, Hector nearly collided with a man of medium height,
obviously older, wearing a flat cap and a loose, brown jacket.
He was standing astride a ball and there was an expression of
affront on his round face as he faced the surging mob. Hector
stopped in his tracks, wincing as the man behind skinned his
left heel, then turned round and held up his hand. 'Watch out
for Mr Vardon, please! Give way for Mr Vardon!'

No disrespect had been intended, and when it was realized that the great man, playing the third, had to protect his
own ball, people slowed to a walk and muttered apologies as
they passed him. Hector lingered to watch him play his shot,
earning a smile and a 'thank you' delivered in a warm, Jersey
accent. Reflecting that the day would come when white lines
round the greens would be seen as inadequate and the fairways
would be completely roped off from spectators, Hector continued his pursuit of Jones and his brilliant score, a little of the gilt
having been knocked off the occasion.

The sixteenth safely negotiated in par, Jones came to the
dangerous seventeenth. Hector decided to watch from a hum-
mock to the right of the fairway, where he saw O.B.. Dancing
about with excitement and apprehension, he was talking to
Bernard Darwin, the golf correspondent of *The Times*.

'I don't know if he'll like leading the field from the beginning,' O.B. told Darwin. 'He's never done it before.' After Darwin

had moved on, he told Hector, 'During a championship, Bob suffers horribly from nerves. He barely touches food before he plays, and eats properly only once he's done for the day. He likes to overtake his opponents, and leading from the starting gun will make him more nervous than ever.' As he spoke, Jones laid his third, a long putt from short of the green, very close.

O.B. continued, 'Mind you, last night Kiltie said he would win, and I've never heard him make forecasts before.' The twinkle returned to his eye. 'Perhaps you should have put some money on him before you drove the bookies off the course yesterday.'

'Are you set to help Tommy?' Hector asked, wanting reassurance.

'You bet. Could you pick me up opposite the Martyr's Monument at six? Tommy will make his own way to your house and we'll see what this famous club can tell us.'

With nothing to do except wait and hope, Hector followed Jones up the eighteenth, where the great old champion and honorary professional to the Royal and Ancient, Andra Kirkaldy, was on duty, holding the pin with serene dignity. Jones completed his round of sixty-eight, five thousand people craning and jostling to glimpse him doing it.

✽   ✽   ✽

Tommy had scrambled on to the sloping roof of the caddie shed behind the eighteenth green to see the end of the lowest round ever played in an Open Championship over the Old. When the final, yard-long putt went down, he tried to clap his hands, but needed to keep a hold so cheered instead. There was no ostentatious gesture but a simple touch of his cap from Jones to acknowledge the excited applause.

Skinning his knee on the way down, Tommy sat on the bench at the back of the caddie shed. His stomach churning, he kept his eye on the front of the Grand. The end of Jones' round was to signal the start of the action.

He was beginning to fret in case something was wrong when Billy came out of the hotel and stood outside, looking round. Tommy hurried across before a guest could call him and together they made their way round to the staff entrance. Billy checked no one was watching then let Tommy in. He locked the door behind them and ran up the back stairs, Tommy close behind. On the fourth floor he stopped and, at a walking pace, went along a corridor until he came to room 415. 'Mr Wethered's room. He's out of the Open, and he left this morning,' Billy whispered. A quiet knock and the door opened. An unhappy-looking girl was inside. Tommy recognized Jean.

'I'd better not lose my job through you,' she hissed, her dark eyes fixed on Tommy. Short and plump, with a white face and light brown hair held in a tight bun, she was the physical opposite of Billy. His expression told Tommy that his feet were getting colder by the minute.

'You'll both be looked after, I promise, and this isnae thieving. It's catching a killer and a thief. Come on.' Tommy tried to encourage them.

'And there's to be a reward?' Jean insisted.

'If we get the thing we think is there, yes.'

'How much?'

'Maybe ten pounds, divided up a few ways,' Tommy answered. He could see in years to come there would be hell to pay if her husband came home without his full wage.

Her expression softened and she looked prettier. 'Well, come on. I havenae a' day,' she said.

Unused to changing his clothes in front of anyone except

family, Tommy blushed as he took off his jacket and trousers. He felt better when he saw Billy's face redden as well. Jean gazed out of the window, which looked out on the buildings behind the hotel, and Tommy thought he saw the hint of a smile. He pulled on the navy blue bellboy's trousers and found the legs were much too long.

'Here, pull yer breeks up,' Jean said, grabbing the trousers by the sides of the waistband and tugging them up sharply. Ignoring Tommy's squeak, she told him to fasten his belt tight while she held the trousers in place. The bellboy's tunic nearly hid this uncomfortable arrangement, and Billy, clad only in well-worn grey underwear, adjusted the pillbox hat.

'Shoes,' Billy said after standing back to inspect Tommy's scuffed, brown boots. His feet slipped easily into Billy's clean black shoes, which felt loose even after the laces had been tied tight.

'We'll go along to the Murnian's suite, and I'll check who's in,' Jean said, assuming command. 'It should be only Mrs Murnian, as Paul's playing. Enda and his wife went out and usually stay away all day. You keep in the vestibule, and if anyone asks, you're there to help me move a wardrobe so I can dust behind it. The clubs are in the bedroom behind suitcases. I've greased the lock on the door from the vestibule to the bedroom, and before I go into the sitting room, I'll unlock it so you can slip in when I give the signal.'

'What'll that be?' Tommy asked.

'I'll ask her if she wants a window open, so you keep listening at the sitting room door. When you hear me ask that, go into the bedroom, get the club and go. Remember to shut a' the doors behind you, and be as quiet as you can. There's a connecting door between the sitting room and the bedroom, and you can hear through it.'

Tommy said, 'I'll bring the club back here, and Billy can take it to Mr Keeler then unlock the staff door. I'll go down the back stairs and slip out.' He looked hard at Billy, who was sitting on the edge of the bed, physically shaking.

It had been easy to be brave in front of Billy, but once out in the corridor following Jean, Tommy felt sick. Could he rely on the sheriff to get them out of trouble if they were caught? He had not been pleased to get the telephone call from his overseer, if sheriffs had overseers. Could Drummond himself end up in jail?

Their arrival at the Murnian suite put a stop to Tommy's imaginings. In the vestibule, Jean silently turned a key in the lock of the door ahead of them then looked round nervously. Tommy nodded. She shut the door from the corridor, and they were in darkness. Tommy heard her take a deep breath then knock confidently on the sitting room door.

'Come!' The harsh, drawled voice commanded her to enter. Alone in the black, confined space Tommy thought of a cell. He put his ear to the door and listened to Enid Murnian's slurred, demanding tones. She needed clean ashtrays, clean glasses; a cushion was not comfortable; the chaise longue had been badly upholstered and hurt her back. Jean responded briefly, politely. How did she do it, Tommy wondered. At last she asked if she could open a window. 'No,' came the reply.

Aware of his own breathing, Tommy turned the handle of the bedroom door. It opened silently and he tiptoed in, blinking. A heavy, musky perfume lingered in the air and he willed himself not to sneeze. Every slight creak of a floorboard made him stiffen. The room was untidy; an expensive-looking black dress and stockings were carelessly draped over a balloon-back chair. He checked that the connecting door was shut then went to the corner where the clubs were propped behind two large suitcases. These were heavy but he dragged them away silently. Inside the leather golf bag were the dead man's clubs. Tommy's heart sank when he looked at them. There were four woods, all stained black, and three had large sole-plates.

With great care, Tommy drew one of the clubs from the bag. It had been made by Walter Hagen's company. Its lack of loft told him it was a driver. He gripped it as if to play a shot and it felt good. He slid it back into the bag and tried a second one. Another Hagen club, it was a more lofted fairway wood. It also felt normal. Taking a deep breath and telling himself not to panic, Tommy pulled out the third club with a big sole-plate. As soon as he gripped it he knew that this was the one. The head seemed unusually light and when the clubhead rested on the floor the face pointed to the right.

Leaning that club against the wall beside the door, Tommy pushed the cases back into position. As he did so, he saw the grip of the club begin to slide. In slow motion, it moved down until it landed on the exposed wooden floor between the carpet and the wall. The rattle of hickory on oak sounded like a drum roll. He snatched up the club, opened the door to the vestibule, and was closing it behind him when he heard the turn of the handle of the connecting door.

'No, Mrs Murnian, there's no one here,' he heard Jean call. A click told him she had locked the door behind him.

Wasting no time yet not hurrying, he walked along the corridor to room 415, where Billy was waiting on tenterhooks. With relief, they swapped clothes then exchanged grins.

'Mind, don't give it to anyone except Mr Keeler, not even to Bobby Jones himself,' was Tommy's final instruction as Billy left him, the club grasped in his hand. After leaving what he hoped was enough time, Tommy went down the staff stair and sneaked out the door which Billy had left unlocked. Looking as innocent as he could, he went over to the scoreboard to see how Dick's seventy-four compared with the rest of the field.

*　　*　　*

'It was the darndest thing I've seen,' O.B. chortled. With Eleanor, Hector and Lavender, he was in the sitting room at Ballochmyle, watching as Tommy painstakingly unscrewed the sole-plate of the odd driver. 'Bob, Big Bob, Kiltie, Jack and I were sitting in Bob's room, all smiling as Bob told us it was the hardest decent score he ever shot. He holed a bunch of putts out there. On the second, he drove into Cheape's bunker and took two to get out. He holed a long putt for five there, but that was nothing to the tramliner he got for three at the long fifth. He was telling us how he kept holing 'em when the tall young bellboy came to the door. "For Mr Keeler," he said, holding up this club. "Let's have a look at it," Bob said. "I must give this only to Mr Keeler," he said solemnly. "You can hand it to Mr Jones," I said. "I was told not to hand it to Mr Jones," he said. We all started laughing and he turned red as a tomato. So I got up, took the club and thanked him with one of your ten bob notes. When he'd gone, I gave it to Bob, and he said it was the worst balanced club he'd ever felt.'

'You can see why,' Tommy said, embarrassed by his friend's ineptitude, at the same time wondering if he would have heard of the ten bob note from either Billy or Jean. He had removed the sole-plate and underneath was a cavity, apparently filled with tight-packed wood shavings. 'Shall I?' he asked, the screwdriver ready to scrape them away.

'Go ahead,' Hector said.

Delicately at first, then more determinedly, Tommy

scratched until a small parcel, tightly wrapped in linen, fell among the shavings.

'You open it, sir,' he said to Hector.

Slowly, Hector unfolded the cloth until two enormous emeralds lay on the table in front of them. A deep, clear green, with smooth, flat facets, they were not identical, the smaller having more sharp points, but they both caught the light in the room and made it dance as Hector picked them up. 'The Eyes of the Fox,' he gasped, noting their slightly oily feel. He replaced them as carefully as if he was handling porcelain.

'The Eyes of the Tiger, really,' Lavender said. 'How many people have died for them? I'm not sure I like having them in the house.'

'They sure are beautiful,' Eleanor whispered, 'But I see what you mean, Lavender.'

'Imagine being the jeweller who had to cut the facets on these babies,' O.B. said, picking up one in each hand and holding them in turn to the light. 'He'd have to have the steadiest hands in the world.'

'Do we tell anyone we have them, sir?' Tommy was anxious to claim the reward. Even shared, it would solve all his money problems.

'Not yet, Tommy,' Hector said. 'We're going to need them to flush out the murderer.'

'Do you know who it is, Hector?' O.B. asked.

'Lavender and I compared notes this afternoon. She has her theory and I have mine. But we're not going to tell you in case we're both wrong. I hope all will be revealed tomorrow. Just ask yourself, who among our suspects had no option but to kill the clubmaker?'

'How do you plan to flush him out, sir?' Tommy asked, trying to keep the apprehension out of his voice.

'If you're happy to keep going, you'll be vital to what I have in mind. But it will be dangerous. You know how a fox will turn on you when cornered?'

Tommy nodded.

'Well, our murderer is just the same.'

'I'll do what I can, sir.' He felt he had no real option.

'Good man, good man.' In a lighter tone, Hector said, 'I hope you can all stay to dinner? Excellent. Mrs Alves was told to expect you. Darling, could you see to drinks for O.B. and Eleanor in the drawing room? Tommy and I have some plotting to do, and he's not going to touch strong drink before he's put that club back together so no one will know it's been tampered with. Only, it'll have these hidden inside.' He fished in his pocket and pulled out two smooth, white, gravel chips which he wrapped in the linen cloth, taking care to retain the original folds.

15

Thursday 14 July

'Mr Murnian, Mr Murnian,' Tommy called after Enda, who was walking up the Scores from the Grand with Vera.

They both turned. 'You're Robinson's caddie, aren't you?' Enda asked.

'Yes, sir. But this has nothing to do with him.'

'What is it, then?'

'It's one of your father's clubs, a Walter Hagen driver that's supposed to stop a hook. I've heard it's missing, sir, and I think I might know where it is.'

Enda's moustache twitched. 'Well speak to my brother.' Vera took his hand and pulled him away.

Tommy stuck his tongue out at their backs then went round the corner to where the sheriff's car was parked in Links Place.

'Nae sign of interest,' he reported. 'I dinnae like him, sir. There's mair life in a workhouse blanket. I dinnae like her either.'

'So it's a pity we can cross them off the list of suspects?'

'Aye. Kind of.' They settled down to wait for Paul to come out of the Grand.

Tommy had felt thick-headed when the sheriff picked him up earlier. He forced down the ham sandwich waiting for him on the front seat, but the ginger beer was good, despite the bubbles. The sheriff seemed fine, though he had drunk quite a lot the previous evening. With his red eyes, he always looked as if he'd been drinking.

The sheriff would not say as much but, from the way he had described his plan to Tommy as he screwed the sole-plate back on the driver, it was obvious that Dick Robinson was a real suspect. Tommy couldn't imagine him killing anyone, even Murnian.

At dinner the talk had been of golf, particularly Jones' great score, but also the number of players who would qualify to play the last two rounds on Friday. Anyone fifteen or more shots behind the leader after two rounds would drop out. At the end of the day Jones led by three shots from a left-handed Australian amateur, Len Nettlefold. Those on seventy-two included Joe Kirkwood, while Percy Alliss and Henry Cotton were flying the Union Jack on seventy-three. Jones and Kirkwood apart, the American challenge had been poor.

The sheriff had been generous with his claret, and Tommy had made them laugh with some of the more repeatable caddie-shed tales. Mrs Alves had glared at him as she had brought in the clootie dumpling. He couldn't understand why the Americans had liked that so much. Mrs Keeler had gone to the kitchen to get the recipe.

'Quick, Tommy. That's him,' the sheriff hissed.

Tommy opened his eyes with a start. Paul was crossing the road on his way to the first tee. Tommy shook himself then ran to catch up. He caught Paul's sleeve and repeated what he had said to Enda.

Paul shook his arm free and glared. 'If that's the same goddam stick I used on nine against Robinson, it's only good for firewood.'

Disappointed, Tommy returned to the car and reported.

'So, unless we've got things horribly wrong, it's either Dick or Lord Terry,' the sheriff said. 'Plan A it is. I'll go out on the course and see you by the caddie shed about half past twelve.'

*   *   *

'Pity,' the weathered, tweed-clad stranger remarked gloomily to Hector as they walked up the eighteenth fairway. 'He adds a wee dash of colour to the place.'

Hector agreed. In strawberry-coloured pullover and hose, Wild Bill Melhorn was hard to miss. After arriving late, in a suit made of animal skins, he had livened up proceedings, particularly with his fine qualifying score on the New. That owed much to spectacular putting, but the magic wand had turned into a stick of rock, and his frailty on the greens had made for depressing watching as he completed his second and last round in the championship. While most of his gallery had melted away, Hector decided to stay with him to the end.

The previous afternoon, after tea, he and Lavender had looked carefully at the evidence once more. Jim's killer was obviously male, and probably quite strong. Hector thought Murnian's killer might have used the flagpole from the ninth to knock him out, then dragged the body to the bunker. Asphyxiating him in loose sand would have required strength if Murnian was regaining consciousness. The killer also knew the course; but for young Colin's wild, early morning hook, several more hours might have passed before the body was discovered. Lavender thought the final act, shooting Murnian with his own gun, demonstrated something approaching real hatred. At the same time, smoothing over the footprints in the bunker then leaving the wallet for Martin Kay to find showed cool intelligence.

Hector pointed out that the McCann murder would also

have required a considerable degree of strength, as the awl was pushed right through the body and into the workbench. The killer had taken his chance and killed with a single, merciless lunge while the clubmaker's back was turned.

They agreed that Murnian must have been killed after quarrelling with Paul and, if the same person killed McCann, the murderer had a busy time between half past eight and ten. The two murder scenes were more than a brisk half hour's walk apart and McCann's body had been warm when Nugent found him. Hector had been sure Sabbatini would not have been physically able to get from one to the other in the time, or to undertake all the components of Murnian's killing. Lavender added that it was very unlikely that Enid Murnian would be capable of killing her husband in that way.

Lavender continued, 'So, what's most likely?'

'Sabbatini told us that Murnian collected precious jewels. Say he was behind the theft of the emeralds. He would enhance his collection, at the same time getting one over on Lord Terry. How would he get them home?'

'Hiding them in a club would be a good way.'

'Exactly. So Murnian was the man in Auchterlonie's who spoke to McCann, and McCann hid the emeralds in the driver. What then?'

'McCann heard about the reward and wanted more money.'

'Perhaps Murnian sent him a way with a flea in his ear and he told Terry,' Hector said.

'Terry would have gone straight to the police,' Lavender shook her head.

'He was desperate to get the jewels back, but he could he have had an insurance fraud in mind – pay Murnian for the emeralds, but do it on the quiet and claim on the insurance? That family seat must take some maintenance.'

'Maybe Terry arranged to meet Murnian out on the course to discuss that. But why would he kill him?'

Hector thought for a moment. 'Maybe Murnian wouldn't play ball.'

'In which case Terry would go to the police. Is it not more likely that Murnian had seen something or someone in the *haar* on Monday when he went to the tobacconist, and when he heard about Jim's murder after the match, put two and two together? The child-killer wouldn't have hesitated to kill Murnian to keep him quiet.'

'But why kill McCann?' Hector lit a cigarette.

Lavender screwed up her face. 'If McCann had sent a note to Murnian wanting more money, whoever killed Murnian might have found it, and when McCann learned of Murnian's death he would have known that whoever visited him before ten was the person who had killed Murnian. Remember, McCann was expecting to be able to repay Nugent at ten, so he must have been confident of getting cash out of someone, almost certainly Murnian, before Nugent visited him.'

Hector nodded. Lavender continued, 'So let's assume Murnian was killed first, probably by the child-killer, and the murderer found a note from the clubmaker in his pocket, demanding more money for hiding the emeralds in the driver, what would each of our remaining suspects have done?'

'All the Murnians were rich enough to buy off McCann. If either Paul or Enda had gone to meet him instead of Ralf, McCann would have thought nothing of it. They would not have needed to kill him. And they would have made it worthwhile for him to keep his mouth shut.'

'So do we discount the Murnian boys as Jim's killer?' Lavender asked.

'I suppose if his father had guessed Paul was the child-killer he might have silenced him. Mind you, that doesn't fit well with all the fuss over Mrs Van Dyke,' Hector said.

Lavender sighed. 'I think you're right, darling. And I can't see Vera staying with Enda if she even suspected he was killing these boys.'

'So, there's Dick.'

Lavender said, 'Let's just suppose that, for all he seems a nice lad, he's our child-killer. Remember, Ralf Murnian heard about Jim's murder after the match between Paul and Dick was over, and he said something to Dick at dinner. Maybe he showed he knew, or was suspicious, and Dick decided he had to bump him off to keep him quiet. He followed him out on the course and murdered him at the far end.'

'He said he was practising on the New, which would be perfect. The ninth green lies between the sixth and seventh of the New. He could have sneaked out from behind a whin bush.'

'Then he found the note from McCann, and reckoned he could make himself rich overnight.'

Hector nodded. 'He could never pretend that Murnian had sent him, or anything like that, but he could have paid McCann something from Murnian's wallet, enough to get McCann to spill the beans about where the jewels were hidden, because the chef was about to come up the road for cash.'

Lavender said quietly, 'Then he killed McCann to protect himself. He could never rely on McCann to keep quiet.'

'And he was capable of doing it decisively because he is a seasoned killer.' Hector shuddered.

'And he won't have been able to get to the Murnian's suite, so he'll be biding his time till he has a chance of seizing the club, probably as the Murnians leave the hotel.'

'Yes. Stealing the club would be very difficult and dangerous for him. And for Terry, don't forget.'

'Yes. Much the same applies to him as to Dick.'

'He says he was practising on the Eden at the time Murnian was killed.' He lit another cigarette. 'So who do you say it was?' he asked.

'Dick.'

'Terry.'

*   *   *

As he watched Melhorn's sad progress, Hector worried for Tommy. It was the same worry he had felt for the men under his command, with one big difference: the troops had been obliged to fight, while Tommy had been virtually press-ganged. There was no way for a lad with his spirit to have said no to what Hector suggested. If anything happened to him...

As Melhorn signed his card, Hector looked out for Tommy.

'Lord Terry walked straight past me into the R and A,' Tommy's voice came from behind him. 'He wouldnae even sign the bairns' autograph books.'

'I'll catch him in the club,' Hector said, over his shoulder. 'Have you seen Mr Keeler?'

'Aye. We know what to do.'

Without turning, Hector strode into the club. He found Lord Terry sitting by himself in the Big Room, smoking and drinking a whisky.

'Bad luck yesterday,' Hector said, taking a seat beside him. Seventy-nine had been a poor score.

Lord Terry's lips twitched in acknowledgement and he took a long drag of his cigarette.

'I gather you had a few hooks,' Hector continued undeterred.

''Fraid so.'

'I think I might be able to lay my hands on a driver that has its face pointing out to the right, so you hook less. It's a Walter Hagen club. Recently spruced up, too. Would you be interested in getting it?'

Slowly, the young aristocrat turned to Hector, his face hard to read. 'I can think of nothing more stupid than trying to use a club like that. It would damage my whole game. There is nothing wrong with my driving that practice won't cure, and I hope to do considerably better today.' He drained his glass, stubbed out his half-smoked cigarette and got up. Without glancing at Hector, he strode off to change.

'Insufferable prig,' Hector muttered as, deflated, he joined a group of members at the big window.

'What's that about pigs, Hector?' Bean Hamilton asked him.

'Your house guest,' Hector said, more loudly.

'I'd fatten him up and eat him, if he were a pig,' the skeletally thin Bean declared, not caring who might hear. 'The bugger's not going to earn a penny in stud fees. Now, who's for a spot of luncheon?'

*   *   *

Warm, early afternoon sunshine, a welcome respite from the *haar* and rain, failed to reach the bench at the back of the caddie shed where Tommy sat fidgeting, waiting for O.B. Keeler to come out of the Grand. He was not the only one who was nervous. Looking about him anxiously, Keeler came out of the hotel and crossed Golf Place, the club under one arm, its head concealed in a long, blue woollen stocking. And this would be the least obvious way of getting the club to the caddie shed, Tommy thought.

'This is what you're looking for, I think,' Keeler said, handing the club over.

'Right, sir. Thank you, sir.' Tommy showed no sign of familiarity. He took the club into the shed, removed the stocking and, unhappily, placed the driver in Dick Robinson's bag.

For Tommy, life as a caddie was simple: so long as you both played by the rules you helped your man any way you could. When he put the driver in Dick's bag, Tommy felt he was letting him down. There was no limit to the number of clubs, and he would not let Dick hit a shot with the Hagen driver. It would not add one shot to his score. All the same, it just felt wrong.

Sombre and tense-looking, with dark shadows under his eyes, Bobby Jones walked out of the Grand, Jack at his shoulder, hugging the clubs to protect them from the throng. Distinctive in a black pullover, it took Jones some time to make his way to the tee. The previous day, Dick had been a few matches ahead of him. Today, the order of play had been reversed.

Jones' gallery was approaching the Swilken Burn when Dick came up to Tommy, a broad smile on his face.

'What have you done to your Scotch weather?' he asked cheerfully.

'They say there'll be a *haar* this evening, sir.' Tommy shook his head.

'Well, let's see what we can do while the sun still shines,' Dick said, and they set about their preparations, Tommy anticipating what club Dick would want, delaying the moment when he would take a proper look at the clubs in his bag.

It was not until they were on the second tee that Dick noticed the extra club. 'What's this, Tommy?' he asked sharply.

'Oh, that. I thought you'd put it in, sir.' The prepared lie came out smoothly.

'Must have been put in by accident. Can you think whose it might be?'

'No, sir. I can't.'

'Well hand it in to the caddie master when we finish.' He took his own driver and smote a huge drive past Cheape's bunker, giving himself a good line to the pin.

'Great shot, sir,' Tommy said, suddenly happy. Dick's reaction had been innocent, after all.

*　*　*

'How did he react?' Hector hissed in Tommy's ear, nearly three hours later, as Dick walked forward to assess his second to the sixteenth.

'It's no' him, sir. I'm to take the club to the caddie master at the end of the round.'

'That's impossible. Lord Terry showed no interest at all.' He smiled as Dick turned back to his ball.

'Afternoon, Sheriff,' Dick said politely, then pulled a spade mashie from his bag and hit a towering iron to within a dozen feet of the hole.

As he watched Dick play in, keeping his distance from Tommy, Hector asked himself what had gone wrong. Coming up the eighteenth, he sidled up to Tommy, who was walking behind Dick, and whispered, 'Make sure he knows it's the Murnian's anti-hook driver.'

As casually as he could, Hector saw Dick putt out then strolled over to the scoreboard. Jones had taken seventy-two for an aggregate of one hundred and forty, but his lead had been cut to two over a young Welshman named Hodson. Kirkwood was three behind, and Henry Cotton's aggregate of one hundred and forty-five was the subject of much excited chatter. A man in front of Hector claimed that Jones had been most fortunate: his drive at the fifth hit a spectator and was deflected clear of trouble. Both Braid and Taylor would complete all four rounds, but the championship would no longer be graced by Harry Vardon's presence. Hector was surprised to see that Larry Nabhotz had also failed.

'Who's he?' Hector heard a man ask as the scorer chalked up 'D. Robinson' among those on one hundred and forty-six.

Hector gave Tommy enough time to rub up Dick's clubs then went to the north side of the clubhouse, where they had arranged to meet.

Smoking his second cigarette, Hector walked up and down impatiently. At length, a downcast Tommy came round the corner.

'It's him, sir,' he said quietly.

'Did you explain about the driver?' Hector asked, excitement surging through him.

'Yes, sir. When I said it was Murnian's, he got real interested and said he'd take the driver to the hotel himself. So I replied, "You willnae find anything valuable in it." He changed, sir. He gave me such a dirty look. And I said, "Bring six hundred pounds to Hell Bunker tonight at ten, and I'll give you the emeralds." His mouth sort of fell open and he said, "Right, and don't dare try and double-cross me." Then he just walked off to the Grand.' The lad began to shake. 'Sorry, sir.'

'Go up City Road and turn right up Doubledykes Road. I'll catch up with you in the car. We'll go to Ballochmyle and prepare for later.'

'Right, sir,' Tommy gulped, suddenly looking less than his age. Head bowed, and dragging his feet, he went back round the corner of the clubhouse.

Out in the bay, a bank of *haar* sat, dark grey and menacing, ready to smother the links in its chilly embrace. Stubbing out his cigarette, Hector remembered officers, including himself, putting rouge on their cheeks before battle. They had to conceal their fear from their men.

*   *   *

Fine droplets settled on his hair, his clothes, his face. Tommy sat, shivering and anxious, on a slope near Hell Bunker, peering into the gloomy murk. As the *haar* swirled, like smoke from an unseen chimney, over the undulations of the links, shapes and shades changed by the second. At times Tommy could make out the mound just short and right of the fourteenth green, a full mashie-niblick away, only for the *haar* to tighten its grip so he could barely see beyond the steep, uneven face of Hell.

Haar held a special dread for him ever since that night, just seven years earlier, when Jeannie had coughed up blood and his mam had sent him out to look for his father in the town's bars. There had been a 'pea-souper' and he had got lost. Crouched against a wall, crying, a big man suddenly loomed over him. 'Are ye feart of the bogey-man, sonny?' he sneered, then pulled a hideous comic face. When, later, he found his way home, his father belted him. Now, beside Hell Bunker, Tommy was feart of the bogey-man again.

At Ballochmyle, everyone had been edgy. When Tommy could not finish his sandwiches he got a kindly smile from Mrs Alves. Grim-faced and constantly rubbing his forehead, the sheriff had left the room and come back with a gleaming, well-oiled gun which he showed to Tommy. 'Service revolver,' he said in a matter of fact way. 'Just in case. It's loaded.' Then he went to the telephone. As Mrs Drummond asked Tommy questions about the golf, the sheriff's voice came from the hall, 'I know it's dangerous.'

In the drawing room, the sheriff poured glasses of claret

and muttered something about 'Dutch courage'. Then they went through the plan, the sheriff doing most of the talking. Determined to get there ahead of Dick, they left early. Before getting into the car, the sheriff grasped his hand. 'Good man, good man,' he said in a funny voice. Mrs Drummond kissed him on the forehead and they were off. Tommy had been pleased when they stopped at the foot of City Road and picked up O.B. Keeler, carrying a niblick. At least they had an advantage in numbers. The sheriff parked at the Eden Course and they walked out to the second then crossed the railway using the wooden bridge.

'We'd best separate now,' the sheriff said. 'We'll carry on and hide in the whins between the third of the Eden and Hell Bunker. You'd better approach as if you'd walked out on the Old.' He shook Tommy's hand once more. 'Well done, lad,' he said curtly.

Holding his niblick awkwardly, Keeler wiped the dampness from his glasses then took Tommy's right hand in both of his. 'You're a fine young man, son,' he said. 'Do what you have to, but keep safe.'

Hell Bunker came into play on the fourteenth, the long par five coming in. Players tried to drive on to a flat plateau known as the Elysian Fields. To the right, over a low stone wall and out of bounds, was the Eden Course, while to the left the deep Beardie Bunkers lurked. Once past the Beardies the fairway widened. At the end of the Elysian Fields the ground fell away sharply, and in that dip Hell, the biggest bunker on the course, sprawled, ready to devour balls struck foolishly or inaccurately.

It was on the rough ground sloping down from the Elysian Fields that Tommy waited. With poor visibility, the fact that the sheriff and Keeler were hiding in the whins to his right did not make him feel much safer. The weather brought them one advantage: without wind, sound travelled, and the sheriff wanted to hear every word that was said. Tommy realized that he was a bit deaf.

For the twentieth time, Tommy felt for the emeralds in his right trouser pocket. He had not wanted to take them but the sheriff said it would be too dangerous not to. His stomach churned, his mouth was dry and his palms sweated. He wished it could be over. A thought struck him and he carefully transferred one of the stones to his left pocket.

As he finished doing this, a tall figure floated out of the *haar* to his left. For a moment it hovered, then moved purposefully towards him. It was Dick, dressed in slacks and wearing a jacket. Like Keeler, he carried a club, though no one would practise in these conditions. Tommy stood up. This was it.

'Hello, sir,' Tommy said, aware of the tremor in his voice.

'Let's walk,' Dick said. Without breaking his stride, he climbed the bank up to the Elysian Fields and continued in the direction of the Estuary.

'Where are we going?' Tommy asked as he followed, aware that every step took them further from the sheriff and Keeler.

'Don't talk,' Dick said curtly.

They carried on in silence. Tommy kept a step behind, as a caddie should. Head down, he counted the yards as Dick's shoes left a trail on the damp turf, his cream slacks soaked round the turn-ups.

A dark hole to the right was the first of the Beardies. Tommy knew exactly where they were. Just then, the *haar* shifted, suddenly allowing a hundred yards' visibility. Dick stopped and looked round. Tommy kept his head bowed, alert in case Dick saw they had company, scared that they might not have. Saying nothing, Dick walked on. Soon they reached the path leading down into the rough hollow in front of the fourteenth tee. Dick paused and looked round again before turning half right past the thirteenth green. As he went down the steep little slope into the grassy hollow in front of the green known as the Lion's Mouth, a grave for timid approach shots, he slipped on the damp grass and fell back, stifling a curse. Athletically, he pushed himself up. Tommy wondered if he should have taken the chance to run.

'This way,' Dick said quietly. They walked on until they reached the area of steep slopes, heather and whin in front of the sixth tee. Sheltered from wind, the *haar* seemed to stick there. Looking round the wild, black shapes, Tommy thought back to the ghost stories his mam had told him, the hideous deaths that St Andrews had seen. His teeth began to chatter, so he clamped his jaws together.

Dick looked round carefully once more, turning his head to listen for the slightest noise.

Apparently satisfied, he turned to Tommy. 'Have you got them?' he asked quietly.

'Yes.' He spoke out loudly.

'Quiet!' Dick hissed. He stood still and alert for a moment then peered into the gloom. 'Then let's see them.'

Tommy braced himself. 'Do you have the money?'

'Of course.'

'I'd like to see it then.' Tommy hoped he sounded braver than he felt.

'You will. Stones first.' He swung the club with his left hand, swishing easily through a clump of grass.

Tommy took the emerald from his right pocket and held it out as if offering food to an animal. His eyes gleaming, Dick seized it and held it up. Then he turned it over in his palm, looking at it carefully from every angle.

'Now the other one.'

'The money.'

Dick's smile had no warmth in it. 'You're a tough one,' he said, then handed over a wad of folded notes.

'I want tae count them.'

'Trust me. The other stone.'

Hands shaking, Tommy tried to count the unwieldy sheets of paper. He got to twenty ten pound notes and saw it was about a third of the pile.

'We don't have all day.' Dick moved impatiently from one foot to the other.

Tommy rolled up the notes and stuffed the wad into his empty trouser pocket. He had to get to the point. 'You killed Hamish McCann, didn't you?'

'What business of yours is that?'

'He wis a friend.'

'Did he tell you about the emeralds in the driver?'

'That's how I knew about them. Insurance, he told me, in case Murnian double-crossed him. You did kill him, did ye no'?'

'Okay, I did. How did you get the driver?'

'A pal in the hotel helped me.'

'How did you know I would want these?' He held up the emerald.

'I told Paul and Enda Murnian I'd heard the club had been stolen and I could get it, but they werenae interested. I thought, if anyone has killed for them, it must be you, and you'll be working out how tae get the driver. The jewels are too hot tae sell here, so you'll take them back to America. I'm no' going to tell on you, sir. I just want the money.'

'Clever boy. Now, that other emerald.' He sounded menacing.

Tommy stepped back, nearly stumbling on a rabbit hole.

He had to get Dick to say more. 'If I did tell, I'd go to jail for handling them. But why did you kill him?'

'Because I had to. McCann would never have kept that secret.'

'Did you kill that bastard, Murnian, too?'

'What if I did?' He stepped forward, holding out his hand for the second emerald.

'You did everyone a favour, sir.' He could not delay any longer and placed the stone in his hand. 'Did you have to kill him as well?'

Dick took time to examine the second stone. He carefully placed the jewels in his left trouser pocket then looked bleakly at Tommy. 'Sure, I had to kill him. He killed my father.'

'What?'

Dick was silent then began to speak in jerky phrases, his voice catching. 'My mom died when I was a baby. I don't remember her. I have only one memory of my dad: men shouting; I was hiding under a table; a man with greasy black hair reached in his jacket and put a tiny metal banana to my dad's head; my dad kept saying "no, no"; there was a bang and my dad kinda crumpled on the floor, blood coming out of his face. That's the only memory I have of him. I was three. Of course there were no witnesses who would speak up and I got sent to an orphanage. The superintendent was Father Clement.' He spat out the name. 'Years later, he told me it was Murnian who shot my dad, but he'd got off with it. I'd always planned on killing him somehow.

'After that match last week, I was even more determined. Tuesday night, I was out on the New Course, practising. I heard voices from the fourth of the Old. It was Murnian and Paul. Boy, was that old bastard giving him a roasting. When Murnian went further out the course, I followed him. I came out of the whins

at the ninth behind him and used the flagstick to knock him
out. But he was awake all right when I smothered him. He suffered. I made sure of that. He was still carrying the tiny metal
banana he'd used to kill my dad. He was just conscious when I
told him what I remembered. Then I pushed his face into the
sand till he stopped breathing. I turned his head so I could see
his evil face and I squeezed the trigger. And I'm mighty proud of
that.' His lips twisted into a humourless smile and he produced
something from his right trouser pocket. There was a click and
he pointed the thing at Tommy. 'This is the metal banana, Murnian's Derringer.'

He paused, savouring the moment, then continued, 'Something made me go through his pockets and I found a note from
McCann. It was about the hundred pounds reward and told
him to bring that to the shop at quarter to ten. I worked out
what was happening and figured I could make myself rich. Murnian had a lot of cash in his wallet. I helped myself to enough
to persuade McCann to talk before throwing the wallet in the
bushes.'

Understanding and terror hit Tommy simultaneously, but
he knew something Dick had said was wrong and he forced himself to think. Remembering the conversation at Ballochmyle on
Monday night, it came to him: Murnian used a Colt at the time
of Dick's father's murder; no three-year-old would see that as
a tiny metal banana. Should he say something or not? How
would Dick react? He probably meant to kill him anyway so he
had nothing to lose.

'But when your dad died, Murnian carried a Colt. You killed
the wrong man,' he blurted out then held his breath.

A startled look passed across Dick's face. 'How do you know
this?'

Tommy had to be careful. 'During the match last Tuesday I

heard Murnian talking about guns tae the sheriff. He definitely said he used to carry a Colt till recently.'

'I thought he and Sabbatini both had Derringers...'

Sabbatini! In an instant, Tommy saw the whole picture. 'Have you never wondered why Mr Sabbatini's so good to you? It's guilt. I bet he shot your father.'

Dick's whole frame shuddered as he breathed deeply. He took a step towards Tommy, his face twisted. 'That can't be true. You are a squalid, ungrateful little liar,' he said. 'You'll have to pay for saying such a thing.' His voice was an octave higher, with an eerie, silky smoothness.

Tommy shrank away from him, his bowels suddenly protesting.

'With pleasure comes pain,' Dick said in the same sinister voice. 'Drop your pants.'

Tommy wished he had kept quiet about the Colt. He stepped back again, but lost his footing and fell back on to a steep, heathery slope.

'This is Murnian's gun and there's a bullet in the second barrel. I'd rather not use it on you. You're a very good caddie, so I want you to live, but drop your pants.'

Tommy knew Dick couldn't let him live. Still sprawled on the bank, he pretended to fumble with his buttons. He had to play for time and hope the sheriff found him. He asked, 'So did you kill Jim?'

'Who?'

'The young boy murdered last week. Jim Tindall.'

'Was that his name?'

'And the boy at Scioto?'

'What's it to you?' He pursed his lips. Using his own voice, he continued, 'At the orphanage, I was Father Clement's favourite. He beat the other boys but not me. He did things to me, things you wouldn't believe. He took me golfing and when he did...But he called the shots. The last time he rode me I was nearly your age.' Looking down on Tommy, he reverted to his high, Father Clement voice. 'I said, drop your pants, or it will be worse for you.' He brandished the club threateningly in his left hand.

Seeing nothing for it, Tommy began to drag his trousers to his ankles. 'Why did you kill the boys? You willnae kill me, will you?'

'I said I won't kill you. You're a good caddie, and you know you can't afford to talk. But these boys were nothing. They'd have blabbed. I had to kill them. That's better. Now take them right off.'

Tommy reluctantly tugged his trousers over his boots.

'Now turn round and kneel on that bank. Ass towards me.'

For a moment, aware of the rough, cold wetness of the heather scratching yet protecting his bare skin, Tommy sat defiantly still. But Dick pointed the little pistol right at his face. Slowly, Tommy rolled on his front and drew his knees under him.

'Legs apart. Head on the ground.' Clement/Dick panted with sexual excitement.

As the damp, dangerous air invaded parts of his body only his mam and he had touched, Tommy lowered his head and grasped at the wiry stems of heather covering the bank. He had never been so afraid, so ashamed. But he was not going to cry out. He braced himself, willing himself not to feel what was about to happen.

Out of the corner of his eye, he saw the club fall to the ground. He could almost feel Dick's eyes fixed on his bum. It made him sick. A hand rubbed his bare skin, making it creep. Fingers slapped and poked. It had to be Dick's left hand. Behind him he heard a click then a fumbling noise. Dick must have put the gun down, but he was surely going to kill him later. This would be his best chance. He took a deep breath then, in a single move, he rolled to his left, twisted and hurled himself at Dick, his hands reaching for his throat. Off balance, Dick fell back, Tommy on top of him. The last person Tommy had fought had been his father. Dick was stronger, quicker and just as vicious. As Tommy held his neck, scared of killing him, scared of not killing him, Dick tried to reach his jacket pocket, but it was jammed under his back. Instead, his right hand found Tommy's balls.

The sudden, unbearable pain made Tommy yelp and he loosened his hold. The next instant, he was on his back, Dick astride him, unable to breathe.

Neither heard the two metallic clicks as the sheriff cocked his revolver, but they both heard his command from somewhere above and behind Dick.

'Put your hands up, Robinson, and turn round!'

Tommy did not move, praying Dick would give up.

'I've killed before, during the War. I'm prepared to kill you if I have to,' the sheriff said. Tommy hoped Dick would believe him. He closed his eyes. The pressure round his neck eased, and the weight on his body lifted.

'You can get up, Tommy,' the sheriff said.

For a moment he did not know where he was or what had happened. Hesitantly, he opened his eyes and looked round, hardly daring to hope. When he saw Dick's back to him, hands in the air, he felt mightily relieved then very embarrassed. He scrambled to his feet, grabbed his trousers, and roughly pulled them on. Almost wishing for an excuse to use it, he picked up Dick's club and went towards the sheriff, who stood on the slope, his revolver aimed at Dick's chest.

'Go into his right jacket pocket and take out the pistol,' the sheriff ordered.

Glaring at Dick, who remained strangely expressionless, Tommy moved round behind him and put his hand in the pocket. As he carefully drew out the Derringer, in a sudden move, Dick dropped his right hand, seized the gun and brought it up to his own mouth. There was a click then a shocking bang. Dick fell back, brushing past Tommy, then lay still on the ground, his arms and legs at crazy angles, blood coming from his gaping lips.

Instinctively, Tommy stepped back from the corpse as Dick's sightless eyes out-stared him. As he tried to take in what had happened, Keeler appeared behind the sheriff.

'What the...I'll be darned...' he said.

The sheriff picked his way down the bank and stared at Dick's body. He was breathing deeply. 'Good riddance, I suppose, but I'd have liked to see him hang.' He turned abruptly. 'Well done, lad. Are you all right?'

'Yes, sir,' Tommy stammered, his hands at his balls, which felt as if they had been nearly torn off.

'Good man. You did well there. Very well.' The sheriff moved towards him, his arm out. Tommy thought he was going to embrace him, but the arm went back to his side. As Tommy blinked away tears, the sheriff cleared his throat. 'You deserve a medal. I heard enough, by the way. Mr Keeler probably caught a bit more of it. Sorry I couldn't intervene earlier. If I had, he'd probably have shot you. We thought we'd lost you, but guessed he'd head out towards the turn. Mr Keeler heard your voice. Then we crept round in a big semi-circle. It was only once you were kneeling that he dropped the club, put the gun in his pocket and began to undo his trousers. Had to strike at the optimum time; what we were taught in the War. You beat us to it, of course. Any real man would have done the same. Can't have been at all pleasant.' He paused to rub his forehead. 'I'll get the police. You two stay here and don't touch anything. There'll be a telephone in the stationmaster's house. I'll go there.' He set off towards the little white house in the railway yard to the right of the seventeenth fairway.

Numbed, Tommy sorted his clothes. Keeler hovered protectively then put an arm round his shoulder. The dam inside Tommy burst and he buried his face in Keeler's jacket, sobbing uncontrollably. After a bit they sat together, trying to make sense of all that had happened.

'Some life Dick Robinson must have had,' Tommy said, sniffing.

'Ah, life,' Keeler replied wistfully, unsure if the dampness he cleared from his glasses came from his eyes or the *haar*.

'"Life's but a walking shadow, a poor player

That struts and frets his hour upon the stage

And then is heard no more."

It's strange how well Shakespeare put it all these years ago. Dick Robinson was a poor player in more ways than one. And the tragedy is he could have been a great golfer.'

'Only six shots behind with two rounds to play. If he'd kept putting well, and Mr Jones had a bad day...'

'Bob was four back with nine to play last year at Scioto, and he won. He knows as well as anyone what can happen to a lead...'

Their comforting talk of golf was interrupted by PC Gemmell's arrival, the sheriff toiling in his wake. Tommy watched as the young policeman steeled himself to reach into the dead man's trouser pocket and withdraw the two emeralds. After that, events passed in a blur. He answered some questions then walked back to the sheriff's car. At Ballochmyle, Mrs Drummond threw open the front door as the car crunched the gravel, obviously relieved to see them and desperate for news. When she heard about Tommy's humiliating ordeal, she gently squeezed his hand. He had to stop himself from crying again. Claret and an omelette made him feel better. Meanwhile the sheriff and Keeler roused the operator then used the telephone. Sergeant McNeill arrived and, a fish out of water in the drawing room, sat on the edge of his chair, used his official voice to ask questions, and did not accuse Tommy of doing anything wrong. They were both conscious of the sheriff's close attention to what they said.

'Inspector McTaggart will know what to do about Mr Sabbatini,' McNeill said as he left.

'There's nothing that can be done, I'm afraid,' the sheriff commented to the others.

After giving O.B. and an exhausted Tommy a lift into town, Hector went to bed, mightily relieved. But Lavender had an awkward question for him before he slept: had he expected Dick would try to rape Tommy?

'If he had managed, I'd never have forgiven myself,' he said.

She left it at that.

16

Friday 15 July

Hector rose early and drove to Cupar full of excitement. As soon as he arrived he talked to Newton, the fiscal, an honourable and just man, who informed him that the Kays and Nugent had already been released with all charges dropped. As Madsen had been fully committed the decision was with crown counsel, but the fiscal had already sent his recommendation to Edinburgh, and only the sexually-based charges should remain.

Anxious to spread the good news himself, Hector asked the telephone operator to put him through to Mr Wilson, Madsen's solicitor, who had been so understandably demoralised just two days earlier. When Wilson came on the line, his voice was flat, the bounce and verve of his first appearance before Hector entirely absent. Breathlessly, Hector brought him up to date then paused, awaiting an enthusiastic response.

'I've only just heard that Dr Madsen hanged himself last night, Sheriff. When his lover betrayed him, he lost the will to live.'

Hector could not find anything adequate to say. 'Sorry,' he muttered.

'That's what everyone will say. Thank you for taking trouble, Sheriff. I don't want to sound ungracious. I appreciate what you've done, but this morning I simply long for the day when people will no longer be judged according to their sexuality. Good morning to you, Sheriff.'

That day will never come, Hector thought as he replaced the receiver. He disliked Wilson's high moral tone, but he had to admit there was a certain justice in what he said.

There was nothing more to be done in Cupar, so, less happy than he had been earlier, he drove to St Andrews to watch the last two rounds of the Open. He had arranged to meet Tommy at the caddie shed prior to tapping Lord Terry for the one hundred pounds due to the person who recovered the emeralds.

He found the boy, alone and unhappy, on a bench behind the shed. Hector sat down beside him.

'What's wrong?' he asked.

'They're saying Robinson...ye ken, buggered me.' Tommy sniffed back tears. 'Everyone's talking about what happened last night. The polis must be telling lies about me.'

Hector scratched his forehead and brought out his cigarette case. 'Have one,' he ordered.

They sat in silence, blue smoke swirling round them before wafting into the breeze. Hector looked at his watch.

'Right, wipe your eyes and follow me,' he said. They made their way into the crowd beside the door of the Royal and Ancient.

Lord Terry had scraped through to the final two rounds and he was one of the last to play, the order of starting being random.

'Lord Terry, you must meet someone,' Hector called as the aristocrat came out of the clubhouse for his first round of the day.

Lord Terry looked Tommy up and down then wrinkled his nose.

Ignoring the disdainful response, in a loud, clear voice, Hector explained why the reward should go to Tommy. 'He successfully fought off Robinson's advances, and thus recovered your family's jewels,' he concluded.

Lord Terry shook his head. 'That's all very interesting,' he said. 'But I have already paid the reward. Inspector McTaggart came to the Hamiltons' and gave me the emeralds as I was having breakfast. He told me one of his officers recovered them from Robinson's body. I was delighted to write a cheque for the Fifeshire Constabulary Widows and Orphans Fund. I gather McTaggart is a trustee.'

'You and McTaggart make a good pair,' Hector said contemptuously. 'This lad risked his life yesterday. He absolutely deserves the reward your father promised. I shall write to the earl and tell him.'

'From what McTaggart said, your boy used his thieving skills then handed the emeralds to a murderer. I'm told the two of them were surprised during an act of sodomy with your boy entirely willing. I don't care to whom you write, but I don't think he deserves any reward.' Nose in the air, he carried on towards the first tee.

Hector seized his arm. 'Inspector McTaggart is a liar. I've caught him lying in court before. I was there last night, and I saw Tommy fight off Robinson as if his life depended on it. Robinson did not manage to sodomise him.' He shouted so the gathering crowd could hear.

Shaking Hector's hand from his arm, Lord Terry pushed his way towards the tee. Unable to see where he was putting his feet, he stumbled on the top of the broad stone steps leading down to the course and fell forward, landing with a loud crack. Everyone present knew at once that he had broken a bone. Unmanly tears in his eyes, and using words someone of his breeding might not be expected to know, he sat at the foot of the steps, holding his right wrist. A lady in a bucket hat covered her child's ears and proclaimed that the aristocracy were not what they used to be.

As others rushed to assist, Hector and Tommy left the scene. Inside, Tommy was still sick. He really needed that money. His balls were sore and it hurt to walk.

'That Indian holy man had some curse,' Hector said then added, 'as McTaggart will find out the next time he gives evidence in my court.'

'Sheriff, Tommy, I wanted to see both of you!' Sabbatini's harsh tones hailed them. 'That was a terrible business last night, awful.' He took Hector by the arm and led them away from other people. He grasped Tommy's right hand in both of his. 'O.B. told me at breakfast what you did.' Tommy wondered how much O.B. had said. 'Believe me, son, I just wanted to help Dick, be a father to him, in a way. I sure am sorry about what's happened. I can't believe he did these things to young boys. And I swear that till this morning I had no idea what Clement was doing to him. No idea.'

'You are still responsible.' Hector's voice was crisp, authoritative. Tommy pulled his hand away.

Hector carried on. 'It was you that killed Dick's father. The little boy hiding under the table remembered someone with greasy black hair and a little curved gun that looked like a tiny banana. Your hair used to be black, I wager, and you've always carried a Derringer. But Murnian used a Colt then, and that looks nothing like a tiny banana. After that, Murnian got you your time in Sing Sing, but not for killing Dick's father. When you got out, you were scared there would be a young orphan looking for revenge, and you wanted to get back at Murnian. You found the orphanage where the boy was and became a benefactor. As a Catholic, that was easy. You persuaded Father Clement to bring Dick up to believe Murnian had got away with killing his father. As it happened, Dick turned out to be a fine golfer, so you sponsored him, all the time fuelling his hatred of Murnian. One day, you hoped he would kill him. And I don't know how much you really care about the other murders.'

Sabbatini had listened impassively. 'My, Sheriff, you have some imagination. I thought you guys went on evidence, not crazy hunches.' He shook his head. 'You know, my doc says I don't have too long left till I go upstairs. As that day gets closer, well, anyone raised as a good Catholic boy feels the need to do some confessing.' He looked from Hector to Tommy. 'I regret a lot of things, and I'm going to regret them more and more. Dick doesn't have to live with all that he's done, but I do.' He stared out over the golf course. In a softer voice, he said, 'I guess he wanted away from me; that's why he needed the emeralds so bad. You know, the last thing he did before leaving the hotel last night was to steal from me. Six hundred pounds.' He sounded sad.

Tommy felt the notes still folded in his pocket were dirty. 'Well here it is. I still have it after he gave it to me for the emeralds.' He held out the bundle.

Sabbatini's eyes widened. He took a step back. 'Keep it, son, with my blessing. You've earned it.' He opened his wallet and handed over a few more notes. 'Wages,' Sabbatini continued. 'Including some for what you would have gotten today. You'll use it better than I will.'

'Take it, Tommy,' the sheriff said. 'If we took money only from people we approved of we'd all be in the poorhouse.' Tommy hesitated then put the cash in his pocket. It would pay off his father's debts with plenty to spare.

'I'm getting out of town now,' Sabbatini said. 'Goodbye, Sheriff. Goodbye, Tommy.' He extended his hand but neither took it. He shrugged then hobbled a few steps towards the Grand. As the sheriff and Tommy exchanged glances he turned and came back to them. Standing close, he said in a steady, quiet voice, 'If I had known Dick was killing these young boys, I'd have put a gun to his head myself.'

Watching him go, bent and defeated, Hector said, 'You know, I think he has found Purgatory already.' He fixed Tommy with his shrieval stare. 'Now, we have unfinished business, young man.'

Reluctantly, Tommy took him to the rough area near the harbour where the silver was. Hector drove nearby and parked. Leaving most of the money with Hector, Tommy got out, returning quarter of an hour later with a heavy bag. He added a five pound note to cover the small sum of money he had stolen while housebreaking. Then Hector drove to the house from which the silver had come. He accompanied Tommy in and introduced him to the elderly Colonel Rollo, who seemed more angry at Tommy than glad to have his silver back. After five minutes Hector cut short the diatribe against modern youth, pointing out that the silver and money would not have been returned had Tommy been in borstal.

Next stop was the St Andrews branch of the Bank of Scotland, where Hector steered the lad through the formalities of opening an account, leaving an astonished teller wondering how a young caddie could have acquired such a large sum legally.

'It's safe as houses in a bank,' Hector reassured him as he drove back to the course. 'Far better than under the mattress.'

Leaving the car in North Street, they walked downhill to the area in front of the clubhouse, each thinking his own thoughts.

'There's one thing I've been meaning to ask you,' Hector said. 'If you'd gone to borstal, what would have become of your mother and sister?'

Tommy turned and looked at him. 'They'd have most likely gone to my mam's sister in Cupar. At the time, I thought that might be best for them.'

'Better than you trying to provide for them? Was that why you didn't explain yourself in court?'

Tommy shrugged, a wry smile on his face.

Hector muttered, '"You're a better man than I am, Gunga Din."'

'What, sir?'

'Just something Kipling wrote. He knew a good man when he saw one.' They walked on in silence. 'With this business finished, we won't see much of each other, but I'd be honoured if you'd caddie for me when I need one,' Hector said.

'All right,' Tommy said, grinning broadly. 'Look, Mr Keeler seems pleased about something.'

O.B. approached from the direction of the Grand waving a piece of paper. He had got a wire telling him that Harris had been given a stay of execution pending a new appeal. His attorney needed affidavits, and he would be in touch with Hector about these, but for the first time he was confident of success.

'And the championship?' Hector asked.

'Four ahead. Bob hit the ball wonderfully this morning, but took seventy-three. A guy with a camera put him off his second on seven. He dumped it into Shell Bunker and took five. I could have strapped that camera guy into Old Sparky myself. Why don't you charge admission here? You did last year at Lytham.'

'The links are Common Land. It would be illegal. Also, there are so many ways to approach the Old, people would get in free anyway.'

O.B. shook his head. 'You Scots are some race. Well, it's been a privilege meeting you two gentlemen. In case I don't see you again...'

'This visit,' Hector interjected.

'Exactly so. Eleanor and Lavender have exchanged addresses.'

'What will this place be like next week, sir?' Tommy asked as they watched O.B. disappear into the crowd that was waiting for Jones to start his final round.

'St Andrews will return to normal. Will we?'

'I dinnae know what my new normal will be like, sir.'

❊   ❊   ❊

Tense, bare-headed and wearing the same black pullover he had worn on the previous day, Bobby Jones started the last round badly. For the third time, he drove into Cheape's bunker on the second. The immense crowd had eyes only for him, and they swarmed frantically to see the action. It took time for the marshals to clear the fairways, and these delays made Jones' nervous state more acute. It was clear that the crowd was now squarely behind the American. His modest manner had won over the doubters. He was the best and the noblest of golfers, the fitting winner and a true gentleman. With him in the field patriotic hopes seemed small-minded. More than that, he cared about this championship to the depths of his being, and because he cared so much for their championship, the St Andrews crowd wanted him to win it. They sensed that they were in the presence of a sort of greatness. But after five holes he was three over fours. As he would have to play the second nine against the wind, things were looking ominous. On the sixth Jones sat on the tee box waiting to play, his shoulders bowed, staring at the ground as if accepting defeat. Head down also, his father left the scene.

But these images were deceptive; Jones inspired himself

into producing a burst of his finest golf. He birdied the sixth then reeled off four consecutive threes from the ninth. By the time he reached the thirteenth green he was two under fours. From there he played home serenely, with fives at sixteen and seventeen the only blemishes. But the tournament had been won. At the eighteenth, Andra Kirkaldy took the pin and Jones tapped in from six inches for his seventy-two. The pent-up tension broke like a dam. Granite faces were cracked by smiles as the Scots cast off their dour reserve. Those present realized this was a man and a moment to celebrate and treasure. They surged on to the green cheering, lifted Jones shoulder high and carried him off the course, his famous putter, Calamity Jane, held protectively in an upraised hand.

Outside the Grand Hotel, Hector encountered Bobby's father and Stewart Maiden. While the champion's coach allowed himself the merest hint of a smile, his father was bursting with pride and relief.

'After he had that dreadful start, I couldn't bear to follow him. I've been fretting by the eighteenth green for the last two hours. Did you watch him?'

'As much as I could, given the crowd. Bob, your son was magnificent,' Hector said, happy for the father as much as the son.

In the end, Bobby Jones won the Open by six shots from Aubrey Boomer and Fred Robson. The Whitcombes, Ernest and Charles, Kirkwood, Cotton and Alliss all finished well up. James Braid finished best of the Great Triumvirate with an aggregate of three hundred and five, twenty shots behind the champion and six better than his old rival, J.H. Taylor. Paul Murnian was far down the field but, of the main suspects, he was the only one to complete the championship.

Accepting the claret jug for the second year running, in

front of a mass of people stretching nearly to the Swilken Burn, Jones said, 'I had rather win a championship at St Andrews than anything else that could happen to me. You have done so many things for me that I am embarrassed to ask one more, but I will. I want this wonderful old club to accept the custody of the cup for the coming year.' The ovation he received brought tears to many eyes, Hector's included. Carried away, some claimed to have found the 'Unofficial King of Scotland'.

'A sporting god and an old, grey town have fallen in love with each other,' Hector declared to Lavender over his second whisky that evening.

'They say opposites attract,' she replied, a distant look on her face. 'I'm very, very proud of you. You may have broken the rules but you did the right thing.' She reached out to hold his hand. 'And at least Sabbatini knows we rumbled him. Oh by the way, this was in the post today.' She handed over an envelope.

'It's from Rory,' he said, looking at the solicitors' letter-head. For some minutes he read then re-read the letter, his brow furrowed, then turned to her. 'Rory's gone into a lot of detail, but it boils down to this: Jake's interest in the estate is conditional, but the conditions don't bite until he is of age. The main condition is that he reaches the age of twenty-one. At that time he must have the Taylor-Smith name. It doesn't matter what he calls himself till then, and in Scotland you can call yourself what you like. He can be Drummond while he's at Glenalmond and change back to Taylor-Smith before he's twenty-one so that he can inherit.'

She breathed deeply. 'The best of both worlds,' she said. 'Darling, I've a favour to ask of you.'

'Anything.' He beamed at her.

'You showed your emotions at Jim's funeral. Could you just show Jake you love him, hug him sometimes? You don't have to be distant, like your father was. Look at Bob Jones and Bobby. Jake may not have your blood in him, but he's the only son you're likely to get out of me, so love him, and do show him that you love him. Please.'

For a moment he stared. Tears welled up in her eyes. She was his rock. He squeezed her hand. He managed to say, 'I'll do my best, old girl,' in a catching voice.

THE END